Crime Files Series

General Editor: **Clive Bloom**

Since its invention in the nineteenth century, detective fiction has never been more popular. In novels, short stories, films, radio, television and now in computer games, private detectives and psychopaths, prim poisoners and overworked cops, tommy gun gangsters and cocaine criminals are the very stuff of modern imagination, and their creators one mainstay of popular consciousness. Crime Files is a ground-breaking series offering scholars, students and discerning readers a comprehensive set of guides to the world of crime and detective fiction. Every aspect of crime writing, detective fiction, gangster movie, true-crime exposé, police procedural and post-colonial investigation is explored through clear and informative texts offering comprehensive coverage and theoretical sophistication.

Published titles include:

Hans Bertens and Theo D'haen
CONTEMPORARY AMERICAN CRIME FICTION

Anita Biressi
CRIME, FEAR AND THE LAW IN TRUE CRIME STORIES

Ed Christian (*editor*)
THE POST-COLONIAL DETECTIVE

Paul Cobley
THE AMERICAN THRILLER
Generic Innovation and Social Change in the 1970s

Lee Horsley
THE NOIR THRILLER

Fran Mason
AMERICAN GANGSTER CINEMA
From *Little Caesar* to *Pulp Fiction*

Linden Peach
MASQUERADE, CRIME AND FICTION
Criminal Deceptions

Susan Rowland
FROM AGATHA CHRISTIE TO RUTH RENDELL
British Women Writers in Detective and Crime Fiction

Adrian Schober
POSSESSED CHILD NARRATIVES IN LITERATURE AND FILM
Contrary States

Heather Worthington
THE RISE OF THE DETECTIVE IN EARLY NINETEENTH-CENTURY
POPULAR FICTION

Crime Files
Series Standing Order ISBN 0-333-71471-7 (Hardback) 0-333-93064-9 (Paperback)
(outside North America only)

You can receive future titles in this series as they are published by placing a standing order. Please contact your bookseller or, in case of difficulty, write to us at the address below with your name and address, the title of the series and the ISBN quoted above.

Customer Services Department, Macmillan Distribution Ltd, Houndmills, Basingstoke, Hampshire RG21 6XS, England

Masquerade, Crime and Fiction

Criminal Deceptions

Linden Peach

© Linden Peach 2006

All rights reserved. No reproduction, copy or transmission of this publication may be made without written permission.

No paragraph of this publication may be reproduced, copied or transmitted save with written permission or in accordance with the provisions of the Copyright, Designs and Patents Act 1988, or under the terms of any licence permitting limited copying issued by the Copyright Licensing Agency, 90 Tottenham Court Road, London W1T 4LP.

Any person who does any unauthorised act in relation to this publication may be liable to criminal prosecution and civil claims for damages.

The author has asserted his right to be identified as the author of this work in accordance with the Copyright, Designs and Patents Act 1988.

First published 2006 by
PALGRAVE MACMILLAN
Houndmills, Basingstoke, Hampshire RG21 6XS and
175 Fifth Avenue, New York, N.Y. 10010
Companies and representatives throughout the world.

PALGRAVE MACMILLAN is the global academic imprint of the Palgrave Macmillan division of St. Martin's Press, LLC and of Palgrave Macmillan Ltd. Macmillan® is a registered trademark in the United States, United Kingdom and other countries. Palgrave is a registered trademark in the European Union and other countries.

ISBN-13: 978–0–230–00658–4 hardback
ISBN-10: 0–230–00658–2 hardback

This book is printed on paper suitable for recycling and made from fully managed and sustained forest sources.

A catalogue record for this book is available from the British Library.

Library of Congress Cataloging-in-Publication Data

Peach, Linden, 1951–
    Masquerade, crime and fiction : criminal deceptions / Linden Peach.
      p. cm. – (Crime files)
    Includes bibliographical references and index.
    ISBN 0–230–00658–2 (cloth)
    1. Detective and mystery stories, English – History and criticism.
    2. Detective and mystery stories, American – History and criticism.
    3. Popular literature – English-speaking countries – History and criticism.
    4. Masquerades in literature. 5. Crime in literature. I. Title. II. Series: Crime files series.

PR830.D4P385 2006
823'.087209—dc22
                                                                          2006045669

10 9 8 7 6 5 4 3 2 1
15 14 13 12 11 10 09 08 07 06

Transferred to Digital Printing 2008

For Angela

Contents

Preface viii

Acknowledgements xvii

1 Mocking Modernity 1
2 Gender and Performance in the Criminal Masquerade 25
3 The Cadaver as Criminalised Text 56
4 Where Does That Criminality Come From? Writing Women and Crime 81
5 Agatha Christie, Dorothy L. Sayers and Sara Paretsky: The New Woman 104
6 Masquerade, Criminality and Desire in Toni Morrison's *Love* 129
7 Writing the Serial and Callous Killer into (Post) Modernity 150

Conclusion 173

Notes 177
Index 181

Preface

Crime hardly exists outside of narrative. The crime we read about, hear about and, indeed, experience is usually placed within a narrative; either for us in the way in which it is reported or by us through cultural or personal perspectives, prejudices or fears. For example, in December 2005, a British newspaper reported the trial of a gang led by a teenage girl who kicked a man to death on the South Bank in London. In a style of street crime that the press were reporting as a new craze, she invited their victim to smile for the mobile phone camera as they took pictures of the incident. Press coverage likened the vicious assault to those in Stanley Kubrick's well-known film, *A Clockwork Orange* (1971), based on a novel by Anthony Burgess. In doing so, the press did not simply report the crime but place it within a larger, cultural narrative, linking the offender to the principal protagonist in Kubrick's film. This particular piece of contextualisation is pertinent to the subject of this book because the association of a contemporary crime to a well-known text from the previous century highlights how the crime itself, carried out for the camera as much as for the thrill, was itself a performance. Indeed, this is the principal motif in *A Clockwork Orange* in which Alex de Large in one incident bursts into an elderly couple's home, kicks the man almost to death and rapes his wife in front of him. For the gang this is entertainment; they wear bizarre masks and Alex himself performs a soft-shoe kick-dance, landing his blows to the rhythm and lyrics of ' "Singin" in the Rain'. The choreographed rape of Mrs Alexander in which Alex slits her clothes from her pants upwards is itself reminiscent of the late-nineteenth-century, brutal serial murders of London prostitutes by a murderer who was never caught and became known as Jack the Ripper. The press coverage of the South Bank murder reinforces the performance dimension of the murder by linking it with a text that interleaves choreographed violence, slapstick, musical cinema and dance. The assaults in that text are in turn associated with ways in which a Victorian killer did not simply commit but perform his murders, making a spectacle of his victims.

Popular culture, the media and even serious literature play a large part in the cultural process by which crime is turned into narrative. But, paradoxically, they also help us to understand how the social and personal configuration of crime is determined. Although focusing upon this process might appear to divert our attention from what we might think of as 'real' crime against persons and property, it highlights an equally important social phenomena: the process by which society confronts and absorbs 'real' crime.

The South Bank murder serves as a useful introduction to many of the themes in this book. It is an example of a type of street crime that has been a prevailing public concern since the nineteenth century but reappears in different guise in different periods, like 'garrotting' in the Victorian period discussed in Chapter 2. It illustrates the significant role the press and the media play in configuring crime. But, most importantly for the theme of this book, it reinforces an aspect of criminality that was overlooked in criminology until about the 1920s: the excitement that criminals derive from it. As Alex says in a voice over in *A Clockwork Orange* he is looking for 'surprise visit[s]' that are 'a real kick and good for laughs and lashings of the old ultra-violence'.

The emphasis in this book is upon an aspect of the psychology of crime that is highlighted in the press coverage of the South Bank murder and in both the novel *A Clockwork Orange* and its film adaptation: masquerade and performance. At one level, crime as performance is pursued in this book on the understanding that it contributes to the fuller socio-psychic explanation of criminality. But the primary interest is in the way in which it provides a literary space in which larger issues pertaining to masquerade, especially the construction of gender and the enactment of gendered social relations, might be pursued.

Studies of modern literary representations of crime have usually focused upon the differences between detective fiction and the crime novel, and between the various subgenres of crime writing. These include private eye fiction, the gangster story, the police procedural narrative, the forensic science case, the criminal psychology story, the serial killer narrative and lawyer procedural fiction. They have each come into prominence at different times, and in the twentieth century their respective popularity usually depended upon the interleaving of book publishing, the movies and television. However, all these particular genres and subgenres are only specific developments within a much larger field: the response of the literary and the popular imagination to crime. In concentrating on 'crime writing', criticism has tended to neglect this bigger picture.

Chapter 1 places the book's principal concerns with masquerade, performance and criminality in a wider perspective in which criminality is seen as mimicking, even mocking, modernity. It argues that, at one level, crime mimics the principal values that underpin modernity: for example entrepreneurship, independence, self-motivation and self-determination. This argument is pursued in relation to texts where criminality is often a mocking expression of the negative extremes of what modernity, if it does not actually champion, does not sufficiently condemn: ruthless competitiveness, self-interest, and desire for power and control. The emphasis throughout this, and subsequent chapters, is upon the slipperiness of the criminal as subject and the way in which criminality, especially where it is associated with mimicry and masquerade, generally occupies a complex and ambivalent place in individual and social discourses.

At one level, the criminal is an inverted image of the ideals of modernity, but at another level he or she reflects back to modernity its more unpalatable aspects. Chapter 1 suggests that the mimicry and masquerade associated with criminality is unsettling because while we think of modernity in terms of ordered societies, it is actually in a state of continuous flux. Criminal masquerade and performance also raise questions about the extent to which so-called 'respectable' society is ultimately a masquerade. These arguments are pursued initially in relation to a range of nineteenth-century texts: Conan Doyle's *The Sign of the Four*; Edward Bulwer Lytton's *Eugene Aram*; and Charles Dickens's *Oliver Twist*. These authors demonstrate how writing about criminality in the nineteenth century was informed by two ostensibly paradoxical trends: conceptualising crime, especially monstrous crime, as alien to modernity while seeking to explain crime in the terms of the scientific or pseudoscientific rationalism that was perceived as informing modernity. In the case of the former, it is argued that crime is seen as returning to mock what denies its existence whilst, in the latter, crime mockingly refuses to be encapsulated by what it in turn subversively mimics. The authors themselves are discussed with reference to contemporaneous criminological ideas and the emphasis upon the urban in nineteenth-century criminology is developed in relation to Whitechapel at the time of Britain's first serial killer. Contemporaneous notions of a dangerous, criminal class are explored in relation to a particular construction of masculinity in the nineteenth century that was sustained by an ethical code that seemed to make involvement in crime for men in certain urban classes and areas inevitable. Chapter 1 concludes with an account of how popular ideas about the rural in relation to the urban, as far as crime is concerned, might usefully be seen as entertaining a kind of masquerade, a thesis which is pursued with reference to the short stories of an acclaimed twentieth-century writer, Leslie Norris, who has not received the critical attention that his fiction deserves.

Chapter 2 explores the 'theatre' and 'performance' associated with a range of criminal activities in relation to gendered, corporeal identity through examples taken from the nineteenth and twentieth centuries: the Victorian swellman, the Victorian female criminal, the prostitute, the mid-twentieth-century gangster and 'hard-boiled' women. The notion of mimicry, as far as the swellman and the pickpocket are concerned, is explored with reference to Dickens's *Oliver Twist* which is the launch pad for a wider discussion about masculinity as performance: first, in terms of the cultural power of the street 'rough', with examples taken from the work of Dickens, Edward Bulwer Lytton, Virginia Woolf and Leslie Norris, and, second, in relation to the representation of the effeminate male in the late nineteenth century. The concept of masculinity as a 'performance' is developed with reference to 'real life', twentieth-century gangsters and fictional portraits in Graham Greene's *Brighton Rock*, F. Scott Fitzgerald's *The Great Gatsby* and Raymond Chandler's *Farewell My Lovely* and is compared with the representation of the dangerous, female criminal. The subject of criminal masquerade in relation to crossing social boundaries and mimicking traditional assumptions about gender is introduced with reference to two late twentieth-century historical novels set in the eighteenth and nineteenth centuries respectively: Emma Donoghue's *Slammerkin* and Sarah Waters's *Fingersmith*. The way in which female criminals have been configured and the way in which assertive women, especially sexually independent women, have been represented and often criminalised is developed further in Chapter 4.

Chapter 3 raises the question as to whether the concept of criminal investigation that developed in the nineteenth century is itself a masquerade. In its emphasis upon logic and deduction, the collection and processing of information and the importance of proceeding in a planned and methodical manner, criminal investigation would seem to be the epitome of modernity, in many respects legitimating the basic principles upon which modernity is based. This chapter argues that, on closer inspection, the emphasis upon logic, deduction and scientific analysis in crime writing is often a kind of masquerade where intuition, coincidence and chance have an equally significant role in solving crime. Indeed, the more general equation of science, and scientifically based disciplines, entirely with logic and deduction is something of a masquerade itself. At its higher levels, science, like the arts, relies upon hypothesis, imagination and intuition. It is also argued that the crime scene and the modern literary text have much in common in that each crime scene, like a literary text, has its own characteristics that will determine how it is approached by an investigator or reader whilst crime writing is often a game between the author and the reader, as indeed the crime scene is frequently stage managed to mislead or make a point to its investigators.

The nineteenth-century representation of the crime scene is examined with reference to two key Victorian detective stories. But the American writer Edgar Allan Poe's 'The Murders in the Rue Morgue', generally regarded as the first modern detective story, introduces the idea that the cadaver is usually situated in an uneasy relation between the identifiable and the unidentifiable and between the comprehensible and incomprehensible. A new interpretation of Poe's story is presented which argues that it reflects back to American society the way in which women were victimised and abused in respectable society. This reinterpretation of Poe's tale develops some of the arguments about a 'dangerous masculinity' from the previous chapters in suggesting that Poe criticises a prevalent, nineteenth-century, American orthodoxy that might be seen as legitimating male assaults on women.

Ways in which what has happened to the corpse often indicts a larger social order that victimises 'difference' and legitimates particular types of gendered power is further explored in relation to a range of twentieth-century crime and literary novels: Colin Dexter's *The Remorseful Day*; Agatha Christie's *The Body in the Library*; Minette Walters's *The Breaker*; Magdalen Nabb's *The Marshal's Own Case*; Suzanne Berne's *A Crime in the Neighbourhood*; Angela Carter's *Shadow Dance*; Patricia Cornwell's *Postmortem* and Robert Bloch's *Psycho*. These texts demonstrate that the most innovative and insightful crime fiction self-consciously positions itself in the interpretative space that the corpse and the text share. They are perceived as taking further the arguments of Chapter 1 that crime writing involves a degree of masquerade and games playing in so far as they exploit the uncomfortably close alliance between the language of the text, which both reveals and conceals, and the body in the text. Moreover, it is maintained that in the location of the corpse in these texts, all kinds of discourses and ideological narratives criss-cross and intersect including the symbolic role that the victim of serious crime has traditionally played in the construction of moral and sexual norms. In twentieth-century writing, crime, it is maintained, is likely to be a vehicle whereby traditional boundaries, cultural assumptions and social norms are called into question. The argument concludes that, in its focus upon the location of the body in social and cultural discourse, twentieth-century crime fiction introduced a new relation between the body, masquerade, forensic dismemberment, and the literary/cultural process itself. The Renaissance witnessed the dissection of the coherent humanist subject, and modernity and postmodernity have become increasingly concerned with the extent to which the coherent humanist subject is, and always was, a kind of masquerade and with the dissection of what was, beneath the illusion of coherence, already in pieces.

Chapter 4 discusses the assertive, independent female as a source of cultural and social concern. It begins with reference to the nineteenth century where, it is argued, that one of the reasons why the conflation of female criminality and sexuality seemed so natural for the Victorians was that its notions of middle-class respectability were dependent on women's suppression of their sexuality. Female desires were secret longings, inevitably shrouded in guilt, and perceived as dangerous to the social fabric of society. As such, they were easily elided with criminality. The contradictory ways in which women as victims and criminals are represented in Victorian detective fiction is explored with reference to Conan Doyle's *The Sign of the Four* and 'A Scandal in Bohemia'; Mrs Henry Woods's 'The Mystery at Number Seven'; Wilkie Collins's 'Who Killed Zebedee?' and Harry Blyths's 'The Accusing Shadow'. It is maintained that most of the crime fiction and criminological writing about female criminality between the First and Second World Wars, approaching it as a socio-psychic rather than purely social, phenomenon, stresses the importance of fantasy. This thesis is developed with reference to the work of the Chicago School of Criminology, particularly the criminologist W. I. Thomas's concept of 'unadjustment' which provided criminology with an explanatory framework for criminality in young, generally sexually-active, women. This concept is used to provide a context in which to discuss a number of contemporaneous works of fiction or 'faction' concerned with 'criminality' among young people between the wars: Edith Thompson's *A Pin to See a Peepshow*; R. Alwyn Raymond's crime faction *The Cleft Chin Murder*; Josephine Tey's *The Franchise Affair*; Agatha Christie's *The Murder at the Vicarage* and *The Body in the Library*; and Graham Greene's *Brighton Rock*. The chapter places particular emphasis upon the influence of American, consumer-oriented, mass media culture. It is argued that writing about female criminality between the wars interlinked the mental suffering of women; the rise of a seductive, American-oriented, consumer society; and the suppression, if not criminalising, of female sexuality and independence as dangerous. This writing is seen as exploring the extent to which the origins of female criminality lay in a reciprocal relation between the inner psychic world and external pressures and forces. It is also seen as establishing the need to approach crime through a socio-psychic and not simply a social reality paradigm.

Chapter 5 discusses Agatha Christie's *The Murder at the Vicarage*; Dorothy L. Sayers's *Strong Poison*; Sara Paretsky's *Indemnity Only*; *Burn Marks*; *Bitter Medicine*; and her non-Warshawski novel, *Ghost Country*. The chapter focuses on Christie's interest in the 'New Women', with whom some parts of society felt ill at ease but who appeared to be acquiring greater self-confidence and to be increasingly sure of their new-found sexuality. Like Christie's *Murder at the Vicarage*, *Strong Poison* is a product of the 1920s when women, and especially young women, acquired greater control of their lives, acquiring new masks to meet the masquerade they faced. But, like Christie's novel, it is haunted by the Victorian culturally sanctioned masquerade of womanhood.

Whilst it may appear curious to place Agatha Christie and Dorothy L. Sayers alongside the hard-boiled, American, feminist, detective writer Sara Paretsky, it is argued that, like Christie and Sayers, Paretsky is concerned to challenge, albeit in a different context, the social and cultural configuration of feminine independence as an inverse mirror image of contemporaneously accepted norms of womanhood. Although Paretsky is known for revisioning the masculine, hard-boiled tradition of crime writing, Chapter 5 explores the extent to which her work looks back to, British feminist writers of the 1920s and 1930s, and especially Virginia Woolf. All three of the crime writers discussed in this chapter explore the active socio-political and socio-psychic pressures that the configuration of women as mother first and female second exert on the independent woman. Juxtaposing these writers highlights the influence of twentieth-century feminism upon them, particularly in their shared concern with the ways in which women can occupy 'alternative' imaginative spaces to those occupied by, and assigned to them. But, read alongside Christie and Sayers, Paretsky's work demonstrates the way in which psycho-analysis became an increasingly important element in feminist crime fiction and in exploring the masquerade which women were coerced into accepting as 'reality' or assumed in order to undermine the larger masquerade of gendered power relations.

Given Paretsky's interest in Woolf's exposure of gendered, social identity as masquerade, the similarities between her feminism and that in the writings of Christie and Sayers are not surprising. However, the stronger psychoanalytic element in her work gives a different twist to the masquerade of femininity compared with theirs. Her Warshawski crime fiction can be seen as employing the hard-boiled tradition at times as masquerade because of the way in which the reader is frequently given glimpses into something that lies beneath the surface.

Chapter 6 is concerned with the African-American Nobel Prize-winning writer, Toni Morrison's novel *Love*. Although not a crime writer like the women authors discussed in Chapter 5, criminality enters into most of her fiction and especially *Love* which is seen as developing ideas and characterisations from her earlier novels *Sula* and, especially *Jazz*. The novel provides an opportunity to explore how the principal motifs of masquerade, performance, 'unadjustment' and criminality are approached from the perspective of an African-American writer. However, this is not to say that there is one African-American perspective on these subjects. The representation of the City in Morrison's *Jazz*, where performance and persona are celebrated, is different from that in black American crime fiction which tends to have a different set of emphases. The trope of performance has a special significance in relation to African-American culture. The development of black music, dance and theatre provided an important impetus for the arts generally and had a special role in configuring American and, particularly, African-American identity. The novel is seen as being involved with masquerade and performance on a number of different levels including gender identity, language, sexual identity and fetishism.

In Chapter 7 the representation of the serial and callous killer is explored with reference to Robert Louis Stevenson's *Dr Jekyll and Mr Hyde*, Marie Lowndes's *The Lodger*, Graham Greene's *A Gun for Sale*, John Banville's *The Book of Evidence*, Angela Carter's 'The Fall River Axe Murders', Bret Easton Ellis's *American Psycho*, Robert Bloch's *Psycho* and William Trevor's *Felicia's Journey*. As narratives of fictitious and 'real crime', serial criminals have proliferated and, in many cases, become more sophisticated, it is maintained, and the emphasis has fallen upon the repetitive methods and the compulsive psychologies involved. In the most sophisticated accounts, the interest has shifted from the horror of the crimes to the performance of the criminal and the masquerades which they assume in undertaking the crimes and in melting back into 'ordinary' society afterwards.

Nineteenth-century accounts of serial criminality demonised the criminal and stressed the horrors of serial killing as is evident in Robert Louis Stevenson's shilling shocker *The Strange Case of Doctor Jekyll and Mr Hyde*. The texts discussed in this chapter highlight how the serial or psychopathic criminal has been represented in terms of different explanatory models of behaviour; one, deriving its metaphysical framework from theology, and concerned with demonising the serial killer and, the other, based on twentieth-century psychoanalytic theory, seeing the callous killer as a product of a dysfunctional childhood. In the twentieth century, interest in masquerade as an essential element in serial criminality developed in tandem with a psychoanalytic approach to, or psychoanalytic profiling of, the serial criminal. In many respects, psychoanalysis has determined the way in which human motivation is approached in many twentieth-century texts and the chapter pursues the thesis of one cultural critic that psychoanalysis became a 'social force' in the twentieth century to such an extent that it actually determined the way the unconscious was represented. The idea that there was a link between criminality and one's early childhood experiences forcefully entered criminological thinking in the late 1930s and the 1940s when an unbroken relationship between child and mother was perceived as essential for the child's future mental health. Robert Bloch's *Psycho* is explored within this framework. In contrast to Bloch's text, *American Psycho* is seen as offering a self-referential approach to criminality that integrates it with the notion of the spectacle upon which late modernity in America appears to be based. The subject of the text is not so much the criminal as determined by psychoanalysis as the criminal determined by the wider, self-referential, cultural field. Within this context, the emphasis in the novel falls, as it does in the final work discussed, William Trevor's *Felicia's Journey*, upon the different masquerades and performances assumed by the serial criminal.

Acknowledgements

References to the primary texts are to the following editions. Page numbers are given in parentheses after quotations.
Margery Allingham, *The Case of the Late Pig* (1937; rpt. London: Vintage, 2005); Jake Arnott, *The Long Firm* (1991; rpt. London: Hodder and Stoughton, 2000); John Banville, *The Book of Evidence* (1989; London: Picador, 1998); Suzanne Berne, *A Crime in the Neighbourhood* (1997; Harmondsworth: Penguin, 1998); Robert Bloch, *Psycho* (1960; rpt. London: Corgi, 1983); Albert Camus, *The Outsider* trans. Stuart Gilbert (1946; rpt. Harmondsworth: Penguin, 1969); Angela Carter, *Shadow Dance* (1966; rpt. London: Virago, 1995); 'The Fall River Axe Murders' (1981; *Black Venus*, 1985; rpt. London: Picador, 1986); Raymond Chandler, *Farewell My Lovely* (1940; rpt. Harmondsworth: Penguin, 1949); Agatha Christie, *The Murder at the Vicarage* (1930; rpt. London: Harper Collins, 1993); 'The Body in the Library' and '4.50 from Paddington' in *Miss Marple Omnibus* (Harmondsworth: Penguin, 1997); Patricia Cornwell, *Postmortem* (1990; rpt. London: Warner Books, 1998); Michael Cox (ed.) *Victorian Detective Stories* (Oxford and New York: Oxford University Press, 1992); Colin Dexter, *The Remorseful Day* (1999; rpt. London: Macmillan, 2000); Charles Dickens, *Oliver Twist* (1837; Harmondsworth: Penguin, 1967); *Great Expectations* (1861, 1868, 1965; rpt. Harmondsworth: Penguin, 1979); Emma Donoghue, *Slammerkin* (2000; rpt. London: Virago, 2001); Arthur Conan Doyle, *The Sign of the Four* (1890; rpt. Oxford: Oxford University Press, 1993); Bret Easton Ellis, *American Psycho* (1991; rpt. London: Macmillan Picador, 2000); F. Scott Fitzgerald, *The Great Gatsby* (1925; rpt Harmondsworth: Penguin Classics, 2000); Graham Greene, *Brighton Rock* (1938; rpt. Harmondsworth: Penguin, 1971); *A Gun for Sale* (1936; rpt. Harmondsworth: Penguin, *Three Entertainments*, 1992); Patricia Highsmith, *The Talented Mr. Ripley* (1955; rpt. London: Vintage, 1999); Chester Himes, *A Rage in Harlem* (1957; rpt. London and New York: Allison and Busby, 1985); F. Tennyson Jesse, *A Pin to See the Peepshow* (1934; rpt. London: Virago, 1979); Marie Lowndes, *The Lodger* (1913; rpt. Oxford: Oxford University Press, 1996); Edward Bulwer Lytton, *Eugene Aram: A Tale* (1832; rpt. London and New York: George Routledge and Sons, 1847); *England and the English* ed. Standish Meacham (Chicago: Chicago University Press, 1970); Toni Morrison, *Love* (London: Chatto and Windus, 2003); *Jazz* (1992; rpt. London: Picador, 1993); *Sula* (1973; rpt. London:

Picador, 1991); Magdalen Nabb, *The Marshal's Own Case* (1990; rpt. Harmondsworth: Penguin, 1991); Leslie Norris, *Collected Stories* (Bridgend: Seren, 1996); Alan Parker, *The Sucker's Kiss* (2003; rpt. London: Hodder and Stoughton, 2004); Edgar Allan Poe, 'The Murders in the Rue Morgue' in *Selected Writings of Edgar AllanPoe* (1967; rpt. Harmondsworth: Penguin, 1970); R. Alwyn Raymond, *The Cleft Chin Murder* (London: Claud Morris Books Ltd., 1945); Sara Paretsky *Ghost Country* (1996; rpt. Harmondsworth: Penguin, 1998); *Burn Marks* (1990; rpt. London: Virago, 1993); *Bitter Medicine* (1987; rpt. Harmondsworth: Penguin, 1988); *Indemnity Only* (1982; rpt. Harmondsworth: Penguin: 1987); Edgar Allan Poe, 'The Murders in the Rue Morgue'; Dorothy L. Sayers, *Strong Poison* (1930; rpt. London: Victor Gallanz, 1947); Robert Louis Stevenson, *Dr Jekyll and Mr Hyde and Other Stories* (1886; rpt. Ware, Hertfordshire: Wordsworth Editions Limited, 1993); Josephine Tey, *The Franchise Affair* (1948; rpt. Harmondsworth: Penguin, 1951); William Trevor, *Felicia's Journey* (1994; rpt. London: Penguin, 1995); Sarah Waters, *Fingersmith* (2002; rpt. London: Virago, 2003); Irvine Welsh, *Trainspotting* (1993; rpt. London: Martin Secker and Warburg, 1996); *The Acid House* (1994; rpt. London: Vintage, 1995); Virgina Woolf, *The Years* (1937; rpt. Oxford: Oxford University Press, 1992).

1
Mocking Modernity

Criminal fictions

Writing about criminality, whether in literature or in criminology, is usually concerned with 'groups' and with 'grouping' individuals together by virtue of their criminality as, for example, serial killers, rapists, vandals, thieves or pickpockets. This has implications for the way in which we might think about a society, a nation or a particular locale as a 'totality'. It hardly needs pointing out that any study of criminality within a social or cultural context is bound to be based upon social divisions and cultural conflicts. But what also needs to be said is that the emphasis in such a study must inevitably fall not simply upon conflict but upon how groups or individuals, classified in terms of their criminal activity, articulate with, challenge, or undermine the dominant discourses that are meant to bind a society or a nation together in a particular way around a particular set of values.[1]

Whilst modern criminology has tended to stress the social causes of crime, some late twentieth and twenty-first century criminologists have argued for more recognition of the phenomenological reasons why people become involved in crime. Crimes such as burglary, theft, shoplifting and vandalism can be seductive, offering something that is exciting, even thrilling.[2] Dickens clearly understood this; in watching the Artful Dodger and Charley Bates at work on the streets for the first time, Oliver Twist experiences 'the blood so tingling through all his veins from terror, that he felt as if he were in a burning fire' (67). Here Oliver tastes the sense of 'life on the edge' that is important to an understanding of why the young especially become involved in certain types of crime. But equally exciting is the opportunity that some crimes, particularly street crimes, provide for masquerade, trickery and performance. On a darker level, this is also true of serious crimes such as serial murder. William Trevor's *Felicia's Journey*, which is discussed in Chapter 7, focuses not on the serial crimes, as do many popular murder thrillers, but on the cat-and-mouse games which the killer plays with one of his potential victims before she sees through his masquerade.

It is with acts of criminality involving mimicry, masquerade and performance that this book is concerned. Although a great deal of criminality is associated with performance, trickery and a kind of 'theatre', 'performance' and 'theatricality' are among the least discussed aspects of criminal behaviour. But before pursuing these aspects of criminality, it is important to acknowledge that they are part of a bigger picture in which criminality might be perceived as mimicking, even mocking, modernity and its principal values: entrepreneurship, independence, self-motivation and self-determination. Criminality is often a mocking expression of the negative extremes of what modernity might be seen as championing: ruthless competitiveness, self-interest and ambition.

As a product also of urban growth and the freedom of movement afforded by social change and technological development, criminality often expresses some of the tensions between modernity and what it displaced. Most obviously, this is manifest in the conflict between increasing cultural permissiveness and greater social freedom afforded by modernity and the restraint, discipline and hierarchy which more conservative forces continued to champion in the interests of social stability. The latter finds expression in the respectable, middle- and upper-class sleuths associated with classic English detective fiction. However, even some of these such as Agatha Christie's Miss Marple, Dorothy Sayers's Lord Peter Wimsey and Margery Allingham's Albert Campion have an ambivalent relationship to modernity. Moreover there are crime stories, including some featuring these detectives, where the proximity of the detective to the criminal is too close for comfort; a motif that Conan Doyle developed through conjuring a Biblical-style struggle between Sherlock Holmes and his brother.

The conflict between the two brothers is symbolic of inner tensions within Holmes himself. Not only would his gifts make him as able a criminal as a detective but he himself, sometimes to his friend Dr Watson's dismay, fluctuates between the anarchic permissiveness ushered in by modernity and more conservative social perspectives. The extent to which this ambivalence might be seen as embedded in society itself helps account for the popularity of Ernest William Hornung's stories about a gentleman criminal, Raffles, who enjoys the privileges of a public school education and an upper-class social position. The Raffles stories first appeared in 1896 and marked a transition in the late nineteenth and early twentieth centuries from an emphasis upon the detective in crime writing to the criminal. But like the tales in which Holmes assumes a variety of disguises, the Raffles stories explore the contradictions within modernity and the way in which criminality might be seen as mocking modernity through the subject of masquerade, in this case of a thief masquerading as a gentleman.

It is a commonplace criticism that the classic English detective story represents a rift in a generally well-ordered society, whilst in the more industrialised, urban modernity of the American, hard-boiled, detective genre, criminality is an index of a more pervasive and deep-rooted corruption. Although the amateur detective story was displaced in the course of the twentieth century by the police procedural narrative, which in its emphasis upon organisation, categorisation and procedures is a more equivocal manifestation of modernity, even that genre is dependent upon bringing modernity face to face with the corruption that seemingly mocks it. James Ellroy's *L. A. Confidential* (1990) and *Tabloid* (1996) are particularly notable examples of this type of work.

Whilst one consequence of envisaging a nation or locale in terms of its criminal activity is to magnify cultural difference, another is to raise questions about the relationship between the dominant discourses of a nation and the complex reality of lived experience within it. Criminology interrogates the nature of the nation within or beneath its rhetoric. In doing so, it invariably encounters that rhetoric, and the language in which it is couched, as a problem. For what might be accepted as the consensus around which the nation state or society is forged is often revealed in criminology or crime writing as contested territory.

The cultural tensions which criminal activity exposes are often those which the rhetoric of nationhood will often deny or mythicise. But the language in which criminality is written is also problematic because of these tensions. This is a characteristic of the representation of crime to which we will return many times in the course of this book. It is evident, as we shall see, in representations of the nineteenth-century street criminal, the female criminal between the wars in Britain; the American gangster of the 1930s, the crime scene and even the serial killer. Criminality in literature, the media and human community generally is usually responded to with ambivalence; a subject of abhorrence, yet a subject of fascination as well. Part of the public's fascination with criminality lies in the way in which it often mimics and consciously or unconsciously mocks dominant, social discourses. Thus, the language in which criminality is written about, whether scientifically or imaginatively, occupies a kind of 'double time' in that, even in the most scientific accounts, it is caught between objectivism and fascination, and between distance and involvement. For the most part, this is because criminologists and authors know that their readers are themselves poised between objectivism and fascination in their relationship to crime.

This study explores the slipperiness of the criminal as subject and the way in which criminality, especially where it is associated with mimicry and masquerade, generally occupies a complex and ambivalent place in individual and social discourses. This is especially the case, as even the few examples above suggest, in relation to 'modernity' or the 'modern'. At one level, the criminals are an inverted image of the ideals of modernity, but at another level they reflect back to modernity its more unpalatable aspects.

A criminalising modernity?

'Modernity' is an elusive and ambivalent concept, generally speaking, synonymous with the city: the expansion of urban environments, the centralising of capital and socio-economic power, and the control which the metropolis assumed over aesthetic conventions. In crime writing, it is often pursued through particular, urbanised settings or invoked from the standpoint of rural, village locations. The specificity assigned modernity in the crime novel is underscored, especially in mid-twentieth-century American writing, with a wealth of detail that often includes everything from food and cars to clothes and body tattoos.

Modern society is usually perceived as underpinned by the Grand Narratives of the West: progress, scientific rationalism, order, democracy and individualism – in short, the Western definition of civilisation. Moreover, it is usually associated with secularisation, capitalism and industrialisation. Criminality is a reminder of everything that these narratives, despite their grand ideals, failed to eradicate and the problems which they in turn created.

In some respects, the penal and criminal reforms of the nineteenth century reflected, and contributed to, the essence of modernity as 'enlightened' civilisation. The prisons that replaced the infamous convict ships moored in the Thames and are well known even today, such as Wandsworth, Brixton, Holloway, and Strangeways are reminders that the modern prison and criminal justice system has its roots in the transformations of the nineteenth century.[3] If we travelled back in time to 1761, the system of criminal justice we would face would be a lot more foreign to us than the one that would confront us if we found ourselves in 1861, the year in which the Offences Against the Persons Act was passed. By then, capital punishment was retained only for murder, treason, piracy, and setting fire to dockyards and arsenals while pillorying, public flogging, the gibbet and the practice of dissecting bodies of executed criminals had ceased.

However, the concept of 'modern', in relation to society, does not just revolve around longings for a better future but anxieties about the emergent social order which is why the mimicry and masquerade of criminality can itself be so unsettling.[4] While we think of modernity in terms of ordered societies, it is also envisaged as in a state of continuous flux. In the nineteenth century, literature and criminology found themselves confronting the consequences of seismic socio-economic and epistemological change. Moreover, when viewed through a social Darwinian lens, the civilised order appeared to be characterised by ruthless competition and the survival of the fittest, a sense of the individual as alienated in a cruel world; and the struggle between conformity and freedom, including sexual freedom.

Some cultural historians argue that the eighteenth-century city was perceived as a model of social order while nineteenth-century metropolitan life appeared increasingly complex and turbulent.[5] Although Hogarth's depictions of eighteenth-century London and the novels of Henry Fielding and Daniel Defoe undermine that simple binarism, the complex and chaotic modernity of the nineteenth century profoundly influenced social theories of the time, including those of crime. This is most obviously the case in what are normally labelled social realist criminological perspectives where crime is essentially the product of the inequalities of modernity. Marxist-realist, criminological perspectives emphasise the tension between the ostensible emergence of a more humane society and an increasingly intolerant, commercial society. This is evident in some of the paradoxes of penal reform in the nineteenth century. Despite the reforms outlined above, punishment was made more severe for offences that were perceived by the media, the public and the authorities as threatening social order. In response to widespread public concern about violent street crime, the 1865 Prison Act retained the treadmill and the crank and, together with the acts of 1874 and 1877, famously instigated a regime of 'hard labour, hard fare, and a hard bed'.[6] In this respect, criminality highlights a fundamental contradiction in modernity, between the ideal of a new, advancing future and the continued presence of more conservative, and often repressive, forces from the past.

At one level, the tension within 'modernity' between social and cultural idealism, on the one hand, and conservatism, on the other, is not surprising. Concerns about urban crime spiralling out of control were especially pronounced in the mid-nineteenth century, when crime writing itself began in response to the growing complexity of modern social life.[7] Indeed, criminology, as much as crime writing, has been driven by anxieties about the complexity and potential uncontrollability of a rapidly expanding, modern, urban society. At the heart of nineteenth-century and much twentieth-century criminology and realist literature there are similar concerns about the purpose of society, the relationship between freedom and social organisation, the balance between social control and individual responsibilities, and the best ways of achieving personal and social stability. However, these are concerns that have to be viewed within a changing wider social and cultural context.[8]

Contemporary criminology has been termed 'postmodern' by some historians of crime for its emphasis upon the relative nature of the concepts of criminality. But such a distinction between a contemporary criminology that recognises the cultural and temporal relativity of crime and criminality and an earlier criminology that did not is not borne out by history. Recognition of criminality as a changing and dynamic cultural concept predates so-called 'postmodernity'.

Cultural trends that inform the representation of crime in literature, criminology and the mass media reflect the demise and emergence of different preoccupations and anxieties. In Britain in the 1980s, there was widespread panic in the United Kingdom over the abuse of children in institutions such as children's homes. In the 1990s, press coverage of the murder of a toddler by older children in Liverpool in the United Kingdom generated interest in the potential criminality of children; in the extent to which the media blurred the boundaries in drama and advertising between childhood and adulthood; and in the ease with which violent and/or pornographic material in magazines, on video and on the internet could be accessed by the young. In the United States, the 1990s saw the growth of anxieties about gun ownership, an increasingly violent society, and the safety of ordinary citizens arising from the widespread reporting of high-school murders. Across the developed world, the end of the twentieth century and the beginning of the new millennium witnessed widespread anxiety, again to some extent generated by the media, about identity theft, computer crime, especially 'hacking', computerised corporate fraud, pornography on the internet and paedophiles masquerading as children in internet 'chat rooms'.

Thus, it is important to recognise the changing social and cultural context in which criminality activity emerges, is represented in literature and the mass media and theorised in criminology. But it is equally important to recognise that despite what appears to be new types of crime and shifts in emphasis in the public perception of crime, there is a core of concerns that has remained reasonably consistent over the last few hundred years. Indeed, some of the ways in which crime and criminality were perceived in the 'true crime' stories in the broadsheets that pre-dated the mass circulation newspapers have survived in modern writing, including the connection of crime with the invocation of primal fears and desires, the role of a perceived 'other' in the formation of a sense of self; and the relevance of narratives about crime to the construction of national and gender identities.

Criminal physiologies

There is a canonical history of criminology which one recent text book has usefully summarised:

> The classical challenge to pre-Enlightenment notions of arbitrary and violent justice; the positive challenge to classical notions of rationality and deterrence; the sociological challenge to positivist notions of pathology and degeneracy; the postmodern challenge to sociological notions of socio-structural causes and remedies of crime.[9]

Literary concern with crime has a complex relationship to contemporaneous criminology, at times articulating its major premises and at other times challenging them. Often, as is frequently the case with novels by Charles Dickens, a single work can confirm some aspects of contemporaneous thinking about criminality and challenge others.

Writings about criminality in the nineteenth and twentieth centuries are informed by two ostensibly paradoxical trends: conceptualising crime, especially monstrous crime, as alien to modernity while seeking to explain crime in the terms of the scientific or pseudoscientific rationalism that was perceived as informing modernity. In the case of the former, crime returns to mock what denies its existence whilst in the latter crime mockingly refuses to be encapsulated by what it in turn subversively mimics. In the early days of criminology, these different approaches were frequently to be found in the same treatise. Moreover, the science of criminology which emerged, albeit in a rather crude form, at the end of the eighteenth and beginning of the nineteenth centuries, embraced two principal approaches: empirical research such as Patrick Colquhoun's *Treatise on the Police of the Metropolis* (1797), an analysis of the activities of the 115,000 criminals in London, and physiological studies designed to identify a 'criminal type'. The hypothesis that it might be possible to identify criminals physiologically has a trajectory which includes physiognomy, reading people's characters through their faces, and phrenology, reading personalities through the irregularities, or 'faculties', on a person's head.

The physiological studies that had most impact upon the cultural representation of the criminal body in the nineteenth century were the deterministic theories of anthropometric criminality inspired by Darwin's theory of evolution. On the basis of a study of almost 7000 criminals, Cesare Lombroso in *L'Uomo Delinquente* (*Criminal Man*) argued that, physiologically, criminals resembled primitive humanity and apes in their large jaws, high cheekbones, square ears and long arms. Lombroso alleged that 'ravishers' might be identified by their short hands, their medium-sized brains, their narrow foreheads and the abnormalities of their nose and genital organs. Assassins, on the other hand, were said to have prominent jaws, widely separated cheekbones, thick dark hair, scanty beards and pallid faces. Swindlers might be identified by their large jaws, their prominent cheekbones, their large body bulk and their pale faces. As a barely human presence in society and mimicking the prehuman, to which they were perceived as a throwback, the criminal appeared to mock the civilising aspects of modernity in which the early Victorians prided themselves. Indeed, this kind of classification informs the description of the Liverpool 'roughs' in Shimmin's *Liverpool Sketches* (1862): they are 'men of short stature, with big heads, broad, flat faces, and thick necks' who wore 'white trousers turned up at the bottom to show their high-laced greasy boots'.[10] However, the 'rough', who, as we shall see, created an intimidating presence through an effective street performance, could not easily be explained away by theories such as Lombroso's.

Although Lombroso's work was criticised within and shortly after his lifetime, he contributed to the widespread Victorian conviction, supported in Francis Galton's *Inquiries into Human Faculty and its Development* (1883), that there was an identifiable 'criminal type'. Moreover, Lombroso's physiological snapshots of criminals cannot be removed from a wider matrix of cultural representations that include colonised peoples of European Empire. His detailed explications of the physiological features of highwaymen, thieves, ravishers, assassins, swindlers and arsonists are redolent of those with which the nineteenth century configured Africans and West Indians.

The interleaving of criminal and racial physiologies, so that the criminal and the colonised are linked as a perceived mocking, prehuman presence within modernity, is evident in one of the most accomplished Victorian, detective novels, Conan Doyle's *The Sign of the Four*. Although drawing upon a number of different modes of writing, it begins as a 'sealed' or 'locked-room' mystery when Sherlock Holmes and Dr. Watson visit the crime scene at Pondicherry Lodge. Thaddeus Sholto has already related how at his father's death, he and his brother saw a face at the window:

> We both stared round at the window behind us upon which his gaze was fixed. A face was looking in at us out of the darkness. We could see the whitening of the nose where it was pressed against the glass. It was a bearded, hairy face, with wild cruel eyes and an expression of concentrated malevolence. (28)

The primitive and animalistic qualities in the Islander's face invoke the conflation of physiology and metaphor, redolent of Lombroso's work, that was emerging in nineteenth-century cultural analysis of difference. To the impressionable Watson, Tonga has 'venomous, menacing eyes' (87), rarely has Watson seen 'features so deeply marked with all bestiality and cruelty' (86–7), and Tonga is said to have had 'a great misshapen head and a shock of tangled, dishevelled hair' (86). Not only does the novel invoke Victorian debates about anthropometric criminality and the origins of humankind in general, but the Victorian notion of a hierarchy of being in which black peoples, specifically, were perceived as closer to the apes than whites: 'his thick lips were writhed back from his teeth, which grinned and chattered at us with half animal fury' (87). The animalistic grin conspicuously, and with a degree of superiority that belies its primitiveness, mocks what looks back at it from the other side of the glass. It is a reminder of the growing fear in late Victorian society of what were increasingly seen as the unvanquished, non-white, colonised peoples and the resilient criminal recidivist.

Tonga's association with an innate evil stands in contradistinction to Small's confessional narrative that concludes the book. Redolent of the morality tale into which coroners and the press often turned a criminal's life story, the white, male criminal's story weaves mitigating circumstance, personal responsibility and mischance. His life's history is a tale of descent from respectability, he 'comes from steady, chapel-going folk, small farmers, well-known and respectable over the countryside' (96). This thumbnail sketch of his family origins encapsulates Victorian values of hard work, respectability, god-fearing sobriety, restraint and perseverance that the criminal often mocked. In his narrative, Small is configured by Watson as a combination of recklessness (he was 'a bit of a rover' who 'got into a mess over a girl' (97), strong will (he took the Queen's shilling), courage and loyalty (he achieves a small command in the volunteer corps) and gullibility (he eventually agrees to the Sikh's criminal plan and ends up committing robbery and murder).

As an end note to this section, though, it is worth pointing out that the concept of a 'criminal physiology' does not end with the nineteenth century. It may be found in the twentieth and twenty-first centuries, in children's cartoons and comic books, war-time propaganda and even advertisements and wall posters designed to sell security products. Its effect, however, is much the same in the twentieth and twenty-first centuries as in the Victorian period. It refocuses modernity from being the assured symbol of the new to being a divided and contested cultural space.

The inverse image

There is no more powerful signifier of the contemporary within culture than the body and no more disturbing signifier of divided and contested cultural space than what is perceived as 'criminality'. Criminality and the 'transgressive' body – one that does not accord with what is perceived as socially acceptable at a particular time and place – are frequently interleaved as sites of cultural anxieties, phobias and mythologies. In some texts, the detective's body is itself 'criminalised' within the dominant discourses of a particular society or community, which is often the case within lesbian, African-American and feminist crime writing. In this case, they become a vehicle for questioning how accepted definitions of criminality and justice are themselves inscribed by wider, social prejudices and cultural preconceptions.

The modern is a product of an encounter with limit and transgression. In this engagement with boundaries, the body is cast as a trope of conflict and anxiety as often as it is celebrated as a site of creation and transcendence. The modern is both manifest in and mocked by the 'transgressive' body. At the heart of writing about crime, whether in literature or criminology, is the sometimes overt and sometimes subconscious dialectic between the body of the criminal and the 'criminalised' body, and between the victim of crime and the victim of criminalising.

Twentieth-century European cultural theory provides us with fresh insights into how the criminal was repositioned in relation to the nineteenth-century social structures. Drawing upon linguistic theory of culture as a system of visual and verbal signs, one European cultural critic has argued that social systems are not only based on the ideals that they profess but their negatives.[11] Thus, in medicine, the ideal is the healthy body but the 'negative' upon which medical discourse is based is the corpse. If we apply such a line of thought to crime and criminality, we could argue that the law-abiding citizen and the offender operate as cultural signs like the body in medicine. In modernity, the ideal is the law-abiding citizen, equivalent to the healthy body in medicine, and the criminal is the negative, equivalent to the corpse. Thus, despite its overt utopian ideals and its tendency to favour human possibility, the discourses of modernity are often based, too, on negative and somewhat reductive phantasms of the individual.

Although the notion that public discourse is based upon negative 'realities' as well as publicly avowed positive ideals acquired prominence in twentieth-century social theory, the concept had previously obtained at least some currency in relation to crime in the Victorian period. In 1885, W.T. Stead, editor of the *Pall Mall Gazette*, drew attention in his editorial to 'the horrible realities which torment those whose lives are passed in the London inferno'. In fact, he suggests that those who interpret modernity in terms of its positive ideals 'live in a fool's paradise of imaginary innocence and purity'.[12]

The extent to which criminality is integral to the modernity which it mocks is the conundrum at the heart of the work of the first 'modern' crime novelist, Edward Bulwer Lytton. Lytton's *Paul Clifford* (1830) and *Eugene Aram* (1832), which are usually read as precursors to Dickens's fiction, provide a counterpoint to the negative representation of male criminality to be found subsequently in the sensation novel and Victorian melodrama. Together with William Godwin's earlier *Caleb Williams* (1794), they might be regarded as more distant forerunners than the sensation novel of modern crime fiction. But Lytton's novels are among the first to explore the ambiguities of modernity through focusing on the figure of the criminal. As he maintained in 'England and the English', he perceived himself to be writing on the cusp of two sociocultural orders: the decline of the older aristocratic society, and the emergence of the modern democratic society.

In *Paul Clifford*, based on the story of an eighteenth-century highwayman, Lytton argues for a socio-legal system that recognises the human potential within the criminal rather than emphasises his depravity. Indeed, following John Gay's *The Beggar's Opera*, Lytton suggests that there is chivalry among thieves, and that highwaymen are no worse than many politicians. The tragedy of the scholarly Eugene Aram is that he succumbs to the more villainous Houseman and, becoming involved in the murder of a vicious rapist, is thereafter caught in a web of guilt, complicity and blackmail. Aram's confession in the death cell is an argument that a portion of the soul can survive the evils and temptations of the temporal world. Lytton's work reflects the importance that criminological debates of his day attached to the individual, and the conviction that the individual is able to act in ways that mitigate the worst failings of society. Paul Clifford and Eugene Aram emerge as deliberately drawn counterpoints to the negative dimensions of modernity. In the final preface to *Eugene Aram*, Lytton insists:

> The guilt of Eugene Aram is not that of a vulgar ruffian: it leads to views and considerations vitally and wholly distinct from those which ... revolt and displease us in the literature of Newgate and the Hulks. (xi)

The reductive view of the criminal to which Lytton is opposed is paradoxically represented in his reference to 'a vulgar ruffian' which is an example of the criminal reduced to a criminological type. Whilst arguing such reductivism at one level, he perpetuates it at another through his distinction between the 'acceptable' criminality of men like Aram and the 'unacceptable' criminality of the 'vulgar ruffian' of Newgate fiction.

The contradictions within Lytton's novels can be better appreciated when we remember that they were written during a period of transition from semi-religious, demonological explanations of criminal behaviour. Instead of seeing the individual as embroiled, for example, in a battle between good and evil, the criminal is perceived as a product of a particular social biography. But, because he was writing in a period of confusion, and was perhaps thinking through his own ideas, Lytton also drew paradoxically upon earlier discourses of criminality that see the criminal in terms of mysterious evil and the demonic: when Houseman first appears at Grassdale, he is represented, as Lytton thought of criminals and the masquerades by which they lived, as the serpent in the Garden of Eden.

Inside the underworld

Like Lytton, Dickens's work distinguishes those who have fallen into crime but who are capable of redemption, such as Magwitch in *Great Expectations* or Nancy in *Oliver Twist*, from 'habitual' criminals, such as Compeyson and Orlick or Fagin and Bill Sikes. In some respects, the insider view of the criminal underworld in *Oliver Twist* is indebted to Lytton's *Paul Clifford* which appeared seven years earlier -Dickens was an admirer of Lytton's work – and to Gay's *The Beggar's Opera* to which Lytton may have pointed Dickens. As in Lytton and Gay's texts the criminals, in this case pickpockets, housebreakers and streetwalkers, speak in their own, frequently mocking, voices. However, an important distinction to be made between *Oliver Twist* and Lytton's early work is that, with the obvious exception of Nancy, the underworld is not sympathetically drawn. It should perhaps be remembered at this point that whereas Lytton based his novels on criminal records, Dickens had observed the London underworld close-up in his work as a court reporter.

Oliver Twist follows Gay's play in blurring the distinction between criminals and non-criminals in order to satirise those who hide behind masks of public respectability. With less emphasis on the thieves' jargon, Dickens pursues Gay's interest in how the language of the criminal classes mockingly inverts the norms of established society. In the following extract from *Oliver Twist*, the criminal fraternity, as in Gay's play, is structured around a gang leader who is also a receiver of stolen goods:

> 'Well,' said the Jew, glancing slyly at Oliver, and addressing himself to the Dodger, 'I hope you've been at work this morning, my dears?'
> 'Hard,' replied the Dodger.
> 'As nails,' added Charley Bates.
> 'Good boys, good boys!' said the Jew. 'What have *you* got, Dodger?'
> 'A couple of pocket-books,' replied the young gentleman.
> 'Lined?' inquired the Jew, with eagerness.
> 'Pretty well,' replied the Dodger, producing two pocket-books; one green, and the other red.
> 'Not so heavy as they might be, 'said the Jew, after looking at the insides carefully; 'but very neat and nicely made. Ingenious workman, ain't he, Oliver?' (109)

The conversation between Fagin and his gang of young pickpockets inverts Victorian values of hard work: Dodger 'produces' the pocket-books and is an 'ingenious workman'. Fagin's admiration of the stolen goods links stealing – stealing is the gang's 'trade' – to craft or art. The notion that stealing is an art has a long tradition in English writing about crime that can be traced to and through Daniel Defoe's *Moll Flanders* where Moll is taught by a 'governess' the 'art' of stealing shop-books, pocket-books and gold watches from ladies. Moreover, Victorian ideals are further inverted in the description of the boys as 'good' and Dodger as a 'gentleman'. This inversion of Victorian values mocks what it turns upside down. Fagin displays the aesthetic appreciation of a craftsman but his interest in workmanship and quality is laced, as it must be even for the craftsman, with thoughts of profit.

The account of the bungled burglary, later in the novel, draws attention to the specialised equipment that Bill Sikes and his companions take with them. It mirrors not only the way in which the industrial classes worked with increasingly specialised tools but were themselves perceived as less than their tools. The consumption of the individual by their specialist skill is encapsulated in Toby's surname – Crackit! Are their tools an extension of themselves or vice versa?

These episodes from *Oliver Twist* suggest that criminality is not only an inverse mirror image of the ideals of modernity but that modernity is the product of a dynamic between its positive and mockingly negative dimensions. This dynamic, like the definition of what constitutes criminality, is at the heart of the way in which power is exercised within society: power, as the French historian Michel Foucault has said, 'is not exercised simply as an obligation or a prohibition on those who do not have it; it invests them, is transmitted by them and through them; it exerts pressure on them, just as they themselves, in their struggle against it, resist the grip it has on them'.[13]

Dangerous masculinities

Twentieth-century European configurations of the way in which power is transmitted through, and puts pressure on, those that do not have it is especially pertinent to the way in which certain forms of masculinity have been represented in relation to criminality. This is evident in the nineteenth-century depiction of juvenile male criminality. As the contemporaneous criminologist Henry Mayhew maintained: 'In tracing the pickpocket from the beginning of his career, in most cases we must turn our attention to the little ragged boys living by a felon's hearth, or herding with other young criminals in a low lodging-house, or dwelling in the cold and comfortless home of drunken and impoverished parents.'[14] The kind of gang with which Oliver Twist becomes involved operated throughout the late Regency as well as the early Victorian period. They consisted usually of males, operated in small gangs, patrolled markets, fairs and shops and were closely identified with well-known receivers, specialising in silk scarves, watches and pocket-books. Although Fagin is based on a Jewish fence of the time, he also recalls the infamous Mrs Diner, of Field Lane, Holborn, who displayed in her shop window numerous silk handkerchiefs, obtained mainly from boy pickpockets, from which identification names and numbers had been removed.[15]

As in the case of the rural criminal communities, which we will come to in a later section, the familiarity with other lawbreakers seems to be the primary factor in maintaining a criminal fraternity based on crime. But while the criminal fraternity provided alternative deviant cultures in the countryside and the city, the urban fraternity was usually perceived as a more complexly structured subculture. Mayhew divided urban criminals who committed robbery into categories such as 'mobsmen' who relied on catch-and-grab and 'sneaksmen' who stole by stealth. The latter committed opportunistic crimes, unlike Bill Sikes who as a housebreaker or 'cracksman' was a higher status criminal. The Artful Dodger's status, and his name, would have come from his ability to work across several of Mayhew's categories, at the same time as he undermines the rigidity of Mayhew's classification of criminals. The Dodger clearly worked as a 'stookbuzzer', stealing handkerchiefs, and as a 'tail-buzzer', stealing snuff-boxes, purses and pocket-books. He also probably stole pins and brooches, as a 'prop-nailer', and watches, as a 'thimble-screwer'. Such detailed classification of criminal 'specialisms' mockingly imitates the increasing, occupational specialisation of modern, industrial society.

Criminality and community

Given the more complex nature of the metropolitan criminal fraternity, it is not surprising that urban experience has primarily informed writing on the importance of 'community' in sustaining criminality. Nineteenth-century interest in how association with criminals encouraged and sustained particular types of male criminality was part of a wider concern with the criminal environment. This approach was developed through the work of French criminologists such as Guerry and Quételet as well as British criminologists such as Mayhew, although the latter's work remained the most significant for British 'criminology' at the time. The academic discipline of jurisprudence, which in some respects might be seen as the forerunner of criminology, spawned numerous studies of crime and its causes in the nineteenth century. But the most prevalent area of interest was in what might be described in today's parlance as the 'ecology' of crime. Of the many works produced in this area, the most influential were Mayhew's *Those That Will Not Work*, the fourth volume of his *London Labour and the London Poor* (1862), and his *Criminal Prisons of London*. The influence of this school of thought pervades Charles Dickens's fiction and his articles although he drew upon numerous literary sources in giving it 'life'. For example, his representation of London's labyrinthine geography appears to be indebted to the portrayal of the Rookeries in Gay's *The Beggar's Opera* or eighteenth-century prints of the Gin Lanes. At the time Gay's work was written and performed, the wealthy had begun to move to the new suburbs in the west of London, leaving the formerly prosperous areas to become sites of degradation and crime, as the following account from *Oliver Twist* illustrates:

> A dirtier or more wretched place [Oliver] had never seen. The street was very narrow and muddy, and the air was impregnated with filthy odours. There were a good many small shops; but the only stock in trade appeared to be heaps of children, who, even at that time of night, were crawling in and out at the doors, or screaming from the inside. The sole places that seemed to prosper amid the general blight of the place were the public houses; and in them, the lowest orders of Irish were wrangling with might and main. Covered ways and yards, which here and there diverged from the main street, disclosed little knots of houses where drunken men and women were positively wallowing in filth; and from several of the door-ways, great ill-looking fellows were cautiously emerging, bound, to all appearance, on no very well-disposed or harmless errands. (103)

The above passage highlights how by the time Dickens was writing *Oliver Twist* the deterministic interconnection of poverty, dirt, drunkenness and crime had become self-evident. Dickens's discussions of criminality reflect a shift in emphasis that occurred in writings about urban crime between the 1830s and the 1840s from economics to mores, so that crime became increasingly seen as one strain of a larger evil bound up with amorality and ignorance. The effect was to drive more of a wedge between the respectable classes and the criminal fraternities at a time when the latter were increasingly seen as mimicking and exposing the masquerade of the former. The observation that 'the sole places that seemed to prosper ... were the public houses' acquires a different slant, and emphasises the different meanings of 'the general blight of the place', if we read 'sole' as 'soul'. While unemployment, overcrowded housing and a general legacy of deprivation were clearly acknowledged as contributory factors, Victorian social observers, so obviously confronted with the negative aspects of modernity, were dismayed by men for whom lawbreaking was mockingly a habitual way of life. In the mid-nineteenth century, it was axiomatic that there was a 'criminal class', variously referred to as the 'dangerous class' or the 'perishing class'.[16] There was frequently a further distinction made between a poor district and the smaller inner part of it which was perceived as an area of habitual criminal activity.

The above passage from *Oliver Twist* once again stresses the association of masculinity with stealing, violence and destruction and the conflation of this pattern of behaviour, notwithstanding the association of the Irish with immorality and crime, with a breakdown of the normal bonds between mother and child. The pointed situation of mothers 'wallowing in filth,' leaving their children unattended, a crude mockery of the Victorian ideals of motherhood, anticipates the way in which twentieth-century sociology linked criminal behaviour among men to the absence of a home-centred, adult female. Dickens also seems to imply that there is an offending type of male who is different from a non-offender. But there is an uneasy tension in Dickens between the predeterminism of nineteenth-century criminologists, such as Cesare Lombroso, who believed criminals to be born bad, and an alternative ecological model, which might itself be seen as a version of predeterminism, that attributes criminal behaviour to an environment which does not share the ethics of a larger respectable society.

The most infamous example of an association of crime with the environment in which it occurred is provided by the serial murders of prostitutes by the so-called Jack the Ripper in the East End of London, to which I will refer several times in the course of this book. The killings occurred between 31 August and 9 November 1888, within a quarter a mile of each other in Whitechapel.[17] Judith Walkowitz has pointed out that the setting of Whitechapel was the first significant element in the Ripper murders because 'by the 1880s, Whitechapel had come to epitomise the social ills of "Outcast London" '.[18] It was a poor, cosmopolitan locale, with a large transient community living in lodging houses. The following account by the wife of Canon Barnett, published in 1918, echoes aspects of the description of 'outcast London' in *Oliver Twist* in that poverty, drink, street violence, crime and a particular type of masculinity are similarly interleaved:

> There were two or three narrow streets lined with fairly decent cottages occupied entirely by Jews, but, with these exceptions, the whole parish was covered with a network of courts and alleys. None of these courts had roads ... Each chamber was the home of a family who sometimes owned their indescribable furniture, but in most cases the rooms were let out furnished for eight pence a night, a bad system which lent itself to every form of evil. In many instances broken windows had been repaired with paper and rags, the banisters had been

used for firewood, and the paper hung from the walls which were the residence of countless vermin. In these homes lived people in whom it was hard to see the likeness of the Divine. If the men worked at all it was as casual dock labourers, enjoying the sense of gambling which the uncertainty of obtaining work gave. But usually they did not work; they stole or received goods, they hawked, begged, cadged, lived on each other with generous indiscrimination, drank, gambled, fought, and when they became too well known to the police, moved on to another neighbourhood.[19]

Like the passage from *Oliver Twist*, Mrs Barnett's account suggests that lawbreaking among men flourishes where there is frequent contact with those involved in illegal activities and where there are strong cultural expectations to assume a 'masculine' role in a community which denies men opportunities for legitimate work and advancement. Thus, Barnett underlines how the men 'stole or received goods, they hawked, begged, fought ... '. When Dickens writes of the public house as being the sole place to prosper in the 'rookeries', and of men and women wallowing in filth, he implies that these people are different from the respectable poor, and must be seen as responsible for their condition. Mrs Barnett associates the 'criminal classes' with 'evil', and an apparent lack of Divinity.

Such a view as Mrs Barnett's of London's lower working-class men was promulgated years earlier than the Ripper murders, in G. W. M. Reynolds, *The Mysteries of London* (1845). He observes that districts such as Bethnal Green were, like Hogarth's gin alleys, labyrinths of dirty and dangerous lanes, in which physical filth and moral squalor mocked respectable London. In his work, such areas of London represent the 'other' upon which modern metropolitan society is based. At one level, urbanisation encouraged a rationality that dismissed rural superstition. Yet countryside lore was often recycled as modern folk myth. These served as vehicles for middle-class anxieties about the dangerous urban places and the criminals who populated them. Reynolds describes Richard Markham's journey into inner London:

[Richard] began to be alarmed. He remembered to have read of the mysterious disappearance of persons in the east end of the metropolis, and also of certain fell deeds of crime which had been lately brought to light in the very district where he was now wandering, – and he could not help wishing that he was in some more secure and less gloomy region.[20]

Interleaving of the urban, modernity and criminality, appealing to a principally metropolitan readership, once established in the nineteenth century became the fulcrum of twentieth-century crime fiction.

Twentieth-century badlands

The emphasis upon the city in twentieth-century crime fiction can be traced back to the social realist novel in England and to the Paris location of the American Edgar Allan Poe's 'The Murders in the Rue Morgue', generally regarded as the first modern detective story. An important link between nineteenth-century London writers interested in crime as an urban-based phenomenon and twentieth-century authors is the London-based novels of Margery Allingham who began writing in the late 1920s. One of her later works, *The Tiger in the Smoke* (1952), concerning London murders committed by Jack Havoc, is clearly based on the Ripper murders. Not only do the killings occur in the autumn but, like Jack the Ripper, he has surgical skill; the murders create a public panic which is exacerbated by the press; and the police handling of the case comes in for public criticism. It is even suggested, as it was of the Ripper murders, that the killings are being committed by a public figure masquerading as Jack. The Dickensian London fog signifies a masquerade that exists on many levels and has to be penetrated before the crimes can be solved.

It is well known that the interconnection of urban poverty, crime and widespread corruption acquired a particular focus and edge in American crime fiction between the wars. This 'hard-boiled' tradition, evident in the work of Ed McBain and Raymond Candler and in black crime fiction in the work of authors such as Chester Himes, had a far-reaching influence on the way in which criminality and modernity were perceived, to which we will return in Chapter 2. Although there is a strong provincial tradition in English crime writing, the influence of the tougher, urban American crime fiction soon established itself in Britain and is evident even in the late twentieth and twenty-first century Edinburgh-based fiction of Irvine Welsh and the crime writing of Ian Rankin.

Cities offered opportunities for experimentation at private and public levels and were where the impact of the latest social, political and intellectual trends were generated or most keenly felt. They had a diversity and pace of change that meant that they were always finally unknowable and their inhabitants could acquire a degree of anonymity that was not possible in the small town and certainly not in the country village.

Indeed, the city became not simply the setting for crime fiction but a character and text in its own right. In several of her novels, the late-twentieth century and twenty-first century, African-American writer Toni Morrison celebrates the masquerade of city life, taking a generally more positive approach to the urban environment than many mid-century, black crime writers, a subject to which we will return in Chapter 6.

Since much criminality, as we said at the outset of this book, is based on masquerade and city life makes duplicity possible, if not actually encouraging it, urban crime writing has either celebrated modernity as always 'becoming' or exploited the tensions between the 'possibilities of becoming' and the social divisions that mitigate against it. In other words, like the nineteenth-century English, social realist novel, twentieth-century writing which is about crime is invariably inspired by the contradictions within modernity, and often in the masquerade itself. In Irvine Welsh's *The Acid House* (1994) Gus McGlone is typically uneasy in 'the Glasgow wide-boy persona he cultivated': 'It was easy to con the impressionable bourgeois who filled the University staff-rooms that he was the genuine article. In somewhere like Govan, it was another matter' (113). In the same novel, other characters cannot see where metropolitan masquerade begins and reality ends. Olly's friends are 'all City Café types ... who wanted to be musicians, actors, poets, dancers, novelists, painters, playwrights, film-makers, models and were obsessed with their alternative careers' (247). The phrase 'Café City types' gives the masquerade away. In urban representation as ostensibly diverse as Chandler's Los Angeles, Mc Bain's fictitious Isola, Irvine Welsh or Ian Rankin's Edinburgh, Alison McNabb's Florence or the tenements of Harlem, it is possible to find the kind of masquerade Mayhew found on the streets of London that mocks modernity even when it tries to legitimate it. The central character in Welsh's *Trainspotting* (1993) finds in an Edinburgh interview panel for a porter's job what he sees as grotesques: 'a mucho spotty punter in a sharp suit, wi dandruff oan the shoodirs like piles ay fuckin cocaine', a 'fat, stroppy-lookin gadge' and 'a coldly smiling dyke in a woman's business suit wi a thick foundation mask, who looks catalogue hideous' (64). In twentieth-century fiction, city and criminal masquerades merge as they did in Mayhew's observations. Chester Himes in *A Rage in Harlem* (1957), to which we will return in Chapter 6, draws attention to Harlem hustlers 'dressed in lurid elegance, along with their tightly draped queens, chorus girls and models ... sparkling with iridescent glass jewellery, rolling dark mascaraed eyes ... smiling with pearl-white teeth' (60).

The arguments that literature and criminology share a concern to understand modernity and that criminality can be envisaged as mocking the ideals of modernity are most obviously supported by urban criminology and crime writing. However, the representation of rural criminality in British literature and criminology is also pertinent to these arguments. Envisaging the rural locale through its, often understated, criminal activity challenges some of the more conventional ways of mythologising the countryside and exposes country life as a kind of masquerade. In fact, although Lytton's configuration of the criminal influenced writers such as Charles Dickens, his preferred focus was upon the interface between criminality and the rural.

Although crime writing and criminology can be seen to some extent as urban phenomena, literature does not treat crime solely as an urban problem. There is a British subgenera of crime writing based on fictive, or at best semi-fictive, rural geography of which Colin Watson's East Anglian Flaxborough narratives, Ruth Rendell's 'Wexford' series, set in the imaginary market town of Kingsmarkham, and W. J. Burley's 'Wycliffe' mysteries, anchored in Cornwall, are among the better known contemporary examples. The works of these writers exemplify how rural criminality is usually associated with the perceived negative aspects of modernity. In fact, they tend to highlight the permeable nature of the boundary between the urban and the rural and between the modern and the traditional. Thus, even in the accounts of rural crime, the discourses circulating in accounts of city crime are often all too evident. An example is Ruth Rendel's *Road Rage* (1997), which involves the building of a by-pass that will destroy an important natural habitant close to Kingshampton. The way this leads to a narrative about environmental terrorism is typical of the Chinese puzzle box structure of much of this type of crime writing, where the emergence of one element of modernity is often a trigger for another which is more serious and more dangerous and has its roots in urban modernity. However, outside of popular, formulaic detective writing, there is not as much literary writing about rural as urban criminality. An obvious exception is the work of the contemporary short fiction writer, Leslie Norris, to whom we will return shortly.

If the urban badlands are the negative 'realities' that mock modernity, in which the criminals are performers in a satanic masque, the rural, at its most romantic and idealised, appears to lie outside modernity. But the rural, perceived as an 'escape' from the urban metropolitan, casts modernity itself within a negative paradigm. That particular view of the countryside is often inverted by those, especially the young, who live there and long for the excitement and anonymity of the metropolis. The configuration of the rural as an 'ideal' is based, on denial at least in the twentieth century, of what many sociologists and criminologists have identified as 'hidden' to all but those who live there.[21] When officially unrecorded crime is taken into account, the countryside and rural communities in the twentieth and twenty-first centuries are often revealed as far less idyllic places in which to live than we might assume. This antiromantic view of the countryside, which sees it as a romantic masquerade created by the city, can be traced back to before the nineteenth century when rural crime was far from hidden in crime statistics.

The 'vulgar ruffian', whom Lytton finds in Newgate fiction, was not to be encountered sauntering in the nineteenth-century countryside. But the countryside could nevertheless, as today, be perceived as a fairly intimidating place. Indeed, historians argue that the malicious destruction of property was a persistent and important dimension of nineteenth-century rural crime. It was often reported in ways that confirmed contemporary prejudices about the ignorance and immorality of country folk and the anti-social behaviour of the new generation of farm labourers.[22] As the nineteenth century unfolded, and the social problems of the countryside increased and became more complex, families and even whole sections of villages were driven to crime. However, the Victorian period then witnessed the popular mythologising of certain criminal figures which in turn made the rural a much more ambivalent social phenomenon. The poacher not only became an accepted part of country life, but was romanticised, alongside others such as gypsies, as a representative of what at the time could be configured as an enviable rural subculture.[23] But what the romanticisation of poaching also did was to legitimate the dependence of the legal, urban trade in meat and game upon it. Thus, the poacher not only mocked but complicated the gentrified respectability and itinerant criminality binary by implicating the rural criminal classes and the urban respectable classes in the same criminal activity.

A divided countryside

The idea that the rural idyll was a kind of intellectual masquerade, hiding a real, much darker countryside, continued into the twentieth century in both criminology and literature. Criminologists and social historians have identified five categories of crime in rural communities and many, but by no means all of them, regularly go unrecognised as crimes because of the particular sensitivities and balance of relationships within the community: assaults (such as clashes between neighbours, family conflicts), destruction of property (tearing down walls, fences, hedges etc.), non-malicious property crimes (theft of farm produce, game, fish), moral offences (drunkenness, vagrancy) and technical crimes (breaches of public health, highways etc.).

Leslie Norris's stories, mentioned above, set in rural Cardiganshire and West Wales, *The Sliding* (1978) and *The Girl from Cardigan* (1988), feature communities where petty crime is ripe. In 'A House Divided', the participant narrator unwittingly fishes illegally in waters owned by someone else and an unscrupulous lawyer, Lemuel Evans, cheats a couple out of their inheritance. In 'A Roman Spring', a couple is caught stealing tiles from a property that they thought no one owned. In 'The Mallard', we are led to believe that a man's birds have been illegally killed and another's property – a row of poplars – is maliciously damaged before he himself is seriously assaulted. In 'Cocksfoot, Crested Dog's Tail, Sweet Vernal Grass', a young man walks out on his job because his employers discover he is an embezzler. In 'The Girl from Cardigan', the Council is so corrupt 'that the Mafia never got a toe-hold among us. Those Italian boys would have starved' (124).

Although these misdemeanours and crimes are not the usual subjects of crime fiction, Leslie Norris's short fiction raises important questions about the nature of crime and about how crime is defined in our society. In many of the above cases, what is a serious crime or misdemeanour from one perspective is highly debatable from another. Or, as in the case of the solicitor Lemuel Evans's sleight of legal hand in 'A House Divided', what is technically lawful is a moral crime. Traditionally, literary representations of crime have mostly associated criminality with the lower and criminal classes. The misdemeanours and minor offences with which Norris is concerned, however, are those in which ordinary people rather than stereotypical criminal types, such as the urban 'rough', are brought into conflict with the law. These include people, like Mr Simmonds in 'The Mallard', who might be surprised to find themselves classed as 'criminals'.

There are three principal premises from modern, left-of-centre criminology with which Norris's stories appear to be in sympathy: there are different levels of sensitivity to certain offences in different communities, that crime is a social phenomenon and so reflects the social setting, and the 'crime' that characterises society is actually only that degree of unlawful activity that law makers and enforcers perceive through the filters of their own social interests, assumptions and even prejudices. Read within this framework, Norris's fiction presents the reader with the kind of countryside that is revealed behind the masquerade when petty crime, typical of rural areas, is taken into account in configuring the rural. This is not to say that Norris simply presents his Welsh villages as dark and dastardly places that mock English romanticisation of the countryside. His stories can be read as an argument against the way in which popular and media conceptions of crime are often based upon pathologising the criminal. His recurring interests are in the crimes and misdemeanours that bring ordinary people into conflict with the law and in the way in which economic forces, traditions and ethics intersect in the circumstances that create particular crimes. His work challenges the pathologising of crime which sees it in absolute terms, associates it with imagined, alien criminal types, and takes it out of specific social and economic contexts. It is, therefore, worth bearing in mind in contradistinction to the emphasis in criminology and crime writing upon urban criminality. It reminds us that alongside the representation of urban criminality, that is easily traceable to Dickens and social realist fiction, there is an alternative, albeit thinner, preoccupation with criminality in the countryside from which emerges a permeable boundary between the urban and the rural.

The concern of this chapter has been with the way in which criminality often mimics modernity but, exposing its excesses and underscoring what it fails to eradicate, it also mocks it. In Chapter 2, the kind of theatre and performance associated with a range of criminal activity is discussed in relation to gendered, corporeal performance and identity.

2
Gender and Performance in the Criminal Masquerade

Victorian street performers

There are many aspects of criminality dependent upon 'performance' and 'theatre' that are related to traditional notions of gender identity. Some of these are explored in this chapter through examples taken from the nineteenth- and twentieth centuries: the Victorian swellman, the Victorian female criminal, the prostitute, the mid-twentieth-century gangster and 'hard-boiled' women.

We do not have to look far in nineteenth-century criminology to find the criminal as performer, enacting a flamboyant style of male display. It is an aspect of the felon that Mayhew (1862) stresses in his essay on pickpockets, referred to in Chapter 1:

> They dress in various styles; sometimes in the finest of superfine black cloth; at other times in fashionable suits, like the first gentlemen in the land, spangled with jewellery. Some of them would pass for gentlemen – they are so polite in their address. Others appear like a mock-swell, vulgar in their manner – which is transparent through their fine dress, and are debased in their conversation, which is at once observed when they begin to speak. (345)

Here we have not only a description of but revelling in the swellman's splendour and his 'performance'. 'Spangled with jewellery', the swellman takes a pride in his appearance that anticipates the new aestheticism and effete masculinity associated with Whistler and Wilde a few decades later. The kind of revelling in fashion which the swellman displays may be seen as a critique of modernity in which it is turned into a spectacle that in turn undermines Victorian utilitarianism. The swellman cocks-a-snook at utilitarianism and parodies modernity's tendency to spectacle. He was an effective parody because pickpocketing itself conflates art, conjury and the carnivalesque. Closely mimicking but also parodying the gentleman, the swellman mocks authority and propriety. This was especially true of those, sometimes with a woman accomplice, who enticed their victims off the main thoroughfares and then 'skinned' them – taking their clothes and leaving them naked.

Dickens's Artful Dodger exemplifies some of the qualities that Mayhew identifies in the swellman. Like the prostitute and thief, Nancy, in the novel, the Dodger is a liminal figure. In appearance, he stands between the criminal world and respectable society and, no longer a child, he is also not quite a man: 'He was a snub-nose, flat-browed, common-faced boy enough; and as dirty a juvenile as one would wish to see; but he had about him all the airs and manners of a man' (100). This description is based on the Victorian physiological definition of the criminal referred to in Chapter 1 – the snub-nose and the flat-brow denotes a member of the dangerous classes – but there is also the deterministic interconnection of dirt, poverty and crime that, for many a Victorian commentator, defined the enclaves of the habitual criminal. However, the primary interest of the text is the mimicry, the way in which he assumes 'the airs and manners of a man': 'He was, altogether, as roystering and swaggering a young gentleman as ever stood four feet six, or something less, in his bluchers' (100).

The way in which the Dodger mimics but parodies the respectable gentleman is taken up in Sarah Waters's *Fingersmith* (2002) which opens with allusions to *Oliver Twist*, in the figure of 'Gentleman', who might be the Dodger in his twenties, and also hints at an elision between fashionable and effeminate masculinity, to which I shall return later in this chapter:

> He set down his bag, and shivered, and took off his sodden hat and gloves and then his dripping greatcoat, which at once began to steam. He rubbed his hands together, then passed them over his head. He kept his hair and whiskers long and now, the rain having taken the kink from them, they seemed longer than ever, and dark, and sleek. There were rings at his fingers, and a watch, with a jewel on the chain, at his waistcoat. I knew without studying them that the rings and the watch were snide, and the jewel a paste one; but they were damn fine counterfeits. (19)

As part of the scam upon which the novel is based, he assumes the mask of a gentleman.

However, Dickens's Dodger and Waters's Gentleman are not only able to mimic and parody the respectable classes, they are able to 'read' bodies. This aspect of the pickpocket is stressed in another contemporary novel, Alan Parker's *The Sucker's Kiss* (2003), which concerns a young San Francisco pickpocket, Thomas Moran, at the turn of the twentieth century:

> It was an easy lift because he had a belly on him as big as a truck, so I figured he was used to bumping into people and would never even notice me. The back of his head was completely square – whether he had a clumsy barber or bad genes, it was hard to tell ... I deliberately showboated a sneeze over his left shoulder, which forced him to shift the weight of his body ever so slightly to his other side, so that I could slip under his jacket and get closer to the wad bulging in his right inside pocket. (62)

In *Oliver Twist*, the reader really sees Brownlow as the Dodger would see him. But Parker takes the petty thief's way of observing the bodies of his/her potential victims further than Dickens, stressing how the 'art' of pickpocketing is rooted in knowledge of the physical body as well as the clothes in which it is dressed. He also develops the way in which Dickens's Fagin parodies an artist's appreciation of a well turned-out object, referred to earlier:

> To my surprise, it wasn't a wallet at all. I slipped it out of the leather case and my jaw dropped lower than my pant cuffs. I was holding a beautiful bible. It was really old – so old that it had gold leaf on the front and thick yellow parchment pages that crackled as I opened them. (63)

Parker's pickpocket, though, thinks differently from his 'fence' who immediately recognises that this is the book on which the Mob swore their allegiance. However, both Dickens and Parker suggest that the artist and the thief share what distinguishes them from the majority of people – an aesthetic appreciation of 'quality'. In both novels, pride in the art and in the quality of the booty are integrated with pride in pickpocketing as a performance without being cancelled out by the association with crime. Moran boasts: 'In the tiny, infinitesimal seconds when his beefy arm moved away from guarding his stash, I had my fingers – just my fingers, never my hand – tightly around the wad inside his pocket' (62). The contrast between the 'beefy arm' of the victim and Moran's deft fingers inverts the usual way in which male criminals and their victims were presented in nineteenth-century fiction and draws attention to the 'style' assumed by the swellmen. However, the way in which the pickpocket is almost effeminised by the 'art' of pickpocketing raises further issues about the semiotics of the criminal body.

Political bodies

The familiar Marxist argument of late twentieth-century cultural historians that bodies are politically inscribed is apposite to the cultural significance of the swellman.[1] His theatricality challenges the way society's power relations have an immediate hold upon the body and exposes how bodies are bound up in complex, reciprocal relations with their economic use. The activities of the street criminals of the nineteenth century resulted from real economic need or greed. But they are also symbolic, challenging the power relations that are invested in the gentleman or gentlewoman's body and in which the subjection of their own body is in turn inscribed. This is probably one of the reasons why Dickens includes a detailed description of Brownlow in *Oliver Twist*: 'The' old gentleman was a very respectable-looking personage, with a powdered head and gold spectacles. He was dressed in a bottle-green coat with a black velvet collar; wore white trousers; and carried a smart bamboo cane under his 'arm' (114). Indeed, the motif of the symbolic inscription of clothes is introduced early in the text:

> What an excellent example of the power of dress young Oliver Twist was! Wrapped in the blanket which had hitherto formed his only covering, he might have been the child of a nobleman or a beggar; – it would have been hard for the haughtiest stranger to have fixed his station in society. (47)

The nature of the relationship between the one who mimics and the one who is mimicked, where the former, often through excess, is almost but not quite the same as the latter, has been of much interest to writers on colonialism.[2] The way in which it provides an opportunity for subversion and parody is as pertinent to a discussion of the swellman as the colonised. As the Artful Dodger who occupies a space that is 'not quite' on many levels exemplifies, mimicry ruptures authoritative discourse partly through its subversive dialectic with the respectable male, and partly through the presence of a subject that cannot be controlled. In Marxist cultural history, the most socially valued body is both a productive body and a subjected body.[3] The Dodger, as an apprentice swellman, redefines what is meant by 'productive' and breaks the link between 'productive' and 'subjected'. This is achieved through knowledge, however intuitive, of the way in which the body operates within a field of gendered, political forces and signifies the precariousness of that symbolic order. However, the swellman, like the colonial subject, for all his parody, remains dependent upon the symbolic order that limits or prohibits his behaviour.

How the female body operates within a wider socio-political field, being dependent upon an authoritative discourse which it frequently subverts, is evident in a number of Victorian detective stories involving a female trickster. They usually involve a respectable man being duped and then metaphorically 'skinned' by a female criminal. The actual crime of 'skinning' referred to earlier, in which a respectable gentleman who had expected sex with a prostitute was left stripped of all his clothes and belongings, is mimicked in *Oliver Twist* when Nancy apprehends Oliver in the street on his way from Mr Brownlow's house, entrusted with books and a five pound note for the book seller. Taken back to Fagin and the gang, with the aid of Bill Sikes, Oliver is stripped of the five pound note, the books and his fine clothes.

Herbert Keen's 'The Tin Box' (1896) is a particularly interesting example of a 'skinning' story for the importance it attaches to masquerade as a performance within a symbolic field in which women are defined and confined. London gent, Perkins, working in an insurance office, is duped by the wife of a forger and swellman who poses as a widow with a five-year-old child. The central trope is the unreliability of the perceived operation of the body within the wider symbolic order. Not only is Mrs Amelia Williams not what she seems but the old beggar who pursues her turns out to be Perkins's friend, intent to save him from making a fool of himself or worse. From the moment that Perkins responds to her widow's weeds rather than to the contradictions she displays, identity becomes unreliable and the boundaries of social relations precarious. Perkins sees Mrs Williams as a 'subjected' body; a stereotypical widow who has not been well catered for by her husband in the event of his death. In fact, as a criminal's moll, she is a 'productive' body, able to move from a position of subjection as a poor widow to one of manipulative, sexual power as a confidence trickster. This is especially evident in the way in which she opens and relocks her supposed husband's tin box with such speed as only to allow Perkins a glimpse of the contents – itself analogous of the brief view we have of her as a fraudster.

From a feminist perspective, Keen's widow takes control of the social discourses that define widows reductively. As such, she is an example of how the Victorian female criminal provides a cultural space in which passive femininity may be reconfigured. The sensation novel provided numerous fictional examples of independent and sexual transgressive women.[4] It also furnished incidences of women writing about female criminality. The fiction of the period, and to some extent the criminological essays, challenge any simplistic notion that women were only driven to crime through poverty, important a dimension as this was. Women also took to crime to subvert oppressive ideologies of the family, sexuality and the home, and economic factors were embroiled with class conflict and social resentment.

Victorian crime fiction is concerned with the subject's capacity to take control over received cultural meanings in constructing their gender identities. Whilst these are concerns of non-crime writing, too, fiction based around criminal behaviour more overtly explores the lines between innovation, performance, masquerade and deception as exemplified in figures such as Magdalen Vanstone in Wilkie Collins's *No Name* who has a talent for mimicry and for acting and Irene Adler in Conan Doyle's 'A Scandal in Bohemia'. In her letter to Holmes, Irene admits that she has been 'trained as an actress', and, encapsulating the threat that duplicity was perceived as posing to the male orientation of the social order, adds that 'Male costume is nothing new to me' (174–5). Thus, Victorian writing about crime provided a space for authors to explore the different ways in which conventional codes determining bodily behaviour were breaking down in the nineteenth century and undergoing a process of transformation. This in turn cast doubts upon the wider symbolic field in which the respectable and the criminal body operated.

Masculine violence as text

In British working-class fiction and social realist criminology of the 1960s and 1970s, crime involving men, is often political. Within a thinly veiled Marxist framework, young, male criminals are depicted as class rebels and the law is perceived as the instrument of an oppressive state. Usually basing their arguments on a reading of eighteenth and nineteenth-century social history, they gave the association between masculinity and criminality in both urban and rural society a particular Marxist inflection which determined the kind of crimes upon which they focussed. Generally speaking, Marxist criminologists and working-class writers emphasised crimes linked to poverty, unemployment and social occlusion such as the destruction of property, low level theft, smuggling and poaching.

From the 1980s onwards, largely through the influence of feminist cultural and social theory and the emergence of gender studies as an academic discipline, 'masculinities' became a legitimate area of research in the social sciences and humanities, open to a much broader range of perspectives. These studies recognised that 'criminality' was linked to issues around, for example, race and gender as well as class and economic inequalities. But what also brought about a seismic shift in the cultural construction of criminal masculinities was the inclusion of particularly unpalatable and unheroic male crimes such as domestic violence and child abuse. However, not only is such a focus upon 'criminal masculinities' still only developing, but the contribution that late twentieth-century cultural theory might make to our understanding of the criminal male has yet to be fully recognised. Something of the new perspective on male criminality that recent gender and body theory might provide can be gleaned from revisiting a type of male criminality that figures in nineteenth-century criminology and fiction but, like the child abuser and the brutal spouse, does not feature much in Marxist histories of male criminality in the 1970s.

It hardly needs to be said that the rapidly expanding industrial cities in Britain, or rather districts within them, such as 'China' or 'The Cellars' in Merthyr in South Wales, became bywords for crime. The 'roughs', as they came to be called, not only inhabited these areas but hung around city corners, earning themselves the title of 'cornermen'. Sometimes, they belonged to infamous gangs such as the Clock Alley Lads of Manchester. Perceived as a problem as much for their supposed involvement with burglary and prostitution as for their attacks on innocent citizens, the 'dangerous classes', as they came to be known, became a spectre that haunted 'respectable' society.[5] Part real and part cultural fiction, the Victorian dangerous classes acted as a social phantasm, returning to those who benefited from an economic system dependent upon social exclusion what was repressed. The extent to which they were a product of, and occupied, both a real and imaginary space is a phenomenon that has not been fully explored.

Transformational power

The Victorian 'roughs' had a power that was greater than they possessed in practice. It is a commonplace knowledge now that the anxiety generated by certain types of crime is often greater than their actual rate of occurrence warrants. Street crime especially arouses public fears because of its unpredictability and stories of incidents that escalated into violence.[6] As much as in the twentieth century, the public perception of crime in the eighteenth and nineteenth centuries was a product of rumour within communities and, later, press reporting.

The part played by community rumour in generating anxiety about crime enters Bulwer Lytton's *Eugene Aram*, referred to in the previous chapter, at a significant point. Aram and his lover Madeline are accosted by one of the villagers:

> Two houses at Checkington (a small town, some miles distant from Grassdale) were forcibly entered last night – robbed, your honour, robbed. Squire Tibson was tied to his bed, his bureau rifled, himself shockingly *confused* on the head; and the maidservant Sally – her sister lived with me, a very good girl – was locked in the cupboard. As to the other house, they carried off all the plate. There was no less than four men all masked, your honour, and armed with pistols. What if they should come here! Such a thing was never heard of before in these parts. (163)

What is important here is the way in which the crime is reported. It is seen as a threat posed by the 'other' – 'four men all masked' – which is itself a product of modernity, 'such a thing was never heard of before in these parts'. The crime confirms and fuels prevalent anxieties about urban criminal activity intruding into normally safe rural communities.

The Victorian press, as much as twenty-first century media, created public panics through their graphic accounts of certain types of crime. An often cited example is the reporting of 'garrotte robbery', in which victims were caught from behind in a stranglehold. The press turned what were relatively few incidents into a social phenomenon. But what has not been explored is the extent to which the reporting of street crime and burglary contributed to the cultural configuration of masculinity and criminality. This can be illustrated with reference to the way in which the Tithe Barn Street murder of 1874 was reported, originally in the *Spectator*, then copied by the *Liverpool Daily Post* and *The Times*.

The Tithe Barn Street murder case had a number of features that newspapers could stress for a middle-class readership. The victim was a married man of twenty-six at the time of the attack which occurred while he was out walking with his wife. Thus, he could readily be configured in the press as the epitome of the Victorian ideal of respectable masculinity. He is alleged to have told the man who threatened him 'to work for his money, the same as he had to', rendering himself a mouthpiece for, and defender of, the Victorian values of independence and hard work.

Features of the reporting of the case anticipate twentieth-century criminological interest in deviant subcultures. What the victim is alleged to have said to his assailant about working for his money implies that Victorian society saw the street criminal as twentieth-century deviant subculture theory sees delinquents from socially deprived areas. They are perceived as turning to crime for otherwise unobtainable material rewards and/or because they have different moral standards from the social norm. The stress in the reporting of the Tithe Barn Street killing upon the victim as a married man walking with his wife sets his masculinity in opposition to that of the attacker and street gangs and cornermen generally. The implication is that 'offending' is a masculine trait when 'masculinity' is removed from the civilizing influence of the wife/mother.

However, the presence of the victim's wife which reports of the Tithe Barn Street murder stressed not only highlights the victim as a respectable male, in opposition to the deviant male subculture, but implies something about his relationship to women. Although one of the men here is the victim, both are participants in a society where men, in relation to women, have most power and where men hold and use the means of violence. Moreover, although one of the men is a victim, the attack reminds us that violence is perceived in criminology as an important element in transactions among men and that the street is often the site for violent exchanges between different types of masculinities.

The cultural significance of the Tithe Barn Street murder is explicable in terms of what in the twentieth-century might be called 'panic theory', concerned with the way actual crime is exacerbated in community and press reports, and the way in which an event can acquire a symbolic significance that far exceeds the event itself. But the murder also exemplifies how the power and influence of the nineteenth-century 'roughs' lay in their capacity as signifiers, in the Victorian press and literature, to challenge the nation's view of itself as modern and progressing. This kind of 'transformational power', as a recent critic has labelled it,[7] depends upon the signifier being culturally, and historically, displaced from the homogenizing narratives of the nation, especially those that equate increasing prosperity and social progress with industrial and urban development. The Victorian cornerman and the rough highlight society's fragmentariness rather than unity. Their power is associated with their capacity to challenge the nation's dominant view of itself.

Thus, the street criminal who frequents twentieth-century British literature as a culturally constructed harbinger of violence, especially sexual violence, looks back to previous centuries. The worrying of women on commercial city streets by male pests was a phenomenon in which the Victorian press seemed to delight. The *Pall Mall Gazette* even printed complaints from men justifying the practice of stalking women by shifting the responsibility to the women themselves for wearing tailor-made dresses that accentuated their false bottoms and stays.[8] That part of Virginia Woolf's *The Years* (1937; rpt. Oxford: Oxford University Press, 1992), covering the Victorian period appears to pitch itself against the press' refusal to condemn male harassment of women on the streets as a criminal activity. The novel dramatises a young, Victorian girl's fear of the threat posed by a male who invokes the cornerman or Victorian ruffian, highlighting how by the second half of the century such a street predator had become for women a Victorian bogey-man. Woolf epitomises the developing concern among feminist writers that the street rough, as a social reality and a cultural phenomena, was part of the way in which a male-dominated society curtailed the mobility of women. The emphasis falls upon how the man intimidates Rose through gestures and sounds that have covert sexual connotations:

> He was leaning with his back against the lamp-post, and the light from the gas lamp flickered over his face. As she passed he sucked his lips in and out. He made a mewing noise. But he did not stretch his hands out at her; they were unbuttoning his clothes. (28)

The kind of intimidating power acquired by the Victorian 'roughs' associated with places such as Merthyr in South Wales has also fascinated some twentieth-century authors writing about later industrial England and Wales. George Orwell, in *The Road to Wigan Pier*, remembers how loud-mouthed London gutterboys could make life a misery for respectable folks afraid to answer back. But this was only one side of the coin. The power exercised by street 'roughs' was also observed by those who became seduced by them. The middle-class narrator of Leslie Norris's short story 'Johnny Trevecca and the Devil' (1978), who comes under the influence of a twentieth-century Merthyr 'rough' is such a case:

> At school I did no more work than was necessary to keep out of trouble, was not co-operative nor unco-operative: I was absorbing David's values, his attitude of suspicion and antagonism toward authority. I came alive only during the evenings when I ranged the wild streets with my new friends. (272–3)

A member of Arthur Thompson's gang, the narrator remembers: 'We lounged past old ladies sitting on kitchen chairs outside their houses ... ' (269). In other words, it is the display of idleness that is important; not 'lounging' in itself but the performance of what is perceived as an anathema to the respectable and the elderly. The twentieth-century respectable classes felt no less intimidated by the street ruffian than their Victorian and Edwardian forebears. His insolent gait and manner of behaving still appeared to mock respectable, working or middle-class sobriety and attitude toward work. Arthur Thompson's gang in Norris's story is depicted as almost stereotypical Victorian 'ruffians':

> Their clothes, frayed and patched, in rough materials, baggy at the knees, their shapeless limp collars, their worn shoes, all set them apart from me. They argued incessantly among themselves, jeering and threatening, their only purpose, it seemed to establish some sort of superiority over one another, however temporary. (269)

In this story, as in Dickens's *Oliver Twist*, it is those who are both 'different' and most powerless who most admire the gang leader: 'Lazily and tolerantly they mocked [Johnny], imitating his gait, sneering at his clothes, making obscene remarks about his sisters, his mother' (270). In other words, Johnny provides them with an opportunity to mock, under their leader's influence, what is perceived as sacred to respectable society, such as family and motherhood, as well as the conventions governing sexual behaviour.

Norris's story highlights an unexplored aspect of British crime history, despite late twentieth-century interest in the interrelationship between socially constructed bodies and identities: the extent to which the male criminal body as cultural signifier articulates with its physical material presence. One of the key developments in cultural studies of masculinity in the 1990s was an alignment of the post feminist approach to masculinity, in which it was seen within a wider a system of gender relations, with an approach which saw masculinity as emanating from men's bodies themselves.[9] At the heart of the cultural presence of the cornerboys, and others like them, is a bodily performance based on a dialect between the corporeal and the cultural.

In much nineteenth and twentieth-century fiction and non-fiction, the masculine gender is not simply associated with but originates in particular postures, certain ways of moving, and muscular shapes and tensions.[10] The different meanings and tensions that various postures can convey, from aggressive assertiveness to insolent loitering, are evident in Dickens's description of the young, street criminals in *Oliver Twist*:

> The three boys sallied out; the Dodger with his coat-sleeves tucked up, and his hat cocked, as usual; Master Bates sauntering along with his

hands in his pockets; and Oliver between them ... The Dodger had a vicious propensity, too, of pulling the caps from the heads of small boys and tossing them down areas, while Charley Bates exhibited some very loose notions concerning the rights of property, by pilfering divers apples and onions from the stalls at the kennel sides, and thrusting them into pockets which were so surprisingly capacious, that they seemed to undermine his whole suit of clothes in every direction. (113)

The tensions generated by the boys' attitudes and the ways in which they communicate through their body language is bound up here with certain ways of movement and even particular attitudes towards sex, evident in the cryptic allusions.

Studies of youth cultures in the 1970s and 1980s interpreted them as a phenomenon based upon the convergence of consumerism and a hybrid personal style. But mid-twentieth-century criminology focused on 'deviant' youth behaviour as part of a continuum of social marginality. This continuum could be traced 'vertically' within a particular period or 'horizontally' across different periods. Within this paradigm, Dickens's representation of the young, male street criminal and the Victorian roughs can be seen as part of a wider, male corporeal display. The representation of the Dodger and his fellow, young roughs stress a 'symbolic creativity' that anticipates twentieth-century youth culture, sharing the way in which a new identity is forged through particular body postures, ways of walking and holding one self, ritualised street talk and certain codes of dress. In each case, we witness what amounts almost to an 'aesthetic of deviance'. Details such as the Artful Dodger's 'cocked' hat, the sauntering and the bullying of small boys, and Charley Bates's audacious filling of his pockets with stolen fruit and vegetables become part of a larger performance designed to configure an intimidating public presence.

Outlawed muscles

The criminal, male body does not exist in its own narrative but in a dialectical relationship with the 'respectable' body. It is especially noticeable that nineteenth-century representations of men from the lower and the criminal classes focused upon their physical, threatening presence when they are juxtaposed with the middle classes. This is evident in Dickens's description of Bill Sikes:

> The man who growled out these words, was a stoutly-built fellow of about five-and-thirty, in a black velveteen coat, very soiled drab

breeches, lace-up half-boots, and grey cotton stockings, which inclosed a bulky pair of legs, with large swelling calves; – the kind of legs, which in such costume, always look in an unfinished and incomplete state without a set of fetters to garnish them. He had a brown hat on his head, and a dirty belcher handkerchief round his neck: with the long frayed ends of which he smeared the beer from his face as he spoke. He disclosed, when he had done so, a broad heavy countenance with a beard of three day's growth and two scowling eyes; one of which displayed various parti-coloured symptoms of having been recently damaged by a blow. (136)

Sikes is an inverted image of Mr Brownlow, who, with his 'powdered head and gold spectacles', is 'a very respectable-looking fellow'. He is described as 'dressed in a bottle-green coat with a black velvet collar; wore white trousers; and carried a smart bamboo cane under his arm (114). On Sikes, the modest 'black velvet collar' becomes a sinister 'black velveteen coat', white trousers becomes 'very soiled drab breeches', the 'powdered head' is replaced with 'a dirty belcher handkerchief' and the cane is exchanged for the stick with which Sikes threatens anything that comes in his way and with which he eventually kills Nancy. Whilst Brownlow appears to have no body as such, the clothes make him, Sikes's clothes seem to be locked in an argument with his burgeoning physical frame.

Dickens's escaped convict, Magwitch, in *Great Expectations*, too exemplifies the dialectic between the physical, masculine criminal body, determined by certain ways of moving and a particular muscular shape, and the symbolic configuration of criminal masculinity. At one level, Magwitch's initial intimidating appearance invokes the Victorian 'rough':

A fearful man, all in coarse grey, with a great iron on his leg. A man with no hat, and with broken shoes, and with an old rag tied round his head. A man who had been soaked in water, and smothered in mud, and lamed by stones, and cut by flints, and stung by nettles, and torn by briers; who limped and shivered, and glared and growled; and whose teeth chattered in his head as he seized me by the chin. (2)

The allusion to children's folktales, which were intended to influence and socialise children's behaviour, foregrounds the intimidation and victimisation of Pip: ' "You young dog", said the man, licking his lips, "what fat cheeks you ha' got" ' (2). Magwitch threatens Pip with his villainous friend, who is more overtly a member of the 'dangerous class' than himself; he will enter Pip's bedroom despite its locked door. Here, the text seems to be deliberately seeking to strike at the core of Victorian middle-class fears of burglary and violent crime.

The description of Magwitch is consistent with the way in which such dangerous places as the Rookeries and Merthyr's China Town were perceived as being beyond the law and the church. Magwitch's appearance opens a subversive, fictive space that becomes filled with nightmare, darkness, chaos and the supernatural through some of the stock characteristics of the late eighteenth and early nineteenth-century Gothic novel. Pip's panorama impresses on the reader a lack of boundaries:

> the dark flat wilderness beyond the churchyard, intersected with dykes and mounds and gates, with scattered cattle feeding on it, was the marshes; and that the low leaden line beyond was the river; and that the distant savage lair from which the wind was rushing, the sea. (2)

Magwitch also invokes other Victorian, male criminal types who held an inverted mirror to the Victorian social order and its championing of sobriety and respectability.[11] The tramp and vagabond were perceived as the epitome of self-indulgence and depravity, lacking the good habit of hard work and the mental attitude of independence and self-help that the Victorians sought to encourage. But, as in the case of the Victorian rough, their power lay in the dialectic between their cultural configuration, which stressed their unpredictability and the fact that they defied the dominant discourses of the day, and their intimidating, physical presence rooted in the way they moved and carried themselves. It was not that they were violent but that they conveyed possibilities of violence.

The tramp and vagabond were also inverted images of the respectable, Victorian male who regularly undertook journeys on business. Travel on business testified to the combination of technological invention, industry and gendered sense of purposefulness at the heart of the Victorian configuration of modernity. It is difficult to find a Sherlock Holmes story that does not involve travel of some sort, by cab or train. Modern forms of travel brought new pickings within easier reach of the criminal, now able to work in different areas and to take advantage of seasonal events and gatherings. But travel also brought together in close proximity to each other, social types who did not normally mix with each other so closely. The social anxiety that this generated is exemplified in one of the least mentioned modes of crime writing in contemporary criticism. The railway murder mystery was extremely popular in the mid-nineteenth century and was eventually responsible for some of the classic, twentieth-century crime stories, such as Agatha Christie's *Murder on the Orient Express* (1934) and *4.50 from Paddington* (1957).

Bearing in mind the way in which the representation of Magwitch alludes to criminalised Victorian social outcasts, an intriguing aspect of Conan Doyle's Sherlock Holmes stories, such as 'A Scandal in Bohemia' and *The Hound of the Baskervilles*, is the frequency with which he disguises himself as a figure, such as a tramp or a Gypsy, whom Victorians regarded as the antipathy of their ideals. Masquerading as figures who are social outcasts, Holmes acquires the kind of power discussed earlier in this chapter in relation to the Victorian 'rough'. Holmes is able to assert an intimidating power, rooted in new-found ways of moving and holding himself. At the same time, his performance relocates him within a different matrix of social conceptions and prejudices from those with which he is normally associated. When the masquerade is revealed, the disclosure is usually welcomed by his companion Watson. So much so in fact as to suggest that the masquerade is intended to offer the respectable Victorian classes a kind of sublimation of their anxieties aroused by the physical and social presence of the itinerant male traveller.

Holmes's masquerades work in the texts at a number of levels. His disguises are often stereotypical in that they are based upon traits by which these characters would have been known to the Victorian middle class. As such, they reinforce the notion of a dangerous, criminal class discussed in Chapter 1. They also suggest that the more the criminal social outcasts are aware of their intimidating power in society, the more they will 'act up' what they know will be intimidating. However, how they are perceived is not simply the result of their performance but their criminalising by society. At a further level, Holmes's masquerades, as suggested in Chapter 1, blur the boundaries between social classes and raise questions about society in general, especially respectable society, in relation to masquerade.

Another kind of danger

The social history and criminology that replaced the over reliance of the 1970s upon Marxist historicism rediscovered the cultural construction of masculinity.[12] From the eighteenth century onwards, it is possible to find in fiction the kind of comparison mentioned earlier of brutish, criminal men with the emergent, respectable male. The latter, by this comparison, seemed more 'feminine'. Indeed, the juxtaposition reflects cultural anxieties at different periods about the way in which new male lifestyles, focused on domesticity, sedentary occupations and regulated sports, seemed to be emasculating the male. This partly accounts for the way in which, for all his respectability, Mr Brownlow in *Oliver Twist* is an ambivalent character, himself taken for a criminal at one point in the novel, and before the law is less effective in his performance than some of the text's criminal classes.

The late Victorian and Edwardian detective story played a key role in realigning masculine and feminine polarities within public life in the light of the apparently emasculated, respectable masculinity. Together with the work of painters such as Whistler, they helped focus debates about gender. Sherlock Holmes himself is depicted at times as the kind of effeminate aesthete with which the British Aesthetic Movement and Whistler's paintings became associated and which in some quarters were seen as an affront to Victorian manly norms. The 'Precocious Beings' of the Aesthetic Movement were satirised in *Punch* in the Cimabue Browns who live in Passionate Brompton and by Gilbert in *Patience* (1881) who refers to a 'Greenery-yellery, Grosvenor Gallery, Foot-in-the-grave, young man'.[13] The effeminate nature of the 'aesthetic male' was reinforced, and at another level undermined, in the 1870s and 1880s through its association with the new, aesthetic female whose 'cultural languor' obsessed poets, painters and the press even more than her male counterpart.[14]

The feminine ideal that emerged through the Aesthetic Movement, characterised by a pale countenance and, often, long, thin nervous hands, provides an interesting commentary upon the way in which Doyle depicts Holmes's physical demeanour and highlights his ambivalent masculinity. At one level, Holmes represents that form of cultured 'bourgeois' masculinity that defines itself against what it perceives as brutish, uncivilised masculinity. In other words, he is the 'bourgeois' ideal of masculinity of which Dickens's Bill Sikes is the opposite. But elements of Holmes's behaviour cast him negatively in relation to the bourgeois, Victorian male, such as his readiness to disguise himself as what were perceived as intimidating male types and his use of cocaine, a practice that appears to undermine normative, 'manly' discipline. However, it is not only the cocaine habit itself which depicts Holmes as the 'negative' of Victorian respectable masculinity. As in *The Sign of the Four*, Doyle uses it to draw attention to Holmes's effeminate body: he has 'long, white nervous, fingers'; raises his eye brows, and later speaks, 'languidly (3 and 15); has 'drooping eyelids' (15) and suffers from the female malady of depression (17). Here, he is redolent of the new feminine ideal which was evident in so many Victorian paintings, such as Frank Potter's *Girl Resting at a Piano* (1880s), in which the young woman appears too weary and/or melancholic to do anything but isolate herself in a dreamlike, pensive state.

Holmes exhibits the two sides of Victorian masculinity: in the energy and single-mindedness he shows while on a case, he signifies the bourgeois manly ideal, but, at other times, the effeminate aesthete.[15] Holmes himself admits in *The Sign of the Four*: 'there are in me the makings of a very fine loafer, and also a pretty spry sort of fellow' (119). When Holmes is 'pretty spry', Watson is often unable to keep up with the pace; more than once he complains of being 'limp'. The counterpoint to his manly impotence is self-indulgent passivity. In response to Holmes's violin playing he 'float[s] peacefully away upon a soft sea of sound' until the feminine alliteration takes him to 'dreamland, with the small face of Mary Morstan looking down at [him]' (69).

As suggested above, in its concern with an effeminate, aesthetic masculinity, Doyle's detective fiction is of its period. An effeminate masculinity is explicitly linked to Whistler in Arthur Morrison's detective story, 'The Ivy Cottage', published nearly six years after *The Sign of the Four*. The murder victim is an artist who, in line with the satire in *Punch* referred to earlier, is 'casual and desultory' (342) and displays the effeminate side of his nature in the 'eccentric but charming decoration, obviously suggested by some of the work of Mr Whistler' (344). This story offers an interesting variant on the sensation novel motif whereby an effeminate artist is usually transformed in the course of the narrative into a more typically robust Victorian male and family man. Morrison's text kills the aesthete twice over; initially by making him the victim of the crime and, eventually, in revealing that he painted the panels not for aesthetic reasons but to disguise the fact that he has removed stolen diamonds. An aesthetic explanation is substituted by one that is much more pragmatic and in keeping with Victorian utilitarianism.

Writing about crime in fiction and criminology in the Victorian period was not perceived as distinct from each other as they are in the late twentieth and twenty-first centuries. Literature and criminology's shared concern to understand 'modernity', referred to earlier, was particularly anchored at this time in the way in which emergent gender identities were configured as the inverse of what society as a whole sought to sanction and encourage. Whilst scholarship has tended to focus upon the representation of the female in this respect, it is evident also in the way in which deviant types of masculinity – such as the 'rough', the cornerman, the street criminal and the vagabond – were configured as inverse mirror images of respectable manly dispositions. But it is also to be seen in the way in which 'negative' masculine types, such as the 'rough' and the cornerman, acquired a 'transformational power' in access of their real social impact. Thus, reading contemporaneous explorations of this phenomenon through recent identity and body theory highlights Victorian interest not simply in inverse mirroring but also in the way in which deviant masculinities, even monstrously violent masculine behaviour, articulate with respectable manly norms and actually calls them into question. This is also true of the twentieth- century gangster. The unveiled emphasis upon the dialectic within Victorian representations of masculinity reveals that what seems to have most worried Victorians was not anxiety about deviant, or even violent, masculinity, but the slippery nature of the male as signifier. In other words, Victorian concern focussed on the unreliability of manly ideals and the permeable nature of the boundaries between different signifiers of masculinity. Again, this is true of mid-twentieth-century gangster fiction.

Mobsters and molls

It may seem a long step from the Victorian street criminal to the twentieth-century American gangster. However, both draw upon melodrama in the polarising of good and evil; in the contrast between the criminal who is capable of redemption and the one who is inherently evil; and in the way in which crime is determined by the environment. Moreover, the street 'tough' of the classic, American gangster story is not a million miles from the Victorian 'rough'. Both exude a masculinity characterised by violence and both are simultaneously admired and feared by the criminal fraternity.

The British Board of Film Censors set up in 1913 was resistant to American representations of a violent, criminal underworld. However, the influence of the gangster genre was eventually seen in a range of British crime fiction from the portrayal of the anachronistic gang leader Pinkie in Graham Greene's *Brighton Rock*, to Carl Hulten in R. Alwyn Raymond's crime faction *The Cleft Chin Murder* (1945), and the young hoodlum in one of the most significant post-war British crime films, *The Blue Lamp* (1950).

The British imagination appears to have been caught by the way in which the American gangster, like the late nineteenth-century outlaws with whom they were associated, acted out a role. The young gang leader Pinkie in Graham Greene's *Brighton Rock*, a British crime novel which is both influenced by, and resists, the American gangster genre, enjoys 'performing' the role of the big-time gangster in down-town

Brighton. He also highlights a difference between the representation of the white gangster and the young, black hoodlum in crime fiction by black writers. Whilst both white hoodlums like Pinkie and black hoodlums like Jake in Herbert Simmons's *Corner Boy* (1957) become 'performers', basing themselves on big-time gangsters, in the case of the latter it is a much shorter lived part of their lives. Jake desires the material success and flamboyance that he sees white society enjoying and, through drug dealing and crime, he acquires a Cadillac but the emphasis is much more upon his dissolution and final isolation in prison.

Like the American gangsters that he imitates, Pinkie has a trademark, designed to instil fear in his victims which he demonstrates to his girlfriend, Rose:

> 'You never seen vitriol?' the Boy said, grinning through the dark. He showed her the little bottle. 'That's vitriol.' He took the cork out and spilled a little on the wooden plank of the pier; it hissed like steam. 'It burns,' the Boy said. 'Smell it' and he thrust the bottle under her nose.
>
> She gasped at him. 'Pinkie, you wouldn't – ' and 'I was pulling your leg,' he smoothly lied to her. That's not vitriol, that's just spirit. I wanted to warn you, that's all. You and me's going to be fiends. I don't want a friend with her skin burned off. (49)

This passage highlights the interrelationship between performance, criminality and the infliction of pain and, although there is no physical injury on this occasion, the kind of violence normally associated with American pulp fiction is brought into a familiar context for many British readers. Such 'theatre' frequents gangster novels. As in the opening episode of Jake Arnott's *The Long Firm* (1999), where it is called 'gameness' (19), it is an important part of breaking someone in order to demonstrate who is the boss. Here fiction and 'reality' becomes blurred. The 1960s British gangster, Eddie Richardson, remembered that hurting people 'was more about proving my manhood. It does make you feel powerful'.[16] While Arnott and Greene's novels, with differing degrees of explicitness, demonstrate what Arnott says is often absent from press coverage of the gangsters – the importance of the 'theatre' of torture to maintaining power – they also suggest the importance of sadomasochistic pleasure obtained not only from the infliction of pain but the masquerade that accompanies it.

A crucial question raised by such moments in gangster fiction is the extent to which the reader is encouraged to relate to what is going on.

The episode involving the vitriol in Greene's novel locks the reader into the violence, especially through the way Rose is traumatised by what Pinkie does. Pinkie's actions are designed to get as much emotional impact as possible from the chemical reaction of the apparent vitriol with wood, while ensuring that the hissing signifies pain and the disintegrating wood suggests burning flesh. The reader is forced, like Rose, into a situation where they are encouraged to project themselves imaginatively into a 'theatre of pain', a place where pain and the infliction of pain become the central point of consciousness.

In the vitriol episode, as in the poker incident that opens Arnott's text, we are made aware of the physical specificity of violence; that it is imposed upon a particular, individual body. This is clearly evident also in the murder scenes at the beginning of Greene's less well-known novel, *A Gun for Sale* (1936) where Raven's mechanised actions are all the more horrifying because of the way the text highlights the humanity of the subjects who are annihilated. But a more subtle illustration of this idea is the cruel joke that the assassin Raven, who is himself overtly conscious of his hare-lip, plays on the hunchbacked Alice. In purchasing a dress to suit a 'perfect' figure, Raven enters a clothes shop and an encounter with a shop assistant whose general appearance and body shape, 'a neat curved figure' (14), makes her indistinguishable from the mannequin she dresses. The hostility between them is literally embodied in their respective bodies. They are not only each conscious of their physical appearances but the way in which their bodies are located within wider signifying systems that invest them with cultural meanings. These meanings determine that different types of bodies occupy different cultural spaces. Thus, Raven is all too aware, or rather made aware, that as a disfigured, not physically impressive, man his presence in the shop is incongruous: 'She wouldn't 'sir' him' (14). Raven demonstrates how the 'freaks' of history – the criminals and the assassins as well as the deformed – serve a disruptive function within the larger discourses of power. 'Deformity' for Greene is also a matter of class: thus, the shop girl is said to have 'lisped at [Raven] genteely' (14).

The American crime novel triggered debate over what was acceptable and unacceptable 'violence' in the 1920s and 1930s in ways that had not occurred in Britain for some time. At one point, George Orwell attempted to distinguish between sadism in the crime thriller from sadism in pornography, claiming that 'unlike most books that deal in sexual sadism, it lays the emphasis on cruelty and not on the pleasure'. But in doing so, he had to confront the wider interconnection, which the American gangster genre at its best explores, between 'sadism, masochism, success-worship, power-worship, nationalism, and totalitarianism'.[17]

The theatrical element within gangsterism was inevitable, highlighting, to adapt Simone de Beauvoir's famous sentence about womanhood, how 'one is not born, but rather becomes, a gangster'. Many of the male gangsters of the 1920s and 1930s sought to re-vision their own biographical histories, together with the cultural history of America, in their own corporeal terms. George Clarence 'Bugs' Moran, who ran the North Side Chicago 'Irish gang', liked to pose for press photographs in an immaculate three-piece suit, expensive fedora and a cashmere coat; 'Big Jim' Colosimo dressed in expensive suits and draped himself lavishly in diamond jewellery; and Al Capone invented heroic tales of how he got the four inch scar on his face which inspired his nick name. According to one of them, it was from a piece of shrapnel while serving in the First World War. British gangsters followed the American lead even a generation later, indulging in what was basically a social masquerade. As one twenty-first century British newspaper columnist, reflecting on 1960s British gangsters like the Kray twins and the Richardson brothers, has said: 'We tend to romanticise gangsters as quasi-heroic figures who keep the streets safe with their rough justice, but only hurt those who deserved it and always loved their dear old mums.'[18] But their mythology was part of a wider masquerade. The Richardsons and their fellow gangsters 'dined in fine restaurants, dressed elegantly and exuded a spurious glamour that made [British] stars such as Stanley Baker and Diana Dors want to befriend them'.[19]

The social and cultural identities of the 'celebrity' gangsters confirmed gender as a fluid process of interpretation and affiliation, able to permit individual possibilities in a culture ridden with conventions and taboos. This provides a new context in which to approach not only the male gangsters but the molls and the women criminals associated with them. For many women criminals and gangster's molls, identity as something one could construct for oneself, and adapt to meet changing circumstances, was crucial for survival in an environment characterised by its unpredictability. But, at another level, women criminals in their performances and, when the circumstances were appropriate, their displays of sexual confidence and adventurousness, also mimicked the behaviour of the New Woman of the 1920s and 1930s.

The representation, including self representation, of male and female gangsters is based upon an understanding of gender identity as a product of both cultural and individual interpretation which the late twentieth-century labelled 'performative'.[20] As a combination of culturally received and self-created meanings, gangsters often reflected back to 1930s society how 'choice' was inevitably a matter of selection from, and adaptation to, various entrenched cultural norms. This was, of course, particularly true for women and some of the female gangsters of the period provided sensational performances in which cultural meanings were received and subverted. Bonnie Parker infamously liked to pose in snapshots as the deadly gun moll. Her photographs served as a direct counter to the way in which J. Edgar Hoover liked to be photographed in action poses as the heroic detective. In one photograph, she dangles a pistol from her hip and clenches a cigar in her mouth. The pose is contentiously ambivalent. The gun dangling from her hips is provocatively phallic while the cigar chewed in her mouth suggests oral sex. But like all her posed photographs, this one is self-conscious; not only in the obvious sense of the word but in her realisation of how the boundaries of the female body are bound up with the limits of social acceptability. In this respect Bonnie Parker was a product of her times.

While from one perspective American gangsters signified the beginning of a new, terrible phase in crime, from another they were romanticised, largely because of their association with the ideals of American society. The first gangster movies to emerge in the 1930s, for example, Mervyn Le Roy's *Little Caesar* (1930), William Wellmann's *The Public Enemy* (1931) and Howard Hawks's *Scarface* (1932), were primarily concerned with the American ideals of individualism, self-reliance and individual wealth. But no other connection assured the romanticisation of the gangster than their involvement in countering Prohibition in the 1920s.

One of the key literary texts linking Prohibition and the gangster in the 1920s is F. Scott Fitzgerald's *The Great Gatsby* (1926). It is well known that in the figure of Gatsby, Fitzgerald combines two mythologies: the secular myth of the self-made man and the Christian fable of the courtly Arthurian legend. The two myths act as a commentary upon each other, forming the basis of discourses in the novel around wealth, success, beauty and femininity. But one of the most important presences in the book is also the vaguest, Dan Cody, a relic of an earlier America, on whom Gatsby's re-invention of himself, and ultimately his 'performance', is based. Through Cody, Gatsby has links to the Wild West, and the kind of self-made hero that Malloy in Raymond Chandler's hard-boiled detective novel, *Farewell My Lovely* (1940), admits that he can barely remember.

Cody is an important presence in *The Great Gatsby* because he anticipates how the popular configuration of the American gangster was to become complicated in the 1930s by the appearance of a new type of criminal who flourished briefly between 1931 and 1936 in the mid-West where outlawry had been something of a tradition since the Border wars of the 1860s.²¹ Although the outlaws of the Old West had been replaced by the mid 1930s with a new style of organised crime, they continued to have a pervasive impact on the Anglo-American imagination. One of the possible reasons for this was a conflict, as in Victorian Britain referred to above, between different paradigms of masculinity. In this case, it was between a respectable, pseudo European, East coast masculinity which, through its emphasis upon self restraint and Christian civility, might be seen as emasculating, and a more overtly masculinist tradition associated with America's expansionist celebration of the frontiersman and the pioneer and defined in terms of a strong physiology.²²

In many ways, the gangsters of the mid-twentieth century recreated the Old West for a new generation more than the Western did. The Western in the early twentieth century offered faith in American myths and ideals, but it often bore little resemblance to the real frontier. The exploits of the hard-boiled gangsters of the 1930s, on the other hand, including infamous names such as Ma Barker, 'Machine Gun' Kelly, Bonnie and Clyde, Pretty Boy Floyd, Dillinger and Baby Face Nelson, and the fiction and movies about them, stressed the precarious position of the weak and the vulnerable, sectional rivalries and exploitation. Indeed, the cities in which they operated – New York, Chicago and Los Angeles – were depicted by the first pulp magazine devoted to crime fiction, *Black Mask*, as the new Wild West.

By the late 1930s, the configuration of the masculine body, on which the American hard-boiled hero was based, and its concomitant monolithic masculinity had been undermined by greater cultural consciousness of the differences which they occluded. Even in the previous decade, *The Great Gatsby* is poised between celebration of the energising, performative nature of identity and a particular performance from which the energy has begun to sap. The narrator Nick Carraway's attraction to Gatsby is undermined by his developing cynicism about Gatsby and his friends. By the time Chandler wrote *Farewell My Lovely*, which alludes at times to *The Great Gatsby*, the monolithic masculinity of Western mythology which Gatsby admired had shed much of its authenticity. Throughout Chandler's novel, the masculine tradition of self-reliance is perceived as coming to an end, reflected in the way in which it is frequently rendered in self-conscious clichés. The novel virtually opens with a fight in a bar redolent of the Western saloon brawl resulting from an encounter with a stranger. As in the Western stereotype, the barman is the frequently acknowledged presence, ominously 'rolling the whites of his eyes' (13), pretending to ignore what's going on, but all the time conscious of the shotgun beneath his bar. But the flatness is deliberate, an indication of how the vitality has seeped from the Western motif. Moose Malloy complains that 'There ain't nothing left of the joint' while the bouncer moves 'wearily, a man suddenly old, suddenly disillusioned' (14). Malloy reminds us of the lawlessness behind the Old West that was often underplayed in the mythology. He is described as 'a man who could take a bank single-handed' (16) while his own description of the bar's former glory invokes the iconoclastic West that stood in contradistinction to family and community values.

In the encounter between Marlowe and Anne Riordan, the hard-boiled tradition is itself treated ironically, in turn suggesting that by the end of the 1930s it had become recognisable as simply that, a convention rather than a bona fide response to life. The tough private investigator emerged in the early 1920s in *Black Mask*, but Carroll John Daly's project of a tough guy detective relating his own narratives was more successfully pursued by, among others, Dashiell Hammett, Frederick Nebel, Raoul Whitfield and Erle Stanley Gardner. Although these writers created a variety of hard-boiled investigators, appealing to a range of readers, they all echoed elements of the frontier myth, sharing a distrust of women, police and politicians, and often living and operating alone. Although the 1930s was the heyday of the hard-boiled detective, with *Black Mask* eventually succumbing to fierce opposition from *Dime Detective* established in 1932, the genre had become highly derivative in two senses. Not only was the formula itself over reproduced but the stereotypes on which it depended soon appeared tired and worn. At one level, the hard-boiled hero was a spectacle, something to be consumed by the reader or the viewer. But by the late 1930s and the early 1940s, the spectacle of masculinity in the hard-boiled tradition, and even the American gangster genre with which it was sometimes interleaved, seemed to be an object of entertainment rather than a subject of awe. In the early days of the genre, the homosocial aspect of the American tough guy survived ridicule because of its association with America's, initially Westward, expansionist vision. By the mid-1930s, it had become more an object of male delight, permitting the articulation of homosocial pleasure.

In *Farewell My Lovely*, Chandler parodies Fitzgerald's Jay Gatsby in the effeminate Lindsay Marriott. The description of his extravagant wealth apes Fitzgerald's novel: Marriott drives ' a huge black battleship of a car with chromium trimmings, a coyote tail tied to the Winged Victory on the radiator cap and engraved initials where the emblem should be' (44). Gatsby's 'gorgeous car' (62), 'with fenders spread like wings' (66), is 'swollen here and there in its monstrous length with triumphant hat-boxes and supper-boxes and tool-boxes, and terraced with a labyrinth of wind-shields that mirrored a dozen suns' (63). But many of Fitzgerald's details have been rewritten to make them more effeminate. Gatsby's 'elaborate formality of speech just missed being absurd' (49); while Marriott has a 'cool supercilious voice' and a phoney affectedness. Gatsby is 'an elegant young rough-neck, a year or two over thirty' (49) who favours caramel coloured suits; Marriott has 'the general appearance of a lad who would wear a white flannel suit with a violet scarf round his neck and a cornflower in his lapel' (45). Gatsby's 'tanned skin was drawn attractively tight on his face and his short hair looked as though it were trimmed every day' (51); Marriott's 'blond hair was arranged, by art or nature, in three precise blond ledges' (45).

Thus, even in the 1920s, when cases of true-life gangsters rewriting their identities were at their most common, the figure of Gatsby, based like Marlowe on Arthurian legend, signifies that the American myth of the self-made hero was losing its vitality. What had once had purpose and authenticity appears a rather shallow performance in the figure of Gatsby, as he swallows his own words in describing himself, leaves sentences unfinished, and uses phrases that Nick says at one point 'were worn so threadbare they invoked no image' (64). Not surprisingly, Gatsby and Marriott, who both meet bloody ends, have to be killed off.

In order to counter the homo-eroticisation of the male body, hard-boiled detective and gangster fiction required a female character focalisation. But as the hard-boiled male hero ceased to be the dominant paradigm of mid-twentieth-century masculinity, he failed to be as convincingly shored up by the female gaze within the text. This was partly because of the increasing redundancy of hard-boiled masculinity itself and partly because the changing socio-economic condition of women between the wars impacted on the literary and filmic representations of the female gaze. In *Farewell My Lovely*, Marlowe presents himself at the scene of Marriott's murder almost as a parody of the hard-boiled hero, to which Anne Riordan who is there before him, responds mockingly, 'Oh – a hard-boiled gentleman' (62), and teases him, 'You ask the answers. He-man stuff' (63). Her explanation that she has been looking at a man is double-edged, for the narrative at this point puts Marlowe, and the hard-boiled hero, in the spotlight. The final sentence of the section is ominous: 'There was no sound anywhere now except our steps and the girl's breathing. I didn't hear mine' (64). The implication is that while Anne represents the future, the hard-boiled detective may be the past.

Chandler's Anne Riordan also exemplifies the hard-boiled fiction's concern with the tensions and contradictions within gender relations. In some respects, she is a female reflection of the hard-boiled male hero. Like the traditional private I, she is a loner – her parents are dead and she does not have a partner. Like them, she can be self-deprecating while uncompromising in acknowledging her stubborn independence: 'I'm just a damned inquisitive wench. But there's a strain of bloodhound in me' (81). While she is presented, and represented as presenting herself, within traditional female contours, these are frequently compromised. She does not wear lipstick, is outspoken and irreverent, and is quick to adopt the hard-boiled drawl. At the end of the novel, she may throw herself at Marlowe, but she does so in a way that mirrors how the detective often unromantically picks up his girl: 'I'd like to be kissed, damn you' (250). At one point in the book, she humorously expresses the real fear that men in hard-boiled fiction have of the women with whom they become involved: 'I bet it's fun to be played by handsome blondes' (248).

In the figure of Anne Riordan, we see the hard-boiled heroine, like the hard-boiled female criminal, displaying a sexuality which is antipathetic to emergent bourgeois norms of femininity, but is also the 'other' in which masculinity must define itself. The interlinking of aberrant sexuality and criminality as a mirror for the way masculinity, as much as femininity, conceives of itself is a recurring trope in a range of crime writing that is not confined to America. It is to be found in the British literature referred to in this chapter and can be traced through the British sensation novel and the work of criminologists such as Henry Mayhew to eighteenth-century crime writings which, in stressing the allure of certain female criminal types for men, imply that it is in their masquerade that male sexuality sees its own masquerade reflected.

In this respect, the female criminal might be usefully seen as a further example of male fetishising of female sexuality which includes figures like the vampire-prostitute, who, too, are based on masquerade and performance. It is perhaps not surprising that in the 1930s, when, as suggested above, there are numerous examples of dangerous female criminals in fiction, film and the news media, the two published works concerned with the Jack the Ripper murders betray the wider social anxiety of the time around dangerous female masquerade.[23] Edwin Woodhal (1937) suggested that the murders may have been a deliberate attempt to find and kill Mary Kelly, a carrier of sexually transmitted disease, by Dr Stanley in revenge for what he believes she did to his son. William Stewart (1939) even more significantly proposed that the Ripper may have been a woman. The conclusion is less telling than the so-called evidence. Stewart argues that 'mutilation is the supreme expression of spitefulness and spitefulness is a vice to which female criminals are addicts' and that history 'records instances of female murderers whose cunning and ferocity transcends that of any male killers'.[24] In 1931, too, Sax Rohmer, author of the Fu-Manchu mysteries about a diabolical villain who seeks to take over the world, published his *Daughter of Fu-Manchu* loosely adapted for the screen the same year as *Daughter of the Dragon*. Stewart's female Ripper and Rohmer's villain's daughter are figures which bring with them a sense of 'theatre' that echoes that displayed by the gangsters discussed above. The way in which assertive women, especially sexually independent women, have been represented in literature and often 'criminalised' is discussed further in Chapter 4.

Post-war tricks

In Daniel Defoe's eighteenth-century novel *Moll Flanders*, one of the earliest examples of literary crime fiction, Moll pretends to be a rich heiress in order to attract wealthy husbands. As we have seen, this kind of masquerade, involving crossing boundaries between one social sector and another, has been a key trope in literary crime fiction ever since. It is has been especially important to understanding much criminal behaviour as an 'art' in the twentieth century.

In Emma Donoghue's incisive, feminist perspective on eighteenth-century prostitution, *Slammerkin* (2000), learning the 'tricks' of the trade is about acquiring performance as well as corporeal skills. A child prostitute is advised by her older mentor:

> Doll blew out a contemptuous puff of air. 'All the street-cullies ask is a pair of open legs, my dear. In the bawdy-houses, gentlemen are paying so high, they expect a girl to roll her eyes in bliss.' She snorted at the idea. (73)

An integral part of the prostitute's performance is her clothes:

> 'It's not us they want you, dolt!' said Doll. 'In those rags, the girl can't let on to be anything but herself. Remember, sweetheart, you should without a week of dinners sooner than pawn your last good gown.' (76)

How clothes enable prostitutes and swellmen to masquerade as more than themselves is also the subject of Sarah Waters's *Fingersmith* (2002), set in the 1860s, in which a young orphan who is brought up by thieves – 'fingersmiths' – is placed as a maid to a wealthy young heiress in an elaborate scam. The novel literally turns on a series of masquerades. The plot is for one of the thieves, Gentleman, to marry Maud, the heiress who helps her uncle by transcribing erotic books, and then for her husband to confine her in an asylum. However, the tables are turned on the maid who is incarcerated instead. It transpires that Gentleman's marriage to Maud has been engineered by Mrs Sucksby who presides over the gang in order to get Maud, who is her daughter, back. Sue and Maud were exchanged as babies so it turns out that the maid, who manages to escape from the asylum, really is the heiress.

In both *Slammerkin* and *Fingersmith*, the masquerade which mimics many of the gendered assumptions of respectable society also challenges conventional boundaries between the ideals and negative 'realities' of English society. In the Victorian period, the point was reinforced in the Cass case of 1887 in which a respectable milliner, Miss Elizabeth Cass, was mistakenly accused of street walking on Regent Street.[25] In *Slammerkin*, the gown itself is an emblem of the Janus nature of respectability. Opening at the front, the slammerkin was as much favoured by prostitutes, because it made plying their trade with street-cullies easier, as by fashionable ladies desiring the latest fashion item. The masquerade of female respectability is also evident in the play which Donoghue's heroine goes to see:

> But soon Mary had got the gist of the play. Mrs Abington was a lady who had switched clothes with her maid, as a sort of joke. It was astonishing, the difference a hat made, or an apron, or a gilt buckle. If you looked like a lady, it seemed, men bowed to you a lot, and if you dressed like a maid, they tried to kiss you behind doors. But what the maid and mistress didn't know was that the gentleman coming to court the lady had done the same swap with his manservant. So they were all liars, and none of them knew who they were flirting with, which made it very funny. (62)

Waters's principal female criminal would agree with Mary: 'When I try to sort out who knew what and who knew nothing, who knew everything and who was a fraud, I have to stop and give it up, it makes my head spin' (110). Like Dickens's *Oliver Twist*, these texts not only stress the 'othering' of fraud, deception and petty crime but the masquerade and performance necessary to carry them out. At one point, in *Fingersmith*, the mistress who is the intended victim of the scam and her supposed maid exchange roles, ironically given the denouement, as she provides her maid with some of her gowns:

> 'Oh, try it, Susan, do! Look, I shall help you.' She came close, and began to undress me. 'See, I can do it, quite as well as you. Now I am your maid, and you are the mistress!' (102)

When the maid Margaret enters the room, she mistakes Susan for the mistress: 'I should never have known you from the mistress, I'm sure!' (102) Donoghue's novel highlights how prostitution serves as a conduit for all parts of society:

> By now there was hardly a corner of the city where Mary hadn't turned a trick, from the pristine pavements of the West End to the knotted Cockney streets where Spanish Jews, Lascar seamen from the Indies, blacks and Chinamen all mingled like dyes in a basin. She'd had coopers and cordwainers, knife-grinders and window-polishers, watchmen and excisemen and a butcher with chapped hands ... Soho Square at five in the morning was a good hunting ground; that was when the lords were finally turfed out of Mrs Cornelys' Select Assemblies. (63–5)

The salient motif in these contemporary, historical crime novels that society is itself a kind of gendered masquerade in which one performance simply articulates with another, is one that runs through twentieth-century literature from modernist novels such as Virginia Woolf's *Orlando* to late-century serial killer fiction discussed in Chapter 6. In Patricia Highsmith's *The Talented Mr Ripley* (1955), the kind of articulation of one false identity with another that provides Donoghue's young prostitute with a valuable insight into respectable society has sinister outcomes. A case of mistaken identity leads the sexually ambivalent Tom Ripley being paid to persuade a profligate playboy, Dickie Greenleaf, to return home to the family business. He soon assumes the role of the Princeton graduate and professional pianist for which he is mistaken by Dickie's father but, when Dickie tires of Tom, who has developed a fixation for him, he is murdered, allowing Tom to assume his identity. Masquerade at the level of the individual signifies, like the play attended by Donoghue's Mary and Waters's allusions to a dramatisation of *Oliver Twist*, a society which is itself a giant performance:

> It was as if something had gone out of New York – the realness or the importance of it – and the city was putting on a show just for him, a colossal show with its buses, taxis, and hurrying people on the sidewalks, its television shows in all the Third Avenue bars, its movie marquees lighted up in broad daylight, and its sound effects of thousands of honking horns and human voices talking for no purpose whatsoever. As if when his boat left the pier on Saturday, the whole

city of New York would collapse with a *poof* like a lot of cardboard on stage. (23–4)

The elision of personal and a wider social masquerade is important to each of these novels, as generally in fiction which probes the role of mimicry and performance in criminal behaviour. It is a means by which the criminal seeks to attain the class–gender–race mobility which they see all around but which is denied them. Writing about criminal behaviour as performance, from the nineteenth to the twenty-first century, uses criminal masquerade to enter and challenge the larger trappings of wealth and class and employs the interweaving of the two to explore the extent to which identity *per se* is based on performance.

The most obvious author to have brought the explicit concern with masquerade and the way in which the body operates within a wider symbolic field in Victorian detective fiction into the twentieth century and to have developed it in relation to both the criminal and the detective is Margery Allingham. In many ways she acts as a bridge between contemporary writing and the Victorian fiction with which this chapter began.

The Case of the Late Pig (1937) opens with an admission by Allingham's detective Albert Campion about his 'valet', Lugg. Lugg, we are told, is a 'parole man' who, when he met Lord Pownes's valet was 'instantly inspired to imitation' (7). This confession introduces the principal tropes of 'imitation' and 'masquerade' which run throughout the novel. The anonymous note informing Campion of Roley 'Pig' Peters's funeral is 'flowery' (7); on the way to the funeral Lugg looks 'like a thug disguised as a plain-clothes man'; and all funerals are seen as having an aspect of masquerade about them. Indeed, it is the masquerade of the funeral that alerts Roley's fiancée to the fact that something is wrong. The crime itself is a confidence trick designed to dupe a conservative firm of solicitors and Lugg himself is almost killed because the corpse of one fat man looks almost like another.

The masquerade motif in *The Case of the Late Pig* is employed throughout the novel to raise questions about public behaviour and social etiquette as masks. At what is ostensibly Peters's funeral, one female mourner is in 'rather flashy black' and an elderly man in a 'topper' is said to have 'stood in a conventional attitude of grief which was rather horrible because it was so unconvincing' (13). When Campion is called to examine a corpse six months later he realises that it is Peter himself who has been 'masquerading' as Oswald Harris who has 'the manners of an enemy non-commissioned officer' (19–20). The investigation and the crime itself depend upon recognising society as a series of masks communicating with each other. As such, the text reflects the mood of the 1930s in which the Great Depression and events in Europe that would eventually trigger the Second World War had undermined public confidence in conventional social structures and the appropriateness of many traditional perspectives.

Allingham acts as a bridge between nineteenth and twentieth-century writing about crime in another sense, too. One of the novel's initial images of Lugg as a thug in a bowler not only confounds conventional, social distinctions but introduces questions about masculine behaviour and definitions of masculinity. Lugg constantly subverts the class relationship between himself and Campion: 'You're a philistine, that's what you are, a ruddy 'phylis' (8). Insisting that he does not want to be called 'Bert', Campion is addressed by Lugg as 'cock' (8). At one point, Lugg complains to his employer: 'You're getting so lah-di-lah and don't speak-to-me-I'm clever, you make me tired' (118). The relationship between Campion and his man-servant is an interesting variant on that between Conan Doyle's Holmes and Watson and between Dorothy L. Sayers's Peter Wimsey and his man-servant. But Allingham's use of the Campion and Lugg relationship to explore issues of masculine identity has echoes of nineteenth-century writing about crime. Lugg, his personal warmth notwithstanding, is always never quite the man-servant and in what Campion admits is his 'imitation' of the 'real' thing there is an element of mockery. This is redolent of the kind of mockery which nineteenth-century writers found even in the mimicry of the street criminals. Indeed, the use of the word 'thug' to describe Lugg has resonances which can be traced back to the Victorian, male street criminals who exerted a representational pressure on the respectable classes both through their physical, public presence and their reporting in the press.

However, crime writing does not only explore the larger symbolic order and its treatment of difference through the representation of the detective and the criminal. Methods of forensic investigation, which can be seen as epitomising modernity, and even the crime scene itself have provided authors with a means of dissecting the symbolic fields in which particular types of gendered power operates. And in many texts, forensic investigation and scenes of crime are exposed as masquerades. This is the subject of Chapter 3.

3
The Cadaver as Criminalised Text

The crime scene as signifier of modernity

In its emphasis upon logic and deduction, the collection and processing of information and the importance of proceeding in a planned and methodical manner, criminal investigation is the correlative of modernity, in many respects legitimating the basic principles upon which modernity is based. The crime scene is the creation of a criminal investigation process based, from the mid-nineteenth century onwards, on scientific scrutiny, analysis and classification. Milestones in forensic science include: the microscopic analysis of blood stains (1813), work on human saliva (1830s), bullet comparison (1835), the identification of poisons in body tissue (1850s), the development of tests for blood (1860s), and the analysis of human hair (1870s).

The kind of specialised analytical and microscopic work on which Conan Doyle's Holmes is often engaged in stories written in the 1880s and 1890s, however obtuse some of his actual projects, constituted the basis of late nineteenth-century forensic medicine. In the opening chapter of *The Sign of the Four*, appropriately entitled 'The Science of Deduction', Holmes reveals himself the author of several monographs on technical subjects, including 'Upon the Distinction between the Ashes of the Various Tobaccos'. Indeed, forensic science is a recurring trope in Victorian detective fiction. In Mary Wilkins's short story 'The Long Arm', the murder victim's daughter divides up the crime scene into small units for detailed examination and a principal plot element is that Sarah might be convicted through traces of blood on her dress.

Scrupulous investigation of the crime scene with the naked eye is the staple of Victorian detective fiction, especially when in many of the Holmes stories and in others such as Arthur Morrison's 'The Ivy Cottage

Mystery' (1895), the solution turns on a small detail or object that the police have overlooked. However, on closer inspection, the emphasis upon logic, deduction and scientific analysis in the literary text is often a kind of masquerade where intuition, coincidence and chance play an equally significant, if not the key, role in solving crime. Indeed, the more general equation of science, and scientifically based disciplines, entirely with logic and deduction is something of a masquerade itself. At its higher levels, science, like the arts, relies upon hypothesis, imagination and intuition.

Deceptive appearances

It is a commonplace idea that the literary scholar and the detective are not so dissimilar, but the crime scene and the modern literary text also have much in common. Each crime scene, like a literary text, has its own characteristics which will determine how it is approached by an investigator or reader. However, often at its heart is masquerade; the detective novel is basically a game between the author and the reader, as the crime scene in real life and many film and television programmes is frequently stage managed to mislead investigators. In British crime writing, Agatha Christie's Miss Marple mysteries are largely based upon the beguiling innocuous façade that the elderly spinster consciously or unconsciously creates. In American television crime drama, the much-watched *Columbo*, featuring a dishevelled, apparently disorganised detective in a crumpled raincoat solving crimes the viewer witnesses at the outset, is wholly based upon masquerade from the detective himself to the orchestrated crime scenes that he slowly deconstructs.

The masquerade that constitutes detective fiction and many real life crime scenes works on another level, too, that is akin to the human mind. Traditionally, Western culture may have stressed the rational, conscious mind but the twentieth century saw a greater emphasis upon the subconscious. This in effect turned some of what we thought we understood into a masquerade, masking the half-understood and often hidden motivators of human behaviour. This is mirrored in crime scenes themselves where each crime scene, like each text, often has its 'out-of-the-way places' in which significant traces might be found – in the crime scene behind mirrors, between seats, or under table tops. The point is well made in Mary Wilkins's 'The Long Arm' in which it is the murder victim's daughter who undertakes a search of the crime scene:

> In searching my father's room, I called to mind that saying of his, and his peculiar system of concealment, and then I made my discovery. I

have argued that in a search of this kind I ought not only to search for hidden traces of the criminal, but for everything which had been for any reason concealed. Something which my father himself had hidden, something from his past history, may furnish a motive for someone else ... I examined the bottom of the bureau, and the undersides of the chair seats .... Then I turned each of the green chairs completely over, and examined the bottoms of the legs. (393)

The literary equivalent is to search for what is in allusions and in the spaces between words and under surface meanings. The investigator might find the real keys at the margins of the crime scene, in the garbage, the laundry bags or discarded food containers; the literary critic often finds that entry to a text is through its margins.

Whilst the crime scene appears to be the exemplar of modernity – of the triumph of logic, deduction and the scientific method – behind the façade the relationship between the two is much more complex. This applies as much to the detective at the heart of the text as to the scene of crime itself. Although the detective is usually perceived as signifying the positive ideal of modernity, this has not always been the case. In the nineteenth century, the figure of the detective had an ambivalent relationship to modernity; initially they were perceived with some anxiety and linked to notions of surveillance and the power of the State. The first full-time force, eventually known as the Bow Street Runners, received a share of the reward for bringing criminals to justice, and supplemented their income by watching for pickpockets at public events and undertaking private investigations. Motivated by personal greed, they were not universally welcomed, and associated with the system of secret police, spies and agents provocateurs that had developed in Europe. Only later in the nineteenth century, did the word 'detective' begin to acquire the mystique and respect associated with the detective of classic crime fiction and even the amateur investigator was more highly regarded than the police detective.

The crime scene as negative image

Beneath its masquerade as a new-found expression of faith in scientific progress, the crime scene signified the uncontrollable and uncontrolled energies of modernity which society sought to contain and direct. However, further aspects of the crime scene challenged the apparently more humane, emergent society of the nineteenth century, referred to in Chapter 1. For, as press coverage of the Ripper murders demonstrated, the educated classes that abhorred capital and corporal judicial punishment apparently derived a kind of secret sexual pleasure from the mutilated corpse at a violent crime scene.[1] This leads us to question whether the detective story is always read for the pleasure of seeing a puzzle set up and solved by logic. The more explicit crime stories may well be read for the violent, and often sexual-violent, details that seep piecemeal into their narrative.

It is generally accepted that the first literary crime scene, in the modern sense, is to be found in Edgar Allan Poe's 'The Murders in the Rue Morgue'. In fact, it is located at the cusp of two criminal investigation methods, one emergent in France and the other well established in America. One of the reasons why Poe may have chosen to locate the story in Paris – and may have chosen to set 'The Mystery of Marie Roget' there, too, even though it was based upon a New York murder – is that the French capital had a major role in the development of nineteenth-century forensic science. It was the home of the French Department of Criminal Police, the Sûreté, whose inaugural head established the first archive of drawings of known criminals, and of Marie Guillaume Alphonse Devergie, one of the founders of forensic medicine. By the middle of the century, the Sûreté was pioneering detective methods based upon a close reading of scenes of crime – the methodology that Dupin uses in Poe's 'The Murders in the Rue Morgue' – and Devergie's *Médecine Légale et Pratique* (1835), which included the examination of violent death through rigorous observation, autopsy, microscopic study and chemical analysis, also anticipates Poe's text. In contrast to what was happening in Paris, most American crime was still solved by questioning witnesses, the other important investigative method employed by Poe's detective.

Based on a story reported in the *Shrewsbury Chronicle*, 22 August 1834, of a baboon trained to climb in windows to steal, the crime under investigation in Poe's 'The Murders in the Rue Morgue' is much more violent than any we normally encounter in detective, as opposed to crime fiction. Like other sealed room mysteries, it relies upon elements of masquerade as the author deliberately misleads and deceives the reader, encouraging them to place the crime scene in a number of narratives that turn out to be false.

The women in the story belong to an all female household; an old lady living with her daughter. This in itself undermined conventional assumptions of what constituted a household at the time and if the fact that no men are mentioned implies something subversive, this is underscored in the text by the rumour that the old lady is rumoured to have told fortunes. From medieval times, fortune telling was deemed subversive because the clairvoyant could predict the death of a leader or the defeat of a nation. But along with mysticism and intuition, also traditionally associated with women, it was marginalised by the post-Renaissance, historically masculinist emphasis upon analysis and logic.

In male-dominated societies, the representation of women is a mirror in which masculinity is reflected and defined. The representation of women in 'The Murders in the Rue Morgue' challenges not simply the nineteenth-century American ideals of womanhood but the way in which it is defined by contemporaneous configurations of masculinity in which men were associated with domination, violence and abuse. Noticeably, the public reaction to the killings in Poe's story come from men who also take the opportunity to comment upon the women themselves in disparaging ways. The tobacconist, describing the old lady as 'childish', reflects the century's tendency to infantilise women whilst allowing men licence to punish, restrict and physically abuse them.

In the real-life and fictional crime scene, various personal histories interconnect by coincidence or design. But the crime scene is the conduit of other histories too: the cultural history of crime; the history of criminal investigation and forensic science; and socio-economic history. What is at stake in the cultural analysis of the crime scene is history itself, or rather the 'textuality' of history which might be viewed as another masquerade. The crime writer, like the crime photojournalist, configures scenes of violent crime that challenge the configuration of history as a linear Grand Narrative of human progress, leaving us with the less palatable sense of the random and perilous nature of human existence. Scenes of serious crime penetrate the 'masquerade' of History, questioning its historical assumptions, our preconceptions about modernity and civilisation, and the way in which we perceive humankind. This is one of the reasons why the London Ripper murders acquired such a prominent place in the public imagination. Theories about the Ripper's identity included hypotheses that he was a doctor, a gentleman or even Royalty, each of which challenged the conventional, hierarchical social structure, whilst suggesting a dangerous interleaving of gender and power beneath the masquerade of modernity to which I shall return later in this chapter.

All crime scenes are re-presented when they become the subject of a narrative, whether in the court room or the literary text. The (re)presented crime scene persuades us to particular views of it through the way in which it is ordered and configured. The fictionalised/fictional crime scene cannot be considered independent of its contemporaneous socio-historical context(s).

The body in the text

The cadaver is situated in an uneasy relation between the identifiable and the unidentifiable and between the comprehensible and incomprehensible. In other words, there is an uncomfortably close alliance between the language of the text, which both reveals and conceals, and the body in the text. Both take us to the border of what is known and what cannot be symbolised.

In 'The Murders in the Rue Morgue', Poe has transferred the familiar violent trope of eighteenth and early nineteenth-century Gothic fiction from its traditional location in the wilderness to the city. In doing so, his tale incorporates ideas about the city which were prevalent in Britain and America at the time. Since the city was impossible to map exactly, there were inevitably dark areas where hideous and unspeakable things were thought to happen, such as the slums of London – Clerkenwell, St Giles, Stepney and Bermondsey. This way of looking at the city mirrors European, colonial cartography that divided the world into the 'civilised' and the 'savage'. The Rue Morgue is a 'by-way', a desolate and miserable looking thoroughfare, a Parisian version of those metropolitan districts that English writers like Dickens associated with crime and violence.

The official line on the Rue Morgue murders is that a crime of this nature could only have been committed by an 'other'. This is in turn used to suggest how the interlinking of crime and 'other' contributes to definitions of individual and national identities. The offender is described as having the shrill voice of 'a foreigner', possibly the voice of a non-European, and hardly an essay on this story does not draw attention to the fact that each witness identifies the criminal as speaking in a language other than his own. At the end of the story, the hypothesis that the murder was committed by a foreigner proves false. As is often the case in detective fiction, the reader realises that the story has been constructed as a large masquerade in which they have been wrong footed. But it is possible that the story is even more complex than some readers might suspect.

Read through the condition of the corpses at the crime scene, 'The Murders in the Rue Morgue', anticipating the English Ripper murders a generation later, becomes a critique of masculine violence. The injuries inflicted on the younger, and significantly more sexually desirable, of the two women in 'The Murders in the Rue Morgue' bear greater scrutiny than they have generally received from critics. There are scratches and marks on her body that appear to be made by fingers; her tongue is partially bitten through; and there is a bruise on her stomach consistent with her being held down by a knee. These injuries are suggestive, albeit in an especially maniac form, of rape, and strangulation, the method by which she was killed, is a sexual form of murder. It is now a commonplace idea, that rape and strangulation are more about control than sexual gratification.

To what extent, then, might we ask, is the murder of the old lady and her daughter symbolic? Death by violence was common in early nineteenth-century New York, often in bizarre circumstances, and the most common cause of the murder of women in New York at this time was domestic violence from men.[2] Whilst echoing familiar domestic homicide narratives of wives savagely battered to death by their husbands within conventional family settings, Poe has departed radically from them. In a more cryptic fashion than the usual domestic murder narrative, 'The Murders in the Rue Morgue' might be seen as reflecting back to society the violence which it frequently visited on women in a variety of social contexts. In other words, the masquerade is outside rather than inside the text; like the domestic murder story, Poe's tale challenges the masquerade of domestic bliss and socially accepted masculine behaviour.

While masculine violence might be reflected in the cadavers in Poe's story, the women, as noted earlier, are also criminalised by some of the witnesses. In other words, as women living together without men, they are somehow implicated in their own violent deaths. One of the most sensational contemporaneous crimes against women, and perhaps the most significant as far as 'The Murders in the Rue Morgue' as a crime story is concerned, was the brutal murder in 1836 of Ellen Jewett, a reputedly beautiful prostitute who worked in a brothel in New York. A nineteen-year-old youth was acquitted of the murder and it was generally assumed that he had been brought to trial to deflect attention from others who visited her; respectable men, or rather men whose real instincts and behaviours were hidden beneath a façade of respectability. The kind of detail which the press employed, often in extensive front page coverage, and which Poe uses in his story, was unusual in crime reporting at this time.

There is further evidence external to the Rue Morgue murders to suggest that Poe was interested in the subject of violence inflicted on women, and especially independent women. 'The Mystery of Marie Roget', published in *Snowden's Ladies Companion* between November 1842 and February 1843, concerns the death of a young woman, the sole child of a widow who worked in a perfume shop, whose body was found in the Seine. It enters into the kind of details to be found in 'The Murders in the Rue Morgue' and in the press coverage of the Jewett murder. The story is based on the true case of Mary Rogers, employed as a cigar girl in John Anderson's cigar store in New York which Poe himself might have visited, whose badly bruised body was discovered in the Hudson River in July 1841.

Mary Rogers's murder highlighted the dangers unscrupulous men posed to women, and especially single women, in mid-nineteenth-century cities. Like the Jewett murder, it exposed the masquerade of masculine respectability. Although two years before her death Mary Rogers was involved in a mystery involving a man, it was her employment in a cigar shop that aroused most controversy. Anxiety around such employment for young women was highlighted by the New York *Weekly Herald*, October 13, 1838:

> The recent affair of the young girl in Anderson's cigar store must lead every reflecting person and every good member of the community to desire that something should be done instantly to remedy the great evil consequent upon very beautiful young girls being placed in cigar and confectionery stores ... Designing rich rascals drop into these places, buy cigars and sugar plums, gossip with the girl and ultimately affect her ruin ... young ladies should attend only in those stores where the customers are ladies.[3]

The language here, though, is double-voiced. In trying to give the affair an urgency pertaining to the moment, it draws on the language of melodrama. But what is clear is that the cigar shop is regarded as a façade.

The cigar girl destabilised ideological assumptions about the city and complicated its socio-geographical boundaries. Women were associated primarily with domestic, family spaces and men with the more dangerous areas of the public sphere. But the cigar girl was evidence that the boundaries were more fluid than this; even middle-class women entered the city for shopping and work. She also reminds us that in the mid-nineteenth century, working-class women in certain public areas risked being seen as 'available'.

Ostensibly, the fictional case of the women in the Rue Morgue, the murder of Ellen Jewett, and the suspicious circumstances surrounding the death of Marie Roget do not have much in common. But they all involve women who, albeit in their different ways, were taking advantage of the new economic and sexual opportunities open to them. Ellen Jewett was generally recognised as being the one in control, not the famous clients who visited her. Their deaths, together with those of other such women in mid-nineteenth-century America, focussed public attention upon the changing roles of women; upon issues of sexual licence and abortion; and upon anxieties about the shifting power structures between men and women.

Particular aspects of 'The Murders in the Rue Morgue' bring the Mary Rogers's story to mind. In both a sailor is implicated. After Mary Rogers's death, the *Herald* reported on 3 August 1841, that while she was missing from the store three years previously it was alleged that she had been seduced by a US Naval officer. Both cases involve an all-female family. When she first went to work in Anderson's cigar store, aged seventeen, Mary lived in a household consisting only of herself and her mother – her father had been killed some years before in a steamboat explosion on the Mississippi. Both stories are linked in the ferocity of the violence which seems to have been visited on the victim. The *Herald*, 4 August 1841, describes:

> Her forehead and face appeared to have been battered and butchered to a mummy. Her features were scarcely visible, so much violence had been done to her. On her head she wore a bonnet -light gloves on her hands, with the long watery fingers peering out – her dress was torn in various portions – her shoes were on her feet – and altogether she presented the most horrible spectacle that the eye could see.[4]

It goes without saying that the victim of serious crime has always had an important, symbolic role in the definition of sexual and cultural norms. More often than not, the victim is a woman, and frequently a woman who has met her fate because she has transgressed ideological and socio-geographical boundaries. Feminist theory has led to new and complex understandings, within crime fiction and criminology, of the cultural significance of women's social location. This in turn has produced a more sophisticated understanding of how social practices determine not only gender differences but identities generally. While the physical location of the body has always been an important motif in crime fiction, twentieth-century writing has tended to emphasise its cultural or socio-geographical placement.

The Orang-utan as signifier

One of the most implausible features of 'The Murders of the Rue Morgue' is that the crime is committed by a large male orang-utan.

Possible reasons as to why Poe chose an ape are not hard to conjecture. In Christian symbolism, the ape is portrayed as amoral and contemptible; it is associated with greed and lechery and, in chains, stands for the devil conquered. But the most significant dimension in cultural representations of the ape is its capacity to parody and mock humankind. The association of the ape with mimicry has been prevalent since the Renaissance, even extending well into the twentieth century through, for example, chimpanzee tea parties in circuses and zoos, and their employment in a British television commercial for tea. Thus, the ape as a parody and mimic of humankind, seems particularly appropriate to the story where the savagery of the animal cryptically reflects the savagery of which men are capable of displaying against women. This would be commensurate with the way in which criminality is often used in literature, as discussed in Chapter 1, to mock modernity. But why did Poe choose not simply an ape but an orang-utan?

A recent critic, pointing out that in America at the time Poe wrote this story the plight of native Americans were very much to the fore, argues that the orang-utan as a 'savage' that has to be contained is analogous of how native Americans were conceived at this time.[5] However, this does not explain why Poe, in a story where attention to detail is important, chose to specify an orang-utan. The orang-utan might be seen as symbolic of a different 'savagery' from that associated with indigenous Americans in the nineteenth century – a white savagery.

Poe may have selected the orang-utan in order to suggest that men beating women in American society was part of a general cultural ethos which could be traced back to the importance accredited the frontier in American mythology. Since the name 'orang-utan' translates as 'man of the woods', it is difficult to think of any other creature as a more appropriate analogy of the American frontiersman. The orang-utan lived alone, with little social organisation, mirroring the mythology about masculinity that developed around the frontier, the chief elements of which were: man alone in contact with the wilderness, self-reliance and independence and a desire to escape the domesticity associated with women. In other words, this particular mythology of masculinity might be seen as an inverse mirror image of Eastern seaboard respectability. It encouraged men, attracted by the myth of the frontier, to think of domesticity as a trap, a curtailment of the freedom of the great outdoors which was their true birthright, and women as a potential threat to it. If the Jewett and Rogers' murders exposed Eastern American, masculine respectability as a masquerade, 'The Murders in the Rue Morgue' may be seen as revealing the masquerade of the frontier. The association of the ape with male violence would undoubtedly appear less cryptic to Poe's contemporary American readers than to twenty-first century readers where in domestic murder narratives, husbands who killed their wives were usually characterised as beasts, savages and madmen.[6]

In Poe's story, the ape kills the women with a cut-throat razor. Seen in the context of the frontier and Eastern seaboard binarism, Poe's choice of murder weapon for his story becomes significant. At one level, the razor, especially as a phallic object, is a symbol of masculinity. But it is also a symbol of the respectability that civilization, and, from one perspective women in particular, imposes on men. The cut-throat razor wielded by the ape assumes further American connotations; it is redolent of the scalping knife, and especially here where one of the women is virtually scalped. But this does not mean that we should think of the orang-utan as analogous of the indigenous American rather than the frontiersman. Although the practice of scalping one's defeated enemies was initially associated with indigenous Americans and with Hispanics, it became linked eventually with Anglo-Americans when Government money was offered for the scalps of indigenous Americans who were deemed troublesome to the colonial enterprise.

Moreover, in indigenous American practice, the taking of the enemy's scalp, symbolic of removing their head, was a way of insulting the defeated. The purchase of the scalps of native peoples by white Americans returned the insult as it were. Thus, the near action of scalping the women in the story can be seen as a symbolic insult to women by (supposedly) a frontiersman (represented by the orang-utan) who would perceive independent women as a threat and an all-female household as an icon of female power. The daughter's body is stuffed up a chimney, and it may be worth remembering at this point that the chimney rock – a tall slender formation of stone – was a sign that the traveller was leaving the American Prairies and entering a new kind of territory, the Wild West. The point in the story where we discover what has happened to the young woman at the crime scene is also the point where we enter a new type of territory as regards the boundaries of crime. The chimney, as Freud was to point out much later, has sexual connotations. If this murder were committed by a man who sees these independent women as a threat, then ramming the body up the chimney, analogous of a man violently entering the female vulva, is a perverse expression of his frustration and fear.

Given that American readers were familiar with the injuries that men might inflict on women through domestic murder narratives, one has to ask, why did Poe choose to write about male violence, if we accept that this is what he is doing, so cryptically? It is very probable that Poe chose to link the Rue Morgue murders to male violence against women in such a cryptic way for two reasons. First, especially in the light of some of the newspaper coverage and popular fiction which tended towards melodrama and sensationalism, Poe might have been wary of producing a more explicit story that could have inadvertently legitimised what he sought to criticise. As a writer interested in contemporaneous notions of beauty and the sublime, he could not but have been aware that, as in his own work, Gothic fiction characteristically linked violence, pain, sexuality and desire erotically together. Second, not all press coverage was sympathetic to Mary Rogers. The New York *Advocate of Moral Reform* (1 September 1841), published by the Society of Ladies, turned her story into a thinly veiled warning to women who turned their back on the House of God, failed to honour the Sabbath and went with profligate men.[7]

Writing the Ripper

The way in which the New York *Advocate* turned the murder of Mary Rogers from a crime that exposed the masquerade of nineteenth-century male respectability into a warning against women who wore their respectability as a masquerade is not untypical of the way in which the female victims of serious sex crimes were and are still configured. This was certainly true of the prostitute victims of Britain's first serial killer in London in the 1880. However, as prostitutes, they were not simply implicated in their own murders, but 'murdered' a second time in the voyeuristic press.

The graphic reporting of the killer who became known as Jack the Ripper stimulated public interest on both sides of the Atlantic in horror fiction. It initiated a trend that was interrupted in Europe by the impact of the First World War when the public lost some of its appetite for body horror. The Ripper's appalling mutilations were usually placed within one of two principal narratives that are not mutually exclusive: a sexual gratification paradigm or a narrative about medical knowledge. But what is as disturbing as the crimes themselves is the way in which objective rational reporting of them itself became a masquerade.

The Star at the time suggested that injuries inflicted on Mary Nicholls, for example, could only be the work of some kind of sex beast or maniac:

> The throat is cut in two gashes, the instrument having been a sharp one, but used in a ferocious and reckless way. There is a gash under

the left ear, reaching nearly to the centre of the throat. Along half its length, however, it is accompanied by another one which reaches around under the other ear, making a wide and horrible hole, and nearly severing the head from the body. The ghastliness of this cut, however, pales into insignificance alongside the other. No murder was ever more ferociously and more brutally done. The knife, which must have been a large and sharp one, was jabbed into the deceased at the lower part of the abdomen, and then drawn upwards, not once but twice. The first cut veered to the right, slitting up the groin, and passing over the left hip, but the second cut went straight upward, along the centre of the body, and reaching to the breast bone.[8]

Although the unfathomable murder is supposedly beyond description, the reporter does his best to cater to the voyeurism of his readers. The account interleaves anatomical fact with interpretation, stressing that the murder must be the action of a maniac and employing words such as 'ferocious', 'reckless' and 'jabbed'. There is an uneasy tension, which was to prove significant in the mythologizing of the Ripper, between brutality – there are 'gashes' even a 'wide and horrible hole' – and the language of the dissection room. There is an uncomfortable elision of surgery, butchery and sexual assault which is also to be found in the reporting of the most horrific of the killings, the murder of Mary Kelly:

The poor woman lay on her back on the bed entirely naked. Her throat was cut from ear to ear, right down to the spinal column. The ears and nose had been cut clean off; the breast had also been cleanly cut off and placed on a table which was by the side of the bed. The stomach and abdomen had been ripped open, while the face was slashed about, so that the features of the poor creature was beyond all recognition. The kidneys and heart had also been removed from the body and placed on the table by the side of her breasts. The liver had likewise been removed and laid on the right thigh. The lower portion of the body and the uterus had been cut out and these appeared to be missing.[9]

Of all the details that might have been selected, the report begins with the information that she was not simply 'naked', but 'entirely naked'. This positions the reader in a particular voyeuristic position in relation to the account that follows. The report interleaves the methodical, echoing the anatomy room, with the manic. The description begins with connotations of sadistic misogynism, the displacement of intercourse and the disfigurement of the face. It concludes with a more neutral, anatomical description.

The link between the butchering of women and the butchering of animals was reinforced by the location of the majority of the murders in proximity to slaughter houses. The police constable who discovered Eddowes' body allegedly reported that 'she was ripped up like a pig in the market'[10] The metaphorical connection was exploited by the press and taken seriously by the police who made a point of visiting butcher's shops. The idea of a man gaining satisfaction from entering women with a knife and going on to abuse them ruthlessly after the first insertion mirrored the way in which some men approached sexual relationships, especially those who made use of prostitutes. The violent abuse of prostitutes might be perceived as an inverse image of caring sexual relationships, but it also serves as a mirror to many so-called 'normal' relationships that are not what they seem. Like Poe's work, and the domestic murder narrative, press coverage of the Ripper murders exposes the salient cultural image of male female relationships, as part of a positive family ideal, as masquerade.

Thus, the voyeurism which was displayed in press coverage of the Ripper murders implicates not only the press but the reading public in the killings. The murderer himself becomes less an 'other' than as first conceived, impelled it would seem by a more extreme form of the misogynism in the reading public to which the press panders. In the graphic press descriptions of the victims what is fantasy in the reading public is brought up against the limits of realisation. Many respectable gentlemen who read those accounts may have been users of prostitutes, some of them frequenting brothels specialising in sadomasochism. Many of them would have been regular abusers as well as users of prostitutes, some of them in the kind of locations to which the Ripper took his victims. Others probably pushed back the boundaries of their fantasies in each one of their encounters. The reporting of the Ripper murders probably reminded some of these men of the sadomasochistic violence of their fantasies.

Thus, the Ripper murders, like the Rue Morgue murders, have roots in wider masculine behaviours and the way in which some men masqueraded as respectable, caring husbands but in reality indulged themselves with prostitutes and committed acts of domestic violence. The masquerade which is an inevitable part of the 'theatre' of courtship and sex has its mirror image in the brothel and the street walker. The prostitute's 'trick' is to be what her client wants her to be or to be interested in his fantasies and desires. For that reason, the figure of the prostitute provides writers with opportunities to explore the fluid relationship between fantasy and reality.

But public anxiety about what went on beneath the masquerade of respectable relationships and respectable male behaviour was nothing as compared to a wider public concern about the masquerade of a caring, interested medical profession. It was not long after the first murder that the Ripper was also suspected of having medical knowledge rather than simply butchery skills. *The Star* at the time of the second murder suggested, erroneously, that organs had been removed from the body but this was certainly the case in some of the murders. This aspect of the killings raised the level of public anxiety over the medical profession using organs from bodies for medical research and teaching. In the murder of Annie Chapman, her intestines were severed from their mesenteric attachments and placed at the shoulder of her corpse while the upper portion of her vagina and part of her bladder were entirely removed.

Twentieth-century cadavers

Although the Ripper murders appalled their contemporaries, from the mid-twentieth century onwards, crime writing has brought readers closer to the violated body, which in both male and female authored texts is usually a female cadaver. That the victim of serious crime is likely to be a woman is true across a range of writing about crime. One can think of Marion Crane in Robert Bloch's *Psycho* (1959), Ghislaine in Angela Carter's *Shadow Dance* (1966), Lori Peterson in Patricia Cornwell's *Postmortem* (1990), Mrs Nugent in Patrick McCabe's *The Butcher Boy* (1992), a family in Lynn Hightower's *The Debt Collector* (1999), and the inhabitants of an entire female community in Toni Morrison's *Paradise* (1998). Very often, the female victims are 'criminalised' and punished for their independence and assertiveness.

Like the Ripper murders in which some authors such as Patricia Cornwell have expressed an interest, the forensic investigation novel provides crime scenes in which what has happened to the female corpse indicts a larger symbolic order for the victimisation and criminal abuse of women. Although novels of this type reflect a trend that in Britain began with P. D. James towards a new-found emphasis upon forensic science, they belong to an older tradition of violent crime fiction that can be traced, through reporting of the Ripper murders, back to Edgar Allan Poe. Here, violence against women exposes, consciously or unconsciously, the wider masquerade of masculine respectability. Like Poe's work they are dependent upon a very old idea: the body as 'text'.

The forensic crime novel highlights how the most innovative and insightful crime fiction self-consciously positions itself in the interpretative space that the corpse and the text share. However, this is not an achievement to which the forensic crime novel alone can lay claim. Indeed, one of the most intriguing deconstructions of the body-as-text/text-as-body can be found in the last novel of what until then had been a traditional and very formulaic, British detective series where it is linked to slippages in, and deferrals of, meaning. Colin Dexter's final Inspector Morse novel, *The Remorseful Day*, in which the tabloid press actually invokes Jack the Ripper but gets the dates wrong – 'Would we still be reading about the Ripper if we knew who it was who murdered and mutilated a succession of prostitutes in the East End of London in the 1870s' (37) – points in a direction of travel which more crime fiction may take in the future.

The Remorseful Day opens with an episode located years earlier than the period in which the investigation of the murder occurs. The reader is led to believe that Morse was once friendly with Yvonne Harrison who, outside her caring professional life as a nurse, is something of a sex addict. She has her own collection of pornographic videos, some of which, it is implied, feature herself, and an enthusiasm for bondage. It would be possible to see Yvonne's life as a nurse as a kind of masquerade behind which she is something very different. But the novel offers a more interesting reading; she is like the bird that the older, dying Morse watches through his binoculars – 'variegated'. This is not to suggest, though, that Dexter is not interested in the concept of masquerade *per se*. Throughout the novel, the reader is teased with the possibility that the cerebral Morse might be something of a masquerade and that he had himself participated in bizarre sexual fantasies with his former nurse. Although this eventually proves not to be true, the contradictory nature of people is a salient trope in the text.

Instead of asking how bizarre is bizarre, the reader of Dexter's last Morse novel is encouraged to ask how strange is S/strange, as it is Chief Superintendent Strange who turns out to have been having an affair with the nurse. Indeed, it is his handcuffs that she is wearing at the time of her murder but in a bondage fantasy with someone else. The clue is there near the beginning of the novel when his secretary thinks of him as 'Strange by name and strange by nature' (43). However, if her death is intended as some kind of retribution for her independent sexuality, as is often the case in crime narratives, Yvonne's sexual practices are not 'othered'. The novel inverts the stereotype in violent crime fiction of the male killer initiating and imposing bondage on his female victim, which is how the police initially interpret Yvonne's murder. Her killer proves to be her outraged daughter motivated by discovering her mother's affair with her own lover.

The suggestion with which *The Remorseful Day* teases the reader – that Morse is a masquerade – is part of a much wider playfulness in the novel that seems intent upon exposing the whole Morse series as a masquerade, which of course at one level the reader always knew it was. As was suggested above, the book is littered with allusions, various kinds of textual errors – from copy editing mistakes in newspaper articles to a spelling mistake on the cross over Yvonne's grave – and slippages in meaning at every level from reports to private conversations. This highly self-conscious text appears to undermine the Morse formula that Dexter established through his previous works. He has even moved the traditional location of the body of his text – in both senses of the word. He has shifted his corpse from Oxford itself to a Cotswold village and from the British detective genre to American (or Americanised) crime fiction in which sadomasochism situates the body in the text and the body of the text at the interface of a number of modes of writing including sexploitation fiction.

Dexter's previous Morse novels appeared to look backward to Agatha Christie; even in *The Remorseful Day*, Sergeant Lewis, like Conan Doyle's Watson the hapless reader within the text, looks forward to 'the prospect of a big, fat juicy puzzle like the first page of an Agatha Christie novel' (52). However, while the body in Agatha Christie's novels was forever turning up in unexpected places – the library and even the vicarage – murder, unlike in *The Remorseful Day*, was still comparatively restrained, motivated by personal greed or ambition, without involving anything especially savage or kinky. But the blurred boundaries between the respectable and the non-respectable fascinated Christie too, in whose work the unnaturalness of woman as woman and the notion of gender as a, sometimes grotesque, performance anticipates Angela Carter's writing, to which I will return in a moment.

In Christie's *The Body in the Library* (1942), there are hints of extreme violence: 'the blue swollen face', 'the distorted cheeks', 'lips looking like a gash', and 'blood-red' nails. Everyone in the story takes the body to be that of a hotel dance hostess called Ruby Keene, except of course Miss Marple who alone notices the victim's bitten nails. She realises that it is the body of a schoolgirl whose charred remains the police thought had been recovered from a burned out car in a totally separate incident. Much of the story is an unravelling of the location of Ruby's body in life, situated in a space she constructed for herself – for she is indeed dead – between her public name 'Ruby Keene' and her so-called real name 'Rosy Legge'.

Since Poe's 'The Murders in the Rue Morgue', literary murder has often positioned the corpse on the edge of boundaries, if not boundarylessness. The British writer Minette Walters's *The Breaker* (1998) contains photographs and a map of the foreshore on which the body is washed up; the Anglo-Italian writer Magdalen Nabb's *The Marshal's Own Case* (1990) is an investigation begun with the discovery of a body on a refuse tip on the edge of Florence; and the American writer Suzanne Berne's *A Crime in the Neighbourhood* (1997) is based upon the discovery of a child's body on wasteland, among 'broken bottles, locust husks, and tangled creeper vines', behind a suburban shopping mall (2).

The location of the body has always been a site of contention, both in terms of detective logic – did the crime occur where the body is found or elsewhere? – and deductive logic, what are the social, cultural and biological truths legitimated/challenged by this particular body? In crime writing, it often highlights the location of the body of the victim in her/his life prior to the murder. The victim on the beach in *The Breaker* turns out to have had a secret life beyond the boundaries of her apparent conventionality. Or it challenges our perception of 'reality'. The body discovered on the Florence refuse tip proves to be that of a pre-operation transsexual and the boy killed behind the shopping mall serves to defamiliarise the ostensibly safe suburbs of Spring Hill.

In the location of the corpse, all kinds of discourses and ideological narratives criss-cross and intersect including the symbolic role that the victim of serious crime has traditionally played in the construction of moral and sexual norms. In contemporary writing, crime is likely to be a vehicle whereby traditional boundaries, cultural assumptions and social norms are called into question. But in its focus upon the location of the body in social and cultural discourse, it has introduced a new interest in the relation of the body to the deconstruction process itself.

At the end of Angela Carter's parodic, Gothic text, *Shadow Dance*, Morris, in many ways the innocent dupe, returns to the basement of a derelict house where Ghislaine lies, murdered by the androgynous Honeybuzzard who had earlier slashed her face:

> The candles were burning low, dribbling wax like running noses, long tears of wax. There was a thick, rich smell of melted tallow .... A collapsible trestle table had been assembled in the middle of the floor ... Naked, Ghislaine lay on her back with her hands crossed on her breasts, so that her nipples poked between her fingers like the

muzzles of inquisitive white mice. Her eyes were shut down with pennies, two on each eyelid, and her mouth gaped open a little. There were deep black fingermarks in her throat. With pity and tenderness, for the first time unmixed with any other feeling, Morris saw her fingernails were bitten down to the quick and how shadows smoothed out the cratered surface of her cheek and how the chopped tufts of golden hair had grown no farther than an inch or so below the ears and how there was soft, blonde down on the motionless flesh of her stomach. (177)

Ghislaine's corpse is laid in mockery of the living, leaking body suggested in the imagery of the candles and the violated body signified by the finger marks and the facial scar. Yet what further locates this body is not the grotesque basement or the makeshift chapel of rest, where Honeybuzzard plays out his own bizarre fantasies on a corpse, but, as in Christie's *The Body in the Library* referred to earlier, the fingernails bitten down to the quick. They situate Ghislaine in a psychotic world from which there was no escape for her, and where desire had been transmitted into death. Once it is deconstructed, the trajectory of Ghislaine's dead body is her suffering body in life, her agony in a matrix of unintelligible drives.

The forensic mirror

The position in which Yvonne Harrison's body is found – by 'position' I mean both the body in situ and as a subject of discourse – reminds us that there is a long tradition in the popular culture of female eroticism of playing with sexual violence. The suggestion that Morse might himself once have been a participant in such sex games takes us back to another aspect of female eroticism, female pleasure, actual or imagined, obtained from enslaving the male. In Daphne du Maurier's *Jamaica Inn*, Mary Yellan takes pleasure in contemplating her uncle standing powerless with his hands bound behind him. But erotic writing targetting heterosexual males deliberately or inadvertently mines sadomasochism for metaphors of the subjection of women to patriarchal, even imperialist, authority.

Yvonne's bondage might also remind us of Patricia Cornwell's debut crime novel, *Postmortem*:

> Lori Peterson was on top of the bed, the blue-and-white spread hanging off the foot of the bed. The top sheet was kicked down and bunched beneath her feet, the cover sheet pulled free of the top corners, exposing the mattress, the pillows shoved to the right side of her head. The bed

was the vortex of a violent storm, surrounded by the undisturbed civility of middle-class bedroom furnishings of polished oak.

She was nude. On the colourful rag rug to the right of the bed was her pale yellow cotton gown. It was slit from collar to hem, and this was consistent with the three previous cases. On the night stand nearest the door was a telephone, the cord ripped out of the wall. The two lamps on either side of the bed were out, the electrical cords severed from them. One cord bound her wrists, which were pinioned at the small of her back. The other cord was tied in a diabolically creative pattern also consistent with the first three cases. Looped once around her neck, it was threaded behind her through the cord around her wrists and tightly lashed around her ankles. As long as her knees were bent, the loop around her neck remained loose. When she straightened her legs, either in a reflex to pain or because of the assailant's weight on top of her, the ligature around her neck tightened like a noose. (14)

Here, as in press coverage of the Ripper murders, an unashamed voyeurism is combined with the precision of an autopsy report. The position of the body, like the body of the text itself, points in two directions at once – towards a precise physical location and toward a signified location. The first signified location is constructed by the sadomasochism inscribed in what is done to the body. The way in which Lori is bound suggests a perverse variation of the foetus, while she is tied not with ropes but cords (suggestive of the umbilical cord), one of which is even severed. The precision in which she is bound turns her into a kind of knot, a knot which Scarpetta has to tie herself, imaginatively, before she can untie it. There is a danger in doing so, for the cord is 'diabolically' bound. For the reader, the danger lies in the knowledge about the psyche and about society that is reflected back to society by this pattern of killings. The disorder of the bed, which stands in contradistinction to the civility of the middle-class bedroom furnishings, suggests chaos within the heart, or rather the masquerade, of suburban America, a recurring motif in Cornwell's work.

At one level, the serial murders in *Postmortem*, like those of the Ripper, become case studies in sexual perversion. The psychological profile that is drawn up of the killer suggests someone who is unable to enjoy 'normal' relationships:

> He's the type to pick up a woman in a bar, have sex with her and find it frustrating and highly unsatisfactory ... . He would gain far more

satisfaction from violent pornography, detective magazines, S&M, and probably entertained violent sexual fantasies long before he began to make the fantasies reality. The reality may have begun with his peeping into the windows of houses or apartments where women live alone. It gets more real. Next he rapes. The rapes get more violent and abusive with each victim. Rape is no longer the motive. Murder is. Murder is no longer enough. It has to be more sadistic. (95)

But through the forensic psychologist, the novel, reflecting a characteristic of modern crime writing, takes the reader from a narrow focus upon the erotic maniac to an analysis of the environment that created him. This includes his personal biography – he may have been abused either physically or emotionally by his mother – and the wider world in which he lives, where an entertainment industry caters to sexual fantasies, violent pornography circulates and casual sexual relationships are the norm. But although Cornwell's novels have increasingly pandered to a wider social and cultural paranoia among the middle classes in the South about how society is developing, the possible links are only suggested and the novel avoids any simplistic causal association between the two. What they do, though, is to perform two acts of mirroring back to society, through the lives of the killer and the victim(s), the kind of culture the west has created beneath its masquerade of progress.

Location of the corpse is equally important in Magdalen Nabb's *The Marshal's Own Case*, referred to earlier, where the Marshal investigates the murder of the transvestite prostitute, Lulu, in Florence whose dismembered body is found on a refuse tip. Nabb's novels take the reader through and behind the masquerade of the tourist and cultured city. In this particular text, details of the Florence transvestite prostitute community, initially described as 'large, but closely knit and virtually closed to outsiders' (42), are gradually leaked into the story. The Marshal's phobias about this community are also the prejudices of middle-class Florence. The autopsy establishes that the victim had been killed and dismembered somewhere else. Thus, the body of the victim has more than one location, mirroring the way in which Lulu had different 'locations', or masquerades, in life, associated with her given and assumed genders.

In *The Marshall's Own Case*, the reader is confronted with what is a recurring motif in late twentieth-century crime fiction and can be traced back to the Ripper murders. The bodies of the prostitute victims in Nabb's Florence and the Ripper's London are located not only where the corpse was found but in the spaces in which sex work is practised. Yet there are symbolic links, in, for example, the location of Lulu's corpse on a refuse tip and the proximity of most of the Ripper killings to the slaughterhouses in London's Whitechapel, between the scene of crime/the scene of the corpse and the location of the body in life; the place of death or of the disposal of the corpse reflects the marginalisation of the prostitute in life.

In the account of Lulu's bedroom, there is a similar dialectic between the order and chaos as in the bedroom of the victim in Cornwell's *Postmortem*:

> The double bed was unmade, but if the room was in disorder it was the disorder of opulence rather than squalor. The crumpled sheets were silk and the open wardrobe was crammed with obviously expensive clothes, including one compartment bulging with furs. (68)

Here we have tension between opulence and the middle-class lifestyle and the sexual practices signified by the disordered bed and the pornographic videos. One part of the autopsy report locates Lulu in the facts of her/his death – blows to the head, the administration of a sleeping draught mixed with red wine, and the dismemberment of the head and the limbs with an electrically powered saw (64). The other side of the report, as it were, locates the victim in her/his fragmentary identity and in the open process of the construction of her/his gender: s/he is anaemic as a result of the constant administration of female hormones, and has artificial breasts of silicone. In order to reconfigure the subject as s/he was in life, the police have first to dismember her/him further in death. The way into her/his identity in life is through her/his organs in the dissection room.

Crime, the cadaver and postmodernity

Perhaps one of the reasons why forensic crime novels have secured such a firm readership is that the twin processes involved in reading them are those which have traditionally been associated with the dissection room. Traditionally, the principal tools of anatomy are the mirror which reflects back to the surgeon what has been dissected and the scalpel that is essential for penetrating beneath the surface and rendering the invisible visible.[11] At one level, the 'culture of dissection' which, as one writer has said, has determined the modern culture of knowledge, means that the reader, the forensic investigator, and the victim all participate in the same ontology.[12]

Like the Renaissance anatomist, contemporary crime fiction's pathologist penetrates the surface, as does the reader, to reflect back to society, as the text does to the reader, what are troubling 'realities'. The Renaissance dissection theatre challenged deeply held beliefs and traditions. In many contemporary crime narratives, conventional life styles, traditional sexual practices and family norms are traduced in what the body reflects back to the reader. In the Renaissance, the process of dissection brought about a reconfiguring of the human body which affected the way in which society as a whole saw its 'reality'. In forensic detective fiction, too, the human body is a place for re-organization.

However, contemporary forensic crime writing brings fragmentation to the table in the form of a dismembered corpse. The dismembered corpse reflects the demise of the knowable, coherent subject in postmodernity, suggesting that the fragmentation of the self is somehow inevitable. But even in modernity, the mutilated corpse, as in the Ripper murders, mirrors the social and psychic fragmentation of the lives of the victims. If we look at these lives outside the imposed moral frameworks of the Coroner's inquests and the police, we are presented not with the dismemberment of a whole person but one whose life was already in pieces.

With the exception of Mary Kelly, generally believed to be the last victim, the majority of the Ripper's victims were middle-aged and a common feature of their biographies is that they were separated from their husbands and had no means of providing for themselves other than by prostitution. Martha Turner, who had been separated from her husband for only a few months, had three children to provide for and Mary Ann Nicholls struggled with a drinking problem. On the night she was killed, like Annie Chapman, she had been turned out of her lodgings. Catherine Eddowes had only been released for less than an hour from Bishopsgate Police Station on the night that she was killed, having been arrested earlier that evening for drunkenness. Elizabeth Stride, born Elizabeth Gustafsdotter in Sweden, had married a carpenter in 1869 and for nearly ten years they kept a coffee house in Poplar. But after her husband and three children were drowned when the steamer Princess Alice sank in the Thames, she found herself on the streets. Kelly's relationship with a man had broken up because she invited another prostitute, who drank heavily, to share her room. Like the others, she had great difficulty paying her rent – in fact, her body was discovered by a man sent round by her landlord to collect arrears of thirty five shillings.

Robert Bloch's *Psycho* (1959), to which I will return in Chapter 6, is a key text in this discussion of fragmentation. The author of a short story,

'Yours truly, Jack the Ripper' (1943), Bloch was himself, like Patricia Cornwell, interested in the Ripper murders. The murder of Marion Crane, who is having extramarital sex with a man for whom she steals from her employer, appears to be an example of the symbolic punishment of the sexually transgressive woman. However, Bloch's novel highlights the difficult and fragmentary nature of Marion's life. She lost opportunities to go to college when her father was killed in a car accident, and to marry when her boyfriend did his national service. The principal image with which she is associated in the early part of the novel is a broken mirror: 'She'd thrown something at the mirror, and then the mirror broke into a thousand pieces and she knew that wasn't all; *she* was breaking into a thousand pieces, too' (15). This scene is recalled when Marion, having stolen her employer's money, looks in her car rear-view mirror as she approaches the Bates's hotel where she is murdered: 'In the mirror after mom died, when you went to pieces – ' (20). It is the emphasis upon the dismemberment of a body that is already dismembered, and not simply the explicit violence, that marks the significance of the shower murder scene. The fragmentary nature of her life is reflected, too, in the way in which Norman Bates gathers her belongings: 'He found the shoes, the stockings, the bra, the panties. ... Now what? Kleenex, hairpins, all the little things a woman leaves scattered around the room. Yes, and her purse' (42).

Thus, the boundary between forensic investigation in modernity and postmodernity is not decisively drawn. On each side of the postmodern fence, a fragmented body reflects a fragmented life. Whereas the Renaissance witnessed the dissection of the ostensibly coherent humanist subject, modernity and postmodernity shares its concern with the extent to which the coherent humanist subject is, and always was, a kind of masquerade and with the dissection of what was, beneath the illusion of coherence, already in pieces. Thus, a pertinent question to ask is, what does contemporary crime fiction, increasingly foregrounding the autopsy, offer the reader against the dismemberment of the self? Its response seems to be based upon what is entirely negative, manifesting itself through motifs of death, dissolution and disappearance.

In contemporary crime fiction, dismemberment is what happens to the body at the hands of the killer, but it is also the 'reality' of the autopsy and a fact of the victim's life. The more that Patricia Cornwell's forensic investigator, Kay Scarpetta, in *Postmortem* insists that she 'knew every inch of Beryl Madison' (5), the more she comes to realise how little she really knew about her and that the Beryl Madison she thought she knew was a masquerade. In the autopsy room, Beryl's body is dissected a second time, but in the investigation of her life she is dissected a third time. In the process, Beryl Madison, at least as far as she has been known to Scarpetta, is slowly annihilated. Contemporary accounts of violent crime, especially in the forensic investigation genre, often point in more than one direction simultaneously. While the medical–legal dimension foregrounds the destroyed body, the moral–emotional discourse in the text seeks to recover the presence of the individual. But, the rediscovery of the individual rarely involves finding a coherent, knowable self. If anything, it achieves a deeper understanding of the nature of the 'self' in its postmodern fragmentation. The presence of the individual is not rediscovered in the traditional coherent subject but in the postmodern fragmented subject.

What also emerges in the biographies of the murder victims from the murdered Whitechapel prostitutes to Bloch's Marion Crane, Cornwell's Lori and Nabb's Lulu, is a fluid and performative sense of gender identity. This is not itself the product of postmodernity but of the intersection of criminality and identity in modernity. The coherent sense of self presented by Marion and Beryl, and initially by Norman Bates and, presumably, Beryl's killer in society, hides a life actually based upon fragmentation and dissolution.

The fragmentary life that is revealed is often, especially in the case of women victims, 'criminalised' as a result of its fragmentation. It is interesting to note how the covers of popular crime novels where criminality and sexuality are interleaved imply the criminalisation of the female victim even before the reader begins the text. Patricia Cornwell's *Postmortem* tries to grab the (supposedly male) reader's attention with the back view of the upper body of a naked woman, apparently standing with her hands bound behind her back with a rope that is routed around her neck. Again the image seems designed not only to appeal to a sadomasochistic fetish but to make a comment on the woman's (perhaps secret) sexuality as there is no suggestion of coercion in this photograph. The criminalisation of female desire and of the sexually independent woman is explored further in Chapter 4.

4
Where Does That Criminality Come From? Writing Women and Crime

The Victorian detective story

Interest in female criminality seems to be most pronounced at times of significant change in the cultural representation and the status of women. There is much evidence of this in the nineteenth century, a period of significant transformation in women's fortunes but one in which crime involving women was a major social concern. The 1850s and 1860s saw the 1857 Divorce and Matrimonial Causes Acts which made divorce more accessible to middle-class women, removed a husband's right to the earnings of a wife he had deserted and returned to a divorced or legally separated woman the property rights of a single woman. The Married Woman's Property Act of 1870 allowed women to keep earnings or property acquired after marriage. In theory, the position of women was further improved by subsequent acts: the Comprehensive Property Act of 1882 entitled divorced women to independent ownership of property and the same property rights as unmarried women; the Matrimonial Causes Act of 1878 provided for separate maintenance for the wife of a husband convicted of aggravated assault; and the Matrimonial Causes Act of 1886 gave women the right to sue their husbands for maintenance.

Despite these positive developments, however, the assertive, independent female remained a cause of cultural and social concern. What was perceived at the time as the sexually transgressive female challenged the Victorian 'ideals' of women as caring mothers and dutiful wives. The presence of women who did not comply with this dominant ideology exposed it as a masquerade and drew attention also to male behaviours behind the middle-class, Victorian façade that were not consistent with Victorian ideology. At the same time the independent female confirmed male anxieties arising from the changing social status of women.

One of the reasons why the conflation of female criminality and sexuality seemed so natural to the Victorians was that its notions of middle-class respectability were dependent on women's suppression of their sexuality. Female desires were secret longings, inevitably shrouded in guilt, and perceived as dangerous to the social fabric of society. As such, they were easily elided with criminality.

At one level, the Victorian detective story focussed upon women as emotionally and intellectually inadequate to deal with male initiated crime in which they became, often unwittingly, embroiled. Conan Doyle's *The Sign of the Four* and 'The Speckled Band' open with a woman seeking the help of the male, consulting detective, who behaves towards her as a benevolent father, and who at this point in the story says more for herself than she does after Sherlock Holmes has taken on her case. Here the caring father/consulting detective echoes the caring father/consulting doctor; she hands her symptoms over to a male authority whom she expects to prescribe the solution.

Generally speaking, the Holmes stories present women in conventional and stereotypical ways. When consulting Holmes, Watson notices that Miss Morstan in *The Sign of the Four* demonstrates the kind of weakness stereotypically associated with the Victorian heroine: '[her] lip trembled, her hand quivered, and she showed every sign of intense inward agitation' (12). Although Miss Morstan initially shows uncharacteristic stamina at Pondicherry Lodge, the scene of the crime, she is soon reconfigured along more stereotypical Victorian lines: 'After the angelic fashion of women, she had borne trouble with a calm face as long as there was someone weaker than herself to support ... in the cab, however, she first turned faint, and then burst into a passion of weeping ...' (48).

At another level, Victorian detective fiction, like the sensation novel, offered a means of acknowledging, if not fully exploring, the female criminal who injected a note of dissent into an otherwise politically conservative genre, as in Conan Doyle's 'A Scandal in Bohemia' and 'The Adventure of the Beryl Coronet'. Victorian crime writing was often unequivocal in the causes of female criminality. In 'The Adventure of the Beryl Coronet' a bogus member of the decaying aristocracy persuades a young woman, with whom he purports to be romantically involved, to be his accomplice in stealing jewels from her uncle who has brought her up as his daughter. However, whilst the female criminal challenged the conventional ideal or masquerade of the quiet, obedient Victorian woman, she confirmed the stereotypical equation of femininity and emotional weakness. In Holmes's summary of his conclusions to Mary's surrogate father, Mary is represented as having been led into criminality by her emotional, womanly nature:

> His wicked lust for gold kindled at the news, and he bent her to his will. I have no doubt that she loved you, but there are women in whom the love of a lover extinguishes all other loves, and I think that she must have been one. (314)

In the elision of her criminality with her female emotional weakness, Mary is very different from Irene Adler in 'A Scandal in Bohemia' in which the duplicity of women is initially perceived as more serious than that of men. The crux of the story is that Holmes is requested by the King of Bohemia to retrieve a photograph from a woman, Irene, with whom he has had an affair showing them together. She intends to ruin him by sending the photograph to the parents of the princess he intends to marry on the day that their betrothal is announced. Irene implicitly suggests that the Victorian ideal of womanhood is a masquerade and, as this motif is unfurled, Irene is cryptically associated with Eve's act of betrayal: she lives in Serpentine Avenue and she recalls Eden's serpent also when she assumes a disguise to follow Holmes. At the end of the story, he coldly quips: 'From what I have seen of the lady she seems indeed to be on a very different level to your Majesty' (175).

It was not the norm in Victorian detective fiction for the female criminal to be perceived as rationale and intelligent. This was partly because, as is now well known, in the nineteenth- and early twentieth century madness was defined in terms of characteristics associated with women: emotionalism, irrationality, hysteria and excess. Thus, slippage between female passion, criminality and madness was common, even in detective fiction written by women. In Mrs Henry Woods' 'The Mystery at Number Seven' (1877), Melinda Valentine, whose surname structures her entire being around love, kills her fellow maid, Jane Cross, out of jealousy and ends up in an asylum. The master of the house is abroad when this crime occurs and never explicitly enters the narrative. Thus, the story might be seen as concerned with the feminine in the absence, literally and metaphorically, of the master signifier.

Initially the story is a variant on the sealed room mystery – Jane is killed in a locked-up house. However, the motifs of locks and keys point towards what is locked up within the female psyche. This is consistent with the way in which the narrative itself is constructed around two incidents that appear to confirm Melinda's mental instability: her murder of Jane in a jealous temper, and her frenzied attack on the cook whom she suspects of having opened her private trunk and discovered a half-written, personal letter.

In contrast to Mrs Woods' story, Wilkie Collins's 'Who Killed Zebedee?' (1881) is more complex. It follows literary convention in eliding female passion and criminality, only to subvert the thesis before reintroducing it. The tale is ostensibly a narrative about a 'sensible' young woman, staying with her husband in a lodging house in the few weeks before they move to Australia, who suddenly becomes insane and kills him while they are in bed together. It is revealed that she was prone to sleep-walking which was regarded as a sign of female instability at the time and suggested that she may have been unconsciously influenced by reading of a woman who had stabbed her husband in a dream.

In the first part of Collins's narrative, a woman is reported to be 'completely prostrated by a terrible nervous shock'. Not unusually, the story introduces the trope of the emotional reliability of women; when the surgeon is asked if he considered her 'to have been a sane woman before the murder took place, he refused to answer positively at that time' (148). But while Mrs John Zebedee is assessed and classified by a male surgeon as in 'nervous shock', the most nervous character in the text is the landlord, who 'so trembled with terror that some people might have taken him for the guilty person' (143–4), unlike his wife and the servants who stoically assume responsibility for dealing with the crime. Here the story appears to challenge Victorian stereotypical associations of femininity with instability and masculinity with stability. However, the real solution of the crime reconfirms the familiar motif whereby female emotional instability and criminality are elided. It turns out that the murder was committed by a housemaid who, coincidentally, found herself in the same house as the man who once promised to marry her.

In these stories, women are explicitly seen as assuming the appearance of caring wife or reliable domestic servant which disguises their true nature which reveals itself in their emotional instability, dream states or jealous tempers. But there were Victorian detective stories that offered no such explanation for women's criminal behaviour, suggesting that the female was innately evil or criminal. Harry Blyth's 'The Accusing Shadow' (1894) is structured around the beautiful Julia Barretti. But once again her appearance is a masquerade; in seducing an ostensibly respectable city gent into marrying her, she is reconfigured as a 'designing harpy' (305). She is the 'shadow' to the other female protagonist, a bright, vivacious and dutiful young woman, who is prepared to sacrifice herself by marrying a man whom she does not love, the same man that Barretti seduced. Whilst the story is explicitly concerned with Barretti's masquerade, it implicitly suggests that the gracious, young woman is herself a masquerade behind which the likes of Barretti may lurk.

Dickens' Nancy

The two poles of Victorian femininity represented in Victorian detective fiction are exemplified in a single character in *Oliver Twist*. Nancy is a criminal and a prostitute, but she is also said in her own way to be 'pure'. Unlike many female criminals in Victorian detective fiction, she speaks for herself about her criminality, as in her dramatic confrontation with Fagin: 'There is something about a roused woman; especially if she add to all her other strong passions, the fierce impulses of recklessness and despair: which few men like to provoke' (166). But her association, as a prostitute and petty thief, with 'roused women' in general has the effect of linking all roused women with criminality, and of associating passion and anger in women with a collapse of those boundaries that maintain social and behavioural norms:

> 'Civil words!' cried the girl, whose passion was frightful to see. 'Civil words, you villain! Yes, you deserve 'em from me. I thieved for you when I was a child not half as old as this!' pointing to Oliver. 'I have been in the same trade, and in the same service, for twelve years since.'
> [....]
> 'Aye, it is!' returned the girl; not speaking, but pouring out the words in one continuous and vehement scream. 'It is my living; and the cold, wet, dirty streets are my home; and you're the wretch that drove me to them long ago, and that'll keep me there, day and night, day and night, till I die!' (167)

In order to describe unleashed passion in women, Dickens draws on Gothic melodrama. In doing so, he appropriates the distraught, sexualised woman type, a stock character of Victorian melodrama, with whom male fear of unbridled female sexuality was associated.

At the same time as Nancy's violence would seem to criminalise all passionate women, she is referred to reductively as a 'girl', unconsciously confirming the Victorian equation of women with emotional immaturity and in need of discipline: 'The girl said nothing more;

but ... made such a rush at the Jew as would probably have left signal marks of her revenge upon him, had not her wrists been seized by Sikes at the right moment'. Her rush at the Jew cannot be read in isolation from the narrator's earlier remarks in the novel about men's fear of 'roused' women. The words 'right moment' betray a sense of relief that Nancy is stopped despite the evident sympathy for her. At the end of the episode Dickens resorts to a clichéd formula from Gothic melodrama: 'she made a few ineffectual struggles, and fainted' (167).

At one level, Nancy, read from a feminist perspective, is an example of the 'reality' that threatens to expose the ideal of Victorian womanhood – the obedient wife and dutiful, caring mother – as masquerade. At another level, she seems to reclaim that ideal. She is angry about what has happened to Oliver and protective of him, while enraged over the way that she has been forced into crime and prostitution. It is as if she wishes to reclaim the innocent child she once was. The white handkerchief which she holds up to heaven in her last moments signifies the purity that Nancy has not quite lost. She is not incompatible with other Victorian literary representations of the female criminal in that the emphasis is upon criminality as a socio-psychic phenomenon – an approach that distinguishes Victorian depictions of female from male criminality where the emphasis tends to be upon more external motivators such as class, environment and material need. It is not surprising that the post-Freudian twentieth century should continue the Victorian interest in female criminality as emanating from within female desire. But in the last century, the emphasis shifted to a more focussed debate as to whether the key to female criminality was to be found among inner or external factors or, alternatively, in a complex dialectic between the two.

Women in a criminalising modernity

In the 1920s and 1930s, the Chicago School of Criminology was indebted to the debate within Sigmund Freud's work between 'innate dispositions', which in a less sophisticated form had preoccupied nineteenth-century criminology, and the influence of external circumstances. But it also pursued issues that dominated twentieth-century psychoanalytic thinking. First, the extent to which fantasy enters into an engagement with the 'real'. Second, since Freud was primarily interested in the inner psychic worlds of women, the extent to which women are implicated in fantasies that, however ultimately oppressive, may be experienced as thrilling, even dangerously exciting.

Most of the crime fiction and criminological writing about female criminality between the First and Second World Wars, approaching it as a socio-psychic, rather than purely social, phenomenon, stress the importance of fantasy. But discussion of women's implication in criminal fantasies raises particular difficulties for the crime writer and criminologist. In popular culture and pulp fiction, the icons of female sexuality became divorced from the individual and, in fetishising women within the male gaze, they cast female sexuality as both desirable and threatening. Thus, although crime fiction's concern with women's involvement in violent fantasies was driven in part by Freud's primary interest in conflicts within the female psyche, it was also a product of the wider fetishising of the female criminal.

The peak in crime writing in the 1920s and the 1930s coincided with an interest in the involvement of women in serious crime that continued until well into the 1950s, in which the emphasis was upon women who became involved with criminals such as the gun-moll and/or women who became criminals through pursuing sexual desires and personal ambitions. Criminological and fictionalised accounts of such women appeared to present the reader with two interdependent approaches to female criminality, focusing either on the criminal activity as a social reality or as a product of fantasy. The Chicago School of Criminology, indebted to Freud's argument that the determining cause of all mental life is to be found in the reciprocal relation between innate dispositions and social experiences, offered a different, integrated approach.[1]

Unadjustment and consumerism

The attempt to identify a socio-psychic dynamic in the case histories of women involved with crime after the First World War was spearheaded by a leading member of the Chicago School of Criminology, W. I. Thomas. He suggested a framework for criminality in young, generally sexually-active, women that is, directly or indirectly, explored in numerous texts of the 1920s and 1930s. These include nearly all the versions of the Bonny and Clyde story; F. Tennyson Jesse's *A Pin to See the Peepshow*; R. Alwyn Raymond's crime faction *The Cleft Chin Murder*; Josephine Tey's *The Franchise Affair*; Agatha Christie's *The Murder at the Vicarage* and Graham Greene's *Brighton Rock*.

Thomas's work, concerned with the relation between mental conflict and misconduct, betrays the influence of Freud in identifying instincts which appear actually to invite death, such as the desire for thrilling experience, and those based on fear that tend to avoid death.[2] In accounting for criminal behaviour, it also follows Freud's interest in instincts that may be too strong or too weak and particular capacities that may be stunted or insufficiently developed.

In moving beyond late Victorian concern with female criminality as a product of the particular nature of the 'female psyche', Thomas also reconfigured the 'angel' and 'whore' binarism which had pervaded writing in the previous century:

> Thus fifty years ago we recognised, roughly speaking, two types of women, the one completely good and the other completely bad, – what we now call the old-fashioned girl and the girl who had sinned and been outlawed. At present we have several intermediate types, – the occasional prostitute, the charity girl, the demi-virgin, the equivocal flapper, and in addition girls with new but social behaviour norms who have adapted themselves to all kinds of work.[3]

In identifying a range of 'types', Thomas shows that he shares Freud's view that external impressions affect different people differently. But the particular emphasis that Thomas places on external cultural forces, as existing in a dynamic with inner drives and impulses, is a product of early twentieth-century modernity. The focus is upon rapid social change and the emergence of a mass media, consumer society. He stresses that criminological investigation must take into account that 'a social evolution is going on in which not only are activities changing but also the norm which regulates the activities'.[4] Thus, while Thomas's concept of 'the unadjusted girl' draws upon the Freudian dynamic between innate disposition and external circumstances, his emphasis falls on the changing norms of social behaviour in which has developed an all-consuming 'impulse to get amusement, adventure and pretty clothes, favourable notice, distinction, freedom in the larger world ... .'[5] Within this framework, he argues that female sexuality can be configured as a masquerade, a means employed by many criminal women to realise material ambitions and desires.[6]

Thomas's use of the word 'girl' is pertinent to the way in which young women are presented in the texts discussed in this chapter. It reflects a distinction increasingly made in Britain and America in the nineteenth and twentieth centuries between male and female juvenile offenders. Criminological writing about juvenile female offenders, betraying the prevalent myth that girls were capable of sexual immorality earlier than boys, was preoccupied with their sexuality.

Woman as consumer and spectacle

In Thomas's work, the Victorian concern with the sexual immorality of the juvenile or young adult female offender is given a different twist in being related to the wider, emergent consumer society and being seen as a kind of masquerade. It is well documented that the city in the first half of the twentieth century became the city of display; consumerism became a matter of spectacle reflected in the new department stores, the new arcades and the large illuminated shop windows. In other words, the city itself as a symbol of modernity was a vast, electronic masquerade.

From the 1840s onwards, the national trend was to replace dwelling places in the cities with shops. Railways brought shoppers into the cities and larger towns from the suburbs and the countryside and eventually omnibuses made it possible for them to travel between different parts of the town. As one social historian has pointed out, the Great Exhibition helped create a middle-class culture in which the signs and symbols of prosperity became enormously important, all too evident in the way drapery shops in the metropolis became known for their well-lit window displays.[7]

A key cultural critic in helping us understand early twentieth-century, consumer culture is Walter Benjamin. Linking Karl Marx's concept of commodity and aestheticism, Benjamin suggested that the nineteenth-century metropolis was a vast 'phantasmagoria'.[8] But, other nineteenth-century commentators, too, saw the shopping areas of London very much in terms of theatricality and spectacle. In 1858, Augustus Sala described Regent Street as an 'avenue of superfluities', and in 1866, the *Illustrated London News* referred to the 'fireflies of fashion' and the 'fashionable loungers' who thronged the shopping streets and arcades.[9] Although they did not have Benjamin's psychoanalytic vocabulary which he derived from Freud, these commentators clearly anticipate Benjamin's notion of commodity fetishism. Mayhew's (1862) essay on pickpockets, significantly conflates woman-as-victim, with sexual desire and the spectacle of consumerism:

> A young lady may be standing by a window in Cheapside, Fleet Street, Oxford Street, or the Strand, admiring some beautiful engraving. Meantime a handsomely dressed young man, with gold chain and moustache, also takes his station at the window beside her, apparently admiring the same engraving. The young lady stands gazing on the beautiful picture, with her countenance glowing sentiment,

which may be enhanced by the sympathetic presence of the nice looking young man by her side, and while her bosom is thus throbbing with romantic emotion, her purse, meanwhile, is being quietly transferred to the pocket of this elegantly attired young man.[10]

At one level, Mayhew anticipates what some late twentieth-century cultural commentators have argued, that the new consumerism made women part of the spectacle itself, linking them to display, artifice and entertainment. However, his reference to the young female victim's 'countenance glowing sentiment' suggests that the energy that invests the commodities with which women have become associated also revitalises the masquerade that they, wittingly or unwittingly, assume.

The amateur prostitute

The ultimate symbol of women as street spectacle and masquerade is the prostitute. The association of assertive female sexuality, and even in some texts the mere suggestion that women have sexual desires and fantasies of their own, with the spectre of prostitution is a recurring trope in the criminalising of independent female subjectivity. A key work suggesting the extent to which this elision had acquired cultural credence by the early 1930s is Gladys Mary Hall's (1933) Study of Prostitution, dedicated to the Association for Moral and Social Hygiene. It highlights the changing attitude amongst women toward sex, coincident with the social upheaval following the First World War:

> Sex assumed a new and individual importance, particularly for women, whose accepted role of sexual submission to masculine needs appeared to be changing to one of challenging demand for the recognition of their own, demonstrated by many in a claim for, or a readiness to experience, sex adventures.[11]

In developing this thesis, Hall, following the historical tendency in psychoanalytic writing to analyse female behaviour against a male norm, suggested that women had begun to assume 'masculine' behaviour patterns and that: 'Female sexual activity now tends to achieve the former self-arrogated masculine level.'[12] She also goes so far as to label sexually promiscuous women 'amateur prostitutes', observing that 'the outstanding feature of present-day prostitution in Great Britain is the reduction in the number of professional prostitutes and the increase in the number of amateurs'. An 'amateur prostitute' is described in the following terms:

> In other words, a man may, at the present time, have opportunities for promiscuous sex relations with girls from among his own social group whom he knows, or whose acquaintance he may readily make; and there are methods whereby, in the course of conversation this fact is conveyed to him. Although he usually pays for his satisfaction, the payment takes the form of a gift, or a dinner, or a motor run; the episode appears less commercial and suggests more of passion and spontaneity than a similar episode with a professional prostitute, and for this reason is usually infinitely more attractive. In addition ... there may be no payment whatever, and the whole episode may be mutually desired and mutually satisfactory.[13]

Conventional 'courtship' behaviour, such as an invitation to dinner or a trip in a car, becomes itself a masquerade of which both parties are at least partly aware and in which each participates. Very little in relationships, and certainly sexual relations, seems to be, if we accept Hall's arguments, at face value.

The concept, or masquerade, of the amateur prostitute is interleaved in writing about crime in the 1920s and 1930s with the notion of 'unadjustment'. Thus, Thomas and Hall's work provide useful contemporaneous reference points against which to explore a number of key texts from that period such as R. Alwyn Raymond's *The Cleft Chin Murder*, Julia Starling's *A Pin to See the Peepshow* and Josephine Tey's *The Franchise Affair*. But Thomas is more interested in emphasising, what we may now take for granted, the role of fantasy in the individual's response to social change and in the spectacle or masquerade of mass consumerism itself.

Women, Passion and Danger

In the 1920s and the 1930s, there were a number of infamous murder cases concerned with the involvement of women in fantasies that were both thrilling and oppressive. One of the most reported of these was the Thompson-Bywaters case on which F. Tennyson Jesse based her novel *A Pin to See the Peepshow* (1934). Edith Thompson's prosecution and conviction rested on her presence at the crime scene and the extent to which she could be described as a participant in it.

Thompson's husband was killed on the evening of 3 October 1922, when they were both returning home from the theatre, by the man with whom she was having an affair, 22-year-old ship's clerk Frederick

Bywaters. Although Thompson had willed her husband's death and had made suggestions in letters to her lover as to how she might murder him, the actual killing was not something that they had planned together. Nevertheless, they were both executed.

By the time Jesse's novel was published, the motif of a woman driven to thinking of killing her husband to free herself was well fixed in the public mind. Towards the end of the 1920s, Ruth Snyder's callous murder of her husband with the assistance of her lover, corset salesman Judd Gray, made headlines around the world if only because each of them went to the electric chair. Even more infamous was the case of Madame Fahmy, described in the press coverage at the time as a 'Parisian Adventuress'. She was actually cleared of murder after having shot her Egyptian millionaire husband, Prince Ali Fahmy, whom she alleged was homosexual and had sexually abused her throughout their marriage.

Not surprisingly, then, the decade opens with Agatha Christie's *The Murder at the Vicarage*, discussed in the next chapter, in which Anne Protheroe, assisted by her artist lover, Lawrence Redding, shoots the husband to whom she has been unhappily married for many years. Cases of women killing husbands to whom they are unhappily married reflect ideas proposed in one of Freud's important papers, ' "Civilised" Sexual Morality and Modern Nervousness' (1908), which provides a critique of the way in which men and women, but especially women, were often socially and sexually entrapped by marriage. However, the reporting of such cases also determined the way in which ideas about femininity, passion and violence might be received in the popular imagination.

The press coverage of the Snyder-Gray case exaggerated several dimensions which were also present in the accounts of the Thompson-Bywaters case. Gray and Snyder each tried to shift the responsibility to the other, but the press seemed to want to believe that Ruth Snyder, 'Granite Woman' as she was called, was the harder of the two, and that Gray was 'Putty Man' in her hands. The dangerous manipulative female, and the associated masquerades that she was supposed to assume, was a familiar trope in nineteenth- and twentieth-century newspapers. She appeared in a variety of disguises in the press in the 1920s and 1930s, ranging from Dot King, the New York courtesan and alleged blackmailer, who was found dead in suspicious circumstances in 1923, to Madeline Roberts who in 1925 procured under-age domestic help to satisfy her employer.

Given press interest in this approach to female sexuality, it is not surprising that Tennyson Jesse sees Julia Starling as standing trial not so much as a murderess but a woman of dangerous sexual appetite. In other words, the public were encouraged by the press to see her, in Thomas's terms, as 'unadjusted' because she had desires that in the Freudian paradigm of the Chicago School of Criminology are innately too strong for her own and society's well-being. Like the press versions of other women criminals, referred to above, Julia conflates femininity, passion and danger. Jesse's novel, unlike the public at Julia's trial, focusses on the reciprocal relation between her inner instincts and external circumstances. It acknowledges the importance of Julia's inner psychic world. In fact, Jesse admitted to her Paris publisher, that having written the opening and closing sections of the novel first, she wrote the rest of the book with a view to probing 'the life of an over-emotional, under-educated, suburban London girl'.[14]

However, Julia is also portrayed as the victim of her middle-class background, and its puritanical interleaving of sexuality and motherhood. Typical of much crime writing between the First and Second World Wars concerned with women and violent crime, Jesse follows the line cast by Freud's paper ' "Civilised" Sexual Morality and Modern Nervousness', referred to above. In *A Pin to See the Peepshow*, Jesse is concerned through social and psychological analysis to extend the boundaries of the murder scene in which Julia's husband is killed into a profile of the struggles and restraints experienced by many suburban women in Julia's position. She exemplifies an intensely alive and imaginative woman who is trapped, in this case within the conventions of class. Jesse herself surmises toward the end of the novel: Julia's 'sin' was that 'she had evaded the womb's responsibilities; while partaking of its pleasures' (392). Elaine Morgan in her Afterword to the 1978 edition of the novel argues that Julia 'lacked most of the old-fashioned virtues that romantic heroines were expected to display; she was selfish, unfaithful, sharp-tongued, and discontented' but also 'fell just as far short of the standards of integrity and independence expected of the New Woman at that date' (405). It is the dialectic between Julia's innate disposition and the gender ideologies embedded in her background environment and in the wider culture that impels the book. The novel demonstrates how crime writing in the 1930s was able not only to make a contribution to feminist criminology but also to intervene against the separation of the psychic and the socio-political.

Like Thomas (1923), but with a more sympathetic reading of the social context of women in the 1930s, Jesse recognises that criminal behaviour, especially among young women at this time, could not be seen only as the product of external influences. It was as important to recognise the role of fantasy in examining the female criminal's conception of herself. The novel's title refers to the peepshow which Julia, whilst at school, pays a pin to view. The peepshow is a white cardboard box with a round hole cut in each end, one covered by red transparent paper:

> The floor of the box was covered with cotton-wool, and a frosting of sugar sprinkled over it. Light came into the box from the red-covered window at the far end, so that a rosy glow as of sunset lay over the sparkling snow ... Julia stared into the peepshow, and it was as though she gazed into another world, where she would go clad in snow-shoes and furs, and be able to tame savage huskies and shoot bears; a world of chill pallor, of an illimitable white sky, both only saved from a cruel rigour by the rosy all-pervading light. (19–20)

Julia seeks this kind of illimitable world through a variety of emotional and, subsequently, sexual relationships. In this respect, Jesse's novel anticipates aspects of the female confessional novel of the late twentieth century in which the central figure's inner journey is focussed on her sexual identity, relationships, marriage and, often, divorce. Julia ends up married to a man whom she finds too dull for her:

> Herbert only wanted to be an ordinary, decent husband and wage-earner; he distrusted the wonderful, and he only knew that his life had turned to nothing in his hands, like withered leaves. He had no joy in his wife, for whom he had once lusted so violently, and for whom he occasionally lusted still. (210)

But the fact that her life was not very exciting did not take from her 'that sub-conscious hope of a glory yet to come ... there still remained the possibility of something exciting, though quite what it might be, she didn't envisage' (159). The 'fairy effect' of the peepshow (212) is transferred to Leo as he talks of having 'ran away to sea' and becomes in her fantasy 'this man who had been about the world, and who knew about things of which she had never heard' (213).

American fantasies

Jesse's representation of Julia Starling is in contrast to Alwyn Raymond's configuration of the Elizabeth Jones's story which traces a young girl from when she was a twelve-year-old attending a respectable Welsh school to her time as 'a broken wreck of an eighteen-year-old girl in Holloway prison nursing a bitter grudge against the society she thinks she was nearly smart enough to beat' (3–4). Like Jesse, he focusses upon a psychological and sociological profile of the female criminal protagonist. But his emphasis upon the way in which she thought she could 'beat' society means that there is a more explicit interest in his book on female masquerade. His crime faction places Elizabeth's criminal behaviour not simply in the context of her Welsh respectable upbringing, but its particular, socio-psychic dimension, suggesting that 'in spite of, or perhaps because of, an upbringing of intense respectability, [she] was sullen and rebellious' (4). The hesitancy here – 'in spite of, or perhaps because of' – implies that Raymond is less sure than Jesse in placing his female protagonist into her background.

What is of primary interest to Raymond, as for Thomas, is the reciprocal relation between external forces and Elizabeth's innate disposition. This is explored through the influences of her boy friend, American-based fantasies, and the wider, again American, consumer culture upon her. Whilst Thomas (1923) actually writes out of American consumer society, Raymond's work is less near the source, being rooted in its perceived influence upon British social life between the wars.

Raymond pointedly observes that what Elizabeth was told by the boy with whom she became disastrously involved resonated with what she had seen in American films and magazines (11). But, unlike Thomas, Raymond sees fantasy as important to the socio-psychic dynamic in both male and female identity at this time. In his fantasies, Carl Hulten assumes a kind of masquerade, modelling himself after the salient, masculine type in American popular culture of the day. These American male types appeared to offer young, impressionable, British men, and rebellious, young women, images of virile, ambitious heroes who pursued their social aspirations against a hostile, social environment. This was an aspect of the Cleft Chin Murder case to which George Orwell drew attention, seeing it as justifying his anxiety about increasing American influence on British popular crime fiction, faction and films:

> Not only is he himself living a continuous fantasy-life in the Chicago underworld, but he can count on hundreds of thousands of readers who know what is meant by a 'clip-shop' or the 'hotsquat', do not have to do mental arithmetic when confronted by 'fifty grand', and understand at sight a sentence like 'Johnny was a rummy and only two jumps ahead of the nut-factory'. Evidently there are great numbers of English people who are partly Americanised in language and, one ought to add, in moral outlook. (72–3)

In other words, British life, according to Orwell, is becoming a vast American masquerade.

Raymond and Thomas stress female identity in the 1920s as being configured with what each perceive as a dangerous cocktail of inflated material aspirations, divergent internalised desires and fantasy. The influence of American crime narrative on their views is evident. In modern crime writing or reporting involving a gangster and moll partnership, the male criminal usually promised to provide the woman with whom he became involved with the excitement and stimulus which her life lacked. He had the capacity to make her think that she was the centre of his world, caused her to question the nature of the society of which she was a member and generally made her feel more 'alive'. Thereafter, she entered his masquerade and became a participant in a life where the boundaries between fantasy and 'reality' became blurred.

One of the features of Elizabeth Jones's life which Raymond stresses is that she 'bought into' an American style of sexuality: 'Now it was silk stockings, high heels, American perfume, flashy jewellery, and all the things that she thought made her "glamorous" ' (6). Orwell, too, stresses that Elizabeth's story is embedded in an 'atmosphere of dance-halls, movie-palaces, cheap perfume, false names and stolen cars' (1946,1965: 13). Raymond and Orwell represent Elizabeth as the victim of a wider American-style consumerism that fetishises the accruements of female sexuality – silk stockings, high heels, perfume and jewellery. But Raymond, like Thomas, recognises that these are icons not only of female consumption but also of feminine aspiration and desire, as well as of modernity itself. Such elements together with the short skirt and the long cigarette holder, along with the oddly awkward pose, constituted the standard icon of the seductress on the lurid covers of numerous American paperbacks in the 1940s and 1950s. What is especially disturbing is how crime writing, in connecting the criminal woman or the moll to any fashionable woman in public, seemed to dismember her visually and in *The Cleft Chin Murder* this is parallel to the perceived psychic and corporeal dismemberment of Elizabeth Jones.

The criminalised schoolgirl

In *The Franchise Affair*, the status quo in a small, sleepy English country town is disrupted when a schoolgirl, Betty Kane, accuses an elderly woman and her daughter who live by themselves of kidnapping her, keeping her as a slave and beating her. The offence with which Marion and her mother are charged undermines the conventional associations of womanhood with motherhood. In the course of the novel, they seek the help of, and are supported by, a local, unmarried solicitor who lives with his aunt and brother. After the case, the women flee to Canada when their solicitor, convinced that the younger of the women will marry him, packs his bag and takes the same flight. Within this conservative framework, and despite the many conservative values embedded in the text, the novel raises disturbing issues and addresses some distressing subjects, even if it does not fully pursue the implications of some of its content.

Even before being charged with abduction, Marion Sharp and her mother are perceived by the community as a disturbing presence. Like the mother and daughter in Poe's 'The Murders in the Rue Morgue', they arouse suspicion and gossip because they live alone without, apparently, the need for men. The ostensible crime scene, the attic in The Franchise where Betty alleges she was held a prisoner and whipped, is beyond the civilised comfort of the main part of the house – it is approached by an uncarpeted final flight of stairs, and has only a truckle bed, a chair and one small, round window – and seems apposite for what supposedly happened there. She is allegedly exposed to a cruelty which in fairy stories is historically associated with wicked witches and step-mothers.

The location of the Franchise itself serves to underscore the alienation of Marion and her mother from the community: 'It had no relation with anything in the countryside ... The place was as irrelevant, as isolated as a child's toy dropped by the wayside' (14). Suggesting that The Franchise is 'irrelevant' to the crime, the narrative implies that it is in its apparent irrelevance that its relevance lies. As in Poe's 'The Murders in the Rue Morgue', the ostensible 'othering' of the crime scene says something about the nature and behaviour of those that would categorise it as alien to them. The threat posed by Marion and her mother's independence and self-sufficiency is underlined by the small detail that they have taken over a property that had been owned by a man as long as anyone can remember. The labels that are directly or indirectly applied to Marion and her mother – witches, gipsies, Fascists – place the suspicion which they generate and the violence which they eventually arouse in a wider context of difference and prejudice. Even their solicitor, their most sympathetic advocate, believes: 'The old woman had a fanatic's face if ever he saw one; and Marion Sharpe herself looked as if a stake would be her natural prop if stakes were not out of fashion' (12).

Whilst Raymond in *The Cleft Chin Murder* is interested in the American fuelled fantasies that lead a young girl to reconfigure herself and become involved in crime, Tey is interested in the wider cultural and social fantasies that determine the way in which crime and particular criminals are perceived and received. The accused women's lawyer tries to convince himself that people from the country would not have chosen to have scrawled 'Fascists' on the Franchise wall. But in expressing their outrage over the women's inhuman treatment of a young schoolgirl, the community articulate a capacity for violence redolent of the way in which the Jews were victimised in Nazi Germany. It is ironic that the protesters wish to visit on the women the same abuse that they are accused of visiting on Betty Kane:

> Rage and hatred spilled over to the paper; malice ran unchecked through the largely illiterate sentences. It was an amazing exhibition. And one of the oddities of it was that the dearest wish of so many of those indignant protesters against violence was to flog the said women within an inch of their lives. (116)

The narrative is woven between other crime scenes in which women behave in ways that challenge the stereotypes of respectable womanhood in the novel but also challenge notions of masculinity: the lounge bar in which Betty, although only fifteen years of age and dressed as a schoolgirl, deliberately picks up the man with whom she has a prolonged sexual liaison and the riverside bungalow in which Bernard Chadwick has unlawful sex with Betty whom his wife violently assaults on discovering her there.

The Franchise Affair betrays the influence of what in the 1930s and 1940s became a familiar motif in popular culture: the linking of female eroticism with sexual, often sadomasochistic, violence. But while the alleged crime, and even the revenge attack on Betty by the wife she wrongs, may 'play' with female sadomasochism, the real crime of sexual intercourse between a man and an under-aged girl, who is dressed initially in a school uniform, is more disturbing. In her green hat, frock and grey overcoat, Betty does not appear to be the type to be found even in the lounge bar of the Midland Hotel. Both Betty as innocent schoolgirl and the respectable Hotel lounge turn out to be masquerades. Betty is 'other' than she appears and the lounge bar is a place where men pick up women.

The lounge bar is an example of how the crime scene, in this case the place where an under-aged girl is picked up for sex, can operate as a destabilising element in society and a literary text, calling into question conventional definitions and boundaries. For example, here the boundaries between 'cheap' and 'respectable', 'prostitute' and 'client', 'child' and 'young woman' are redrawn. It reminds us that behind Milford's High Street is Sin Lane. While one hypothesis in the novel is that 'sin' is a corruption of 'sand', locals prefer the more obvious interpretation of the name. The two hypotheses when read together imply that sin, like sand, is destabilising.

The man with whom Betty leaves the hotel to have sex admits that she soon convinced him that she 'looked a pretty sleek little outfit' (238). The choice of the word 'outfit', whilst referring ostensibly to Betty's apparent experience, draws attention to the school uniform that she was wearing in the hotel lounge. At one level, it signifies 'youth and innocence, speedwell and campfire smoke and harebells in the grass' (228) and middle-class, family respectability. At another, especially in popular erotic culture, it is fetishised, fuelling cultural fantasies about schoolgirls in uniform. Faced with a charge of having sex with a fifteen-year-old girl, Chadwick swears on oath that he thought he had been picked-up by 'an inexperienced child of sixteen' (238). While the boundary between fifteen and sixteen is a legal one, it is not an obvious moral one. Chadwick still thinks of her as a 'child' and becomes comfortable about having sex with her when she convinces him that she is no virgin although still, even in his mind, a child.

Given the cultural significance which the schoolgirl acquired in school stories at the turn of the century, perhaps the conflation of the tropes of dangerous female seductress and fetishised schoolgirl was inevitable. One writer on school fiction has argued: 'The new girl – no longer a child, not yet a sexual adult occupied a provisional free space. Girls' culture suggested new ways of being, new modes of behaviour, and new attitudes that were not yet acceptable for adult women.'[15] As a schoolgirl, Betty appears to be a criminalised version of a definition of girlhood, and ultimately womanhood, prevalent in interwar schoolgirl fiction. According to one study, in this world of girls, 'to be assertive, physically active, daring, ambitious, is not a source of tension ... girls "break bounds", have adventures, transgress rules ... codes [are] broken, secret passages explored, disguises penetrated'.[16] The anxiety surrounding such a depiction of womanhood was popularised, while Josephine Tey was working on this novel, in Ronald Searle's St Trinians cartoons. Published initially at one a month, they were first published in book form in 1947. As is clear from the ironic title of the second book, *The Female Approach* (1949), they portrayed the girls boarding school pupil as not only violent and out of control, swigging gin and smoking cigars, but as embodying – quite literally in their short skirts and suspenders – an unadjusted, female identity and sexuality that was to be feared. The first full-length novel which Ronald Searle wrote with D. B. Wyndham, published a few years later, was called *The Terror of St Trinians*.

Another trope in the account of the relationship between Betty and Chadwick is the extent to which female desire is made dangerous, even criminalised, by outside forces. This is evident in the lounge waiter's account of what happened in the hotel:

> Don't you believe it. He hadn't even thought of her when he sat down there. I tell you, sir, she didn't look that sort. You'd expect an aunt or a mother to appear at any moment and say: 'So sorry to have kept you waiting, darling.' She just wouldn't occur to any man as a possible. On, no; it was the kid's doing. And as neat a piece of business, let me tell you, sir, as if she had spent a lifetime at it. (112)

His view of what he now sees as a masquerade echoes Thomas's (1923) concept of an 'occasional prostitute', referred to earlier, one aspect of which was the way in which she was said to employ her 'charm' as 'an asset, a lure, which she may use as a means of procuring entertainment, affection and perhaps gifts.[17] This contemporaneous interpretation of 'unadjustment' provides a useful framework within which to read Tey's novel. The key perspective on Betty's criminality is provided by the barrister Kevin who actually employs Thomas's terminology: 'crime begins in egoism, inordinate vanity ... with an egoism like Betty Kane's there is no adjustment. She expects the world to adjust itself to her' (222). Betty is contrasted with ' a normal girl ... [who could work things out] in sobs or sulks or being difficult, or deciding that she was going to renounce the world and go into a convent, or half a dozen other methods that the adolescent uses in the process of adjustment' (222).

The misleading nature of the novel's 'crime scenes' – the ostensible crime scene turns out to be the product of a mischievous story while the true crime scenes, a hotel lounge bar and riverside bungalow, are seemingly innocuous locations – underscores the concern in the text, and in the representation of Betty herself, with the unreliability of appearances. The novel invites the reader to compare the different versions of Betty that emerge across the different crime scenes. For example, the reader is encouraged to compare the demure, young schoolgirl who innocently takes tea in the Midland Hotel with the young woman that Mary Chadwick finds in their holiday retreat:

> I went in and found her lying on the bed in the kind of negligée you used to see in vamp films about ten years ago. She looked a mess and I was a bit surprised at Barney. She was eating chocolates out of an enormous box that was lying on the bed alongside her. Terribly nineteen-thirty, the whole set up. (244)

The swift movement of this scene typifies the text as a whole. This is a novel where for much of the time we are uncertain as to who is the offender and who is the victim. Initially, it is a scene of seduction, but it becomes a scene of crime because Barney is involved with an underage girl and because of the unlicensed savagery with which Mary beats her, only relenting when she believes the girl has knocked herself unconscious. The initial scene which Betty sets up is, as Mary observes, clichéd, but this only reinforces the extent to which Betty assumes masks to meet the faces that she meets. The question poised is how far these masks relate to her fantasies or the fantasies of others about her. At best only half-glimpsed, the real Betty is difficult to define. As Marion's solicitor observes in the courtroom:

> The result of wide-set eyes and placid brow and inexpressive small mouth always set in the same childish pout. It was that physical construction that had hidden, all those years, the real Betty Kane even from her intimates. A perfect camouflage, it had been. A façade behind which she could be what she liked. There it is now, the mask, as childlike and calm as when he had first seen it above her school coat in the drawing-room at The Franchise; although behind it its owner must be seething with unnameable emotions. (241-2)

Betty Kane turns out to be a myriad of Betty Kanes. The principal crime scene in the novel, exposed as a sham when Marion discovers that one could not see from the attic what Betty describes, likewise becomes an assemblage of different scenes.

The elision of boundaries in this novel, especially the one between social reality and fantasy, is emphasised in the way in which Betty herself operates as a signifier both within and outside the novel. Looking at the text in a wider socio-cultural context, Betty Kane, as suggested above, draws into the work several motifs that increasingly figured in the representation of young women and crime in popular culture between the World Wars: the 'unadjusted girl' and the schoolgirl. However, History has given Betty Kane's name an ironic inflection. In the 1950s, it became the name of Batgirl, an athletic, independent and adventurous eighteen-year old who lived for a while in her Batwoman aunt's mansion and accompanied her in her exploits. In fact, the name Betty would have had several ironic inflections for interwar readers able to recall the classics of schoolgirl fiction, especially L. T. Meade's *Betty: A Schoolgirl* (1895) and her subsequent *A Sweet Girl Graduate* (1891). The plot of *The Franchise Affair* echoes elements of those in which adventurous young women in schoolgirl fiction became involved with kidnapping or prospective kidnapping, isolated houses and gypsies. Not only does the plot revolve around kidnapping, but the isolation of The Franchise is stressed throughout, and Marion Sharp is 'given to bright silk handkerchiefs which accentuated her gipsy swarthiness' (9).

The ironic link between Tey's Betty Kane and Bat-girl may not be coincidental. The name Betty Kane is one to conjure with. It would have been impossible for a 1940s reader not to think of Betty in relation to Grim Natwick's Betty Boop, the female protagonist of the first animated cartoon for adults. Making her debut as a dog in *Dirty Dishes* (1930), she appeared in human form in a series of pre-censorship, American cartoons including *She Wronged Him Right* (1934). By 1930s standards, Betty Boop in short skirts and revealing cleavage was an 'unadjusted girl'. She epitomised a promiscuity and liberated female sexuality that after the 1933 Hollywood code was repressed. What is especially intriguing for Tey's Betty Kane, however, is that Betty Boop was based on Helen Kane who rose to fame in Broadway musicals of the 1920s, and epitomised female sexuality in the Roaring Twenties with her song 'I wanna be loved by you' (1928). This song gave the 'Boop-boop-a-doop' to female sexuality and a few years later Betty Boop. But Betty Boop's legacy could be found in the sexual and erotic films of the 1930s and 1940s featuring platinum blondes and cool seductresses. When Mrs Chapman describes finding Betty in their holiday home, she recalls her 'lying on the bed in the kind of negligée you used to see in vamp films about ten years ago ... Terribly nineteen-thirty, the whole set-up' (244). The language – 'vamp', 'tramp', 'floo[sey] – emphasises why she finds Betty different from her husband's all other women; she is the 'unadjusted girl', the 'amateur prostitute'.

Betty Kane as an example, in Thomas' (1923) language, of an 'unadjusted girl' can also be usefully compared to the 'unadjusted girl' who apparently lies dead in Agatha Christie's *The Body in the Library* (1942):

> The flamboyant figure of a girl. A girl with unnaturally fair hair dressed up off her face in elaborate curls and rings. Her thin body was dressed in a backless evening-dress of white spangled satin. The face was heavily made-up, the powder standing out grotesquely on its blue swollen surface, the mascara of the lashes lying thickly on the distorted cheeks, the scarlet of the lips looking like a gash. The finger-nails were enamelled in a deep blood-red and so were the toe-nails in their cheap silver sandal shoes. It was a cheap, tawdry, flamboyant figure – most

incongruous in the solid old-fashioned comfort of Colonel Bantry's library. (18)

Christie provides us with an example of how, in the 1930s, attention to fantasy in writing about women's involvement in crime shifted from focussing upon private fantasies which helped explain an individual's criminality to the wider cultural fantasies in which crimes and criminals were perceived. It turns out that the body in the library is the body of a schoolgirl believed to have been burned in a burnt out car. She has been made up to look like the figure of a murdered dance hostess by a criminally ambitious woman, Josephine Turner. So what we have is a schoolgirl who is murdered and then made to look like an 'adjusted' girl, then placed in a library. This can be read on many different levels. The made-up body is both the cultural 'other' to the schoolgirl, yet also an 'other' within the schoolgirl. It reminds us that the schoolgirl is associated with 'adjustment' and 'unadjustment', but the made-up corpse serves as a macabre warning of what can happen to the 'unadjusted' girl.

Christie's narrative, like those of Jesse, Raymond and Tey, and in common with criminological thinking at the time, uses crime as an entrance to female desire. In both crime fiction and criminological writing, the elision of criminality and female desire leads to an interlinking of the mental suffering of women; the rise of a seductive, American-oriented, consumer society; and the suppression, if not criminalising, of female sexuality and independence as dangerous. Despite the way this led inevitably to an uncomfortable regulation of femininity, it suggested that the origins of female criminality lay in a reciprocal relation between the inner psychic world and external pressures and forces. It also established the need to approach crime through a socio-psychic and not simply a social reality paradigm.

5
Agatha Christie, Dorothy L. Sayers and Sara Paretsky: The New Woman

The Private Eye

Ostensibly, it may appear curious to place Agatha Christie and Dorothy L. Sayers alongside the hard-boiled American, feminist detective writer Sara Paretsky. But, like Christie and Sayers, Paretsky is concerned to challenge, albeit in a different context, the social and cultural configuration of feminine independence as an inverse mirror image of contemporaneously accepted norms of womanhood. Although Paretsky is known for revisioning the masculine, hard-boiled tradition of crime writing, her work looks back to British, feminist writers of the 1920s and 1930s, especially Virginia Woolf.

Paretsky suggests that she developed her interest in the kind of independent femininity exemplified by her private detective from reading Virginia Woolf. The essay in which she reveals her indebtedness to Woolf begins by challenging the Victorian ideal of womanhood. The independent woman who emerged, and re-emerged, during different periods of major cultural change from the late-nineteenth century and into the 1920s, was often configured, even in the 1930s work of Christie and Sayers, in opposition to this Victorian concept. Paretsky sees the Victorian ideal of womanhood largely in Woolf's own terms, focussing upon her concept of the 'angel in the house' which in Woolf's work itself is often configured as a socio-psychic masquerade. But, as Paretsky acknowledges, it is one which is deeply embedded in the highly gendered, cultural fabric of American as well as British society. It has a trajectory that can be traced back much farther than the nineteenth-century England and haunted the twentieth-century American era in which Paretsky grew up: 'Women have been wrestling with that Angel for many centuries. It is a difficult phantom to overpower because it speaks in so many voices and with so much authority behind it.'[1] Paretsky, like Christie and Sayers, envisages women's writing in relation to the many versions of the voice identified by Woolf 'telling [women that [they] should not have a mind or wish of their own'. Despite admitting that in the twentieth century 'we find enough women writing that we no longer see ourselves as odd', drawing on Woolf, she identifies, like Christie and Sayers, an 'active pressure to keep women doing such things as belong to women'.[2]

Thus, Paretsky's novels, like the work of these earlier twentieth-century English women crime writers, can be read in terms of this 'active pressure' while she herself can be seen as sharing their objectives 'to kill the Angel, to figure out what women really want, what our stories are'.[3] The emphasis in Paretsky's novels themselves, as in the language here, is upon struggle and discovery. The private 'I' in the Warshawski novels is not simply a role model for women but, as in Woolf, Christie and Sayers in their different ways, a literary device for exploring the complexity of the female subject.

All three writers explore the active socio-political and socio-psychic pressures that the configuration of women as mother first and female second exerts on the independent woman. Juxtaposing these writers highlights the influence of early twentieth feminism upon their concerns with bonds between women; with the way women can occupy 'alternative', imaginative spaces to those traditionally assigned them by society; and with the diverse subjectivity of women, reflected in the eclectic cast of female characters in their fiction. But, read alongside Christie and Sayers, Paretsky's work demonstrates the way in which psychoanalysis became an increasingly important element in feminist crime fiction and in exploring the masquerade which women were coerced into accepting as 'reality' or assumed in order to undermine the larger masquerade of gendered, power relations.

The turbulent twenties

From the perspective of Britain in the 1920s and 1930s, it was not simply that women were acquiring a new sense of themselves, but that the times themselves lacked a discernible sense of direction. This in itself might account for the popularity in a turbulent period of a genre, like the English detective story, whose denouement often appeared to confirm the status quo in terms of social and moral values. However, it is worth bearing in mind once again that the detective story is something of a masquerade. Setting false trails for the reader and presenting them with what is not as it might appear, the detective thriller has at its heart duplicity and performance; not only on the part of its characters but the author, too.

The appearance of the denouement of the crime mystery to uphold the dominant social values belies, and is in turn undermined by, the interest in the crimes themselves, and in what are departures from the status quo, that are drip fed into the narrative. The denouement might seek to reassert what is frequently challenged in the body of the text, but its capacity to wipe the slate clean again, to encourage the reader to pretend that all the upheaval never occurred, has often been overrated in criticism. It is possible to argue that the conservative framework of the English detective story pandered to cultural anxieties about women who rejected the social roles imposed upon women. But this is not always the message conveyed by the female body of the text. The voice of Anne Protheroe, the adulteress and criminal, in Christie's *The Murder at the Vicarage* is more 'real' than the voice of the 'quiet, self-contained woman' (24) she had pretended to be and had always been taken for. Lettice appears to assume the voice of a 'spoilt brat' who is tired and exhausted. But she is also associated with tennis which encoded the larger changes in women's lives; through such sports women presented themselves in active and assertive roles involving movement, intellectual agility and physical power. At the end of the text, we realise that, having been convinced of her stepmother's guilt, Lettice has been indulging in a masquerade, hiding her true, sharp intelligence.

The English middle class between the wars, as presented in Agatha Christie's work, was not a coherent group. Despite the denouement of the novels, in which the reader may feel returned to the ideals, sympathies and complacencies of rural England, the new, fragmented England that is revealed in the text, where classes, genders and generations are divided against themselves remains. The England which too many critics of Christie's work have argued that her ostensibly conservative texts reaffirms is left much more difficult to believe in at the end of many of them than at the beginning. At the end of the novels, it is often revealed as much more of a socio-cultural masquerade.

Throughout the Miss Marple novels, there is an interest in 'new women' who appeared to be acquiring greater self-confidence and to be increasingly sure of their newfound sexuality. Indeed, most of the women in *The Murder at the Vicarage* belong to this category: Griselda Clement, Estelle Lestrange, Lettice Protheroe, Gladys Cram and even the maid, Mary, who is ambitious to move on to better things. However, there are important differences between these women. Gladys Cram, who is regarded as 'common' by Griselda, has had to work for her independence and resents Lettice who appears to have been born advantaged and to have no sense of responsibility. The location of the body in the vicarage is typical of Christie's mischief. It embroils the vicarage in a scandal and undermines the conservatism that the vicarage traditionally represents, which is never finally re-established even at the end of the text. The initial impression given to outsiders of this English rural village is of its complacent confidence at the heart of the country, in both senses of 'heart' and 'country'. However, impressions of the village as a rural idyll are gradually revealed to be a masquerade behind which lies a deeper 'reality' of personal ambitions, social antagonisms and pent-up, individual desires.

The site of the murder draws attention to the subversive nature of this particular vicarage. Griselda Clement most obviously embraces the new sexuality. Apart from suggesting to the village gossips that Lawrence Redding is painting her in the nude, she teases her husband with the prospect of having an affair with him. Her relationship with her husband is not what readers might typically think of as existing between a vicar and his wife, as she regularly reminds him:

> It's so much nicer to be a secret and delightful sin to anybody than to be a feather in their cap. I make you frightfully uncomfortable and stir you up the wrong way the whole time, and yet you adore me madly. (9–10)

Griselda can assume a variety of voices, resisting those who would wish to impose a singular identity upon her. At the end of the novel, she appears to be transformed into the kind of domesticated wife and mother he purports to want her to be; in other words, the socially determined ideals of womanhood and motherhood which the vicar's wife is traditionally a signifier. Griselda promises to try 'to be very sober and Godfearing in future', having bought two books on Household Management and one on Mother Love (220). However, all this is undermined by her quips: 'Godfearing in future – quite like the Pilgrim fathers' and 'a real "wife and mother" (as they say in books)'. It is also challenged by her direct commentary on the manuals that she has just bought: 'They are all simply screamingly funny – not intentionally, you know. Especially the one about bringing up children' (220). Here Griselda is not simply rejecting the conventional mother figure but the husband/father who determines women's destiny in terms of familial duty and motherhood.

Anne Protheroe's refusal to behave in ways that are expected of her is most obviously linked, of course, to assertive female sexuality. She has an affair to escape her dreary marriage and to find love and sexual fulfilment. Unlike the vicar's wife, as suggested above, she has always presented herself as a 'quiet, self-contained woman' (24). However, the image that she has projected, like the village itself, proves to be more illusion than reality. Her 'public' identity has been posited on the suppression of her 'true' self. Her liaisons with Lawrence take place primarily in his studio which not only becomes a transgressive, sexual space but gives their affair a particular aetiology; artists' models have been traditionally associated with promiscuity and prostitution, women working in the latter often calling themselves 'models'. But despite Anne Protheroe's affair, the woman with the most overt, sexual presence in the novel is Estelle Lestrange whose effect on Reverend Clement is noticeable: he finds himself 'struck anew by the marvellous atmosphere that this woman could create' (105). But Estelle Lestrange's sexuality is literally 'strange' and thereby disturbing to him: he sees her as 'sphinx-like', 'incongruous and baffling' and a 'mystery'. In other words, she is an example of the sexually independent women who, as we saw in Chapter 4, were associated in social commentaries of the time with a masquerade in which it was sometimes difficult even for the women themselves to distinguish between performance and 'reality'.

The novel follows the thesis that was very much in the air in the 1930s, and entered into much criminological thinking, that there was a link between sexual promiscuity and crime involving women. As we argued in Chapter 4, it was regarded as axiomatic that when women stepped out of their conventional roles as dutiful wife and mother and asserted themselves socially and sexually, the space that they entered was one that was, or was likely to become, a criminal one. Gladys Cram becomes implicated in the criminal activities of Dr Stone, the archaeologist, and Lettice, Estelle Lestrange and even Griselda become suspects in the murder. Anne Protheroe, of course, is a murderer. The way in which female ambition, ruthlessness and criminality were often interleaved even in fiction written by women is encapsulated in another story, *The Body in the Library*, referred to earlier where murderer, Josie Turner, is described by Miss Marple as 'a hard-headed, ambitious young woman' (79). There was often the assumption that criminal women were more 'masculine' than the socially determined ideals of womanhood allowed. Against this background, it is ironic that Colonel Protheroe is murdered in a plot which involves the actor Lawrence Redding assuming a female voice. 'Ironic', because he is murdered by his wife who presumably had been adopting a particular 'female' voice, at least in the latter stages of their marriage, in order to disguise her adultery.

The suggestion in *The Murder at the Vicarage* that the 'quiet, self-contained woman' is herself a masquerade makes the novel's focalization especially significant. It is narrated by the vicar whereby women are defined according to a suburban, church-based gaze as respectable, god-fearing and maternal. However, Clement's perspective is confused and unreliable; not only because he does not know what is going on but also because his responses are contradictory even to himself. Twice he describes Anne as a 'quiet, self-contained woman' but he also sees her as a 'desperate woman' and a 'desperate creature'. The subtext here is that he has as much difficulty coming to terms with her adultery as his own different view of her as a woman. In recognising that she has breasts, a flushed face and quick-breathing, he reconfigures her as a sexual person. He is almost like a child who grows up to suddenly realise that their mother has a sexual identity.

Christie's spinster

Given the way in which women were becoming increasingly visible within, and associated with, the thrilling, dangerous public spaces of the city, the location of the Miss Marple stories in what is a physically rural, but mentally suburban village seems anachronistic. However, Christie's narratives need to be disentangled from their rural England-cum-suburban contexts as she herself frequently employed irony in the novel to do so. Indeed, Miss Marple herself, the principal agent of the irony in the text, takes the New Woman seriously. For example, she swiftly recognises that Lettice, even though she appears rather patronisingly to call her a 'child' at one point, is not 'half as vague as she pretends to be. She's got a very definite idea in her head and she's acting upon it' (49). In referring to Lettice as 'that child', she ventriloquises, with irony, the dismissive views of the village gossips. The choice of the word 'acting' may also be deliberately subtle, suggesting not only decisiveness on Lettice's part but the masquerade that she has assumed.

The figure of Miss Marple herself is clearly important as a trope in which conventional assumptions about gender are contested. Christie had toyed with the creative possibilities inherent in the motif of the spinster in *The Murder of Roger Ackroyd* with the figure of Miss Shephard, the doctor's sister, and in *The Mystery of the Blue Train* (1928) where Katharine does eventually avoid life-long spinsterhood through an unlikely marriage. But it was not until *The Murder at the Vicarage* that

Christie seems to have seen the possibility of using the spinster figure as an anchor in a work that explores the relationship between modernity and the changing nature of femininity.

One of the quirks of the Miss Marple stories is that when she is first introduced in *The Murder at the Vicarage* she is, as Agatha Christie admitted, in her late sixties. Apart from the fact that she is too frail to become actively involved in the detective work in *4.50 from Paddington* and to do her gardening in *The Mirror Crack'd from Side to Side* (1962), she does not seem to change much. In making Miss Marple an elderly lady, though not quite as elderly as she would be if we take the chronology seriously, Christie presents us with a female protagonist who would have been born in the mid-nineteenth century when the first women's suffrage bill was presented to Parliament, brought up in the late Victorian era, and able to observe and comment upon the changing behaviours and appearances of women in the twentieth century. In the 1920s, the increased presence of unmarried women turned them into a trope of the female independence that challenged the male domination of social structures and control of the wider public sphere. But their presence also established a tension between the independent woman of the older generation and the younger generation of 'new women'. This is exemplified in Griselda's attack on Miss Marple, that 'She's the worst cat in the village', especially given her husband's response as the narrator, 'Griselda, as I have said, is much younger than I am' (8). Christie's fiction does not simply reconfigure the spinster through Miss Marple, who seems content in her spinsterhood and intellectual superiority to those around her. Through the different generations and examples of independent women represented in her fiction, Christie explores the definition of independence – genuine independence in her fiction is linked to emotional and intellectual maturity – and how independence of various kinds affects the relationship between generations and classes of women.

The village into which the Miss Marple texts place the 'New Woman' provides a means by which Christie can use Miss Marple as a vehicle for exploring the concept of female independence as it unfolded in Britain between the wars. In many respects, it affords a better context in which to take the 'new women' seriously than the metropolis for, although accepting of the 'New Woman', the city also tended to cast her as masquerade and to simplify her as part of the spectacle of consumerism. In fact, the film production assistant Basil Blake's female companion in *The Body in the Library* can be seen as a satire on the commoditisation of the 'New Woman': 'Out of [the car] tumbled a young woman dressed in flapping black-and-white pyjamas. She had scarlet lips, blackened eyelashes, and a platinum-blonde head. She strode up to the door, flung it open, and exclaimed angrily ... '(27). She also exemplifies how women have tended to be associated with modernity in ways that confirm male control of it and confirm culture as a sphere of primarily male influence. This is satirised in Basil Blake's own masquerade which is based upon an inflated sense of his own importance and upon the way in which his women companions appear to participate in his charade. In *The Murder at the Vicarage*, the sexual and independent women who seek to free themselves of the cultural masquerade of woman as Woman are set in opposition not only to Clement's implicit Church and suburban-based conservatism but the candid, institutionalised misogyny exemplified by Blake and even more blatantly by Inspector Slack, who believes that 'women cause a lot of trouble' (177) and act in 'a silly way' (72), and Melchett who laments that there are 'too many women in this part of the world' (50). Their views are themselves satirised rather than confirmed by the play of irony within the text.

Examining within its ostensibly conservative framework the extent to which women in the 1920s and 1930s sought to free themselves of the social masquerade of womanhood, Christie's fiction is more accepting than many critics have acknowledged of how women found themselves in different kinds of relationships and arrangements to that of the traditional, Victorian family: living alone, sometimes in temporary accommodation, in lodging houses or with women friends. *A Murder is Announced* (1950) features two lesbian spinsters living together, one of whom wears short, man-like hair, corduroy trousers and a battle-dress tunic. *The Murder at the Vicarage*, which privileges the successful marriage between the vicar and Griselda and Griselda's as a contrast to the unhappy marriage in which Anne finds herself, suggests that the traditional model of the family has to be flexible enough to recognise that a family has to have more than one centre. In this sense, Christie's fiction looks back beyond Conan Doyle's Sherlock Holmes narratives, with which it is often placed in some kind of continuum as classic English detective fiction, to the sensation novel with which it shares concerns about the way in which female desire was subject to patriarchal, social control and containment.

Assessing women's modernity

Christie's stories frequently ask whether in the twentieth century things have really changed for women or whether the apparently more liberated world for women is something of a masquerade itself. This helps explain an enigma in one of her best known works, *4.50 from Paddington*. In deciding whether or not to pursue the mystery, Miss Marple takes the kind of approach that readers might associate with modernity: 'Dispassionately, like a general planning a campaign, or an accountant assessing a business, Miss Marple weighed up and set down in her mind the facts for and against further enterprise' (546–47). This way of going about things ostensibly locates Miss Marple and *4.50 from Paddington* in the twentieth century. Yet, at times, the story itself looks back to nineteenth-century Gothic melodrama which appears totally at odds with the mid 1950s the period in which it was written. Indeed, one of the brothers in the family who own Rutherford Hall, the estate where the victim's body is discovered, wryly observes: 'Granted a strange young woman has got herself killed in the barn at Rutherford Hall (sounds like a Victorian melodrama) ... ' (583). Despite the distancing irony here, the influence of Gothic melodrama, which was the first genre to probe the ambivalence lurking behind the façade of modernity, is as evident in the description of Rutherford Hall itself as in Pondicherry Lodge. Christie's house is approached through an 'imposing pair of vast iron gates', the lodge is 'completely derelict', and, almost in a mirror image of Pondicherry Lodge, 'a long winding drive [leads] through large gloomy clumps of rhododendrons up to the house' (556). There is a similar sense of neglect, 'the stone steps in front of the door could have done with attention and the gravel sweep was green with neglected weeds' (556). When she gets to the door, Lucy Eyelsbarrow, who is there at Miss Marple's instigation, has to pull on 'an old-fashioned wrought-iron bell' and, in keeping with the Gothic melodrama, 'its clamour sounded echoing away inside' (556).

However, Rutherford Hall appears to be more of a Gothic masquerade than Pondicherry Lodge and does not sit as comfortably within its Gothic framework. At one level, it takes us back to the decade from which *The Sign of the Four* emerged, and to the heyday of Victorian modernity: 'It was built by a man called Crackenthorpe, a very rich manufacturer, in 1884. The original Crackenthorpe's son, an elderly man, is living there still with, I understand, a daughter' (555). This is the kind of family that was not uncommon in the Victorian period; it was impossible for many unmarried women to leave the family home unless they married. The Victorian motif is enhanced by the revelation that the father, as his daughter Emma admits, can be 'a little – difficult sometimes' and as Lucy surmises 'an old tartar' (558).

In some respects, Christie's story is comparable to Margery Allingham's novel *Police at the Funeral* (1931) which also exposes the masquerade of outdated, Victorian social structures and values. Set in a decaying family mansion, the Gothic motif draws attention to the oppression and, indeed, brutality within a former 'respectable' household dominated by the spirit of the old patriarch John Faraday and the domineering matriarch, Caroline Faraday. But Christie's household is not quite as remote from the modern world as Allingham's.

In juxtaposing the 1950s and the mid 1980s, Christie is asking us to consider whether things have really changed for many single women. In other words, where is the masquerade? In the Gothic mansion or in its ostensibly modern rooms? Significantly, as Lucy is taken through the overtly Gothic house, she is brought to 'a pleasant sitting-room, with books and chintz-covered chairs' (557). The fact that the very evident 1950s sitting room is located in the centre of a Victorian house suggests that the 1950s is not so removed from the 1880s as one might like to think.

At one level the two periods are comparable. The 1880s saw a renewed emphasis upon domestic life as the centre of Victorian, middle-class society. In the 1950s, after the Second World War, women were encouraged through government campaigns and advertising of all kinds to return home and think of themselves as housewives and mothers rather than part of a female workforce. Lucy herself refuses to accept the pigeon-holing of the 1950s. Having obtained a First Class Mathematics degree from Oxford University, and deciding that she did not want to teach, she embarked on her own business – undertaking short-term, domestic engagements – which seems a parody of the good wife and mother scenario projected at the time. In a decade which promoted the family car in advertisements with the man sitting in the driving seat, Lucy's own 'small car' is a signifier of her independence. The fact that it is small also sets it in opposition to the family car and, by implication, Lucy herself in contrast to the family. It is a symbol of her physical as well as her intellectual mobility that were more typical at the time of single men than women; she likes, and lives for, money.

Strong poison

The Murder at the Vicarage was published in the same year as Dorothy L. Sayers's *Strong Poison*. Unlike Christie's novel, it does not have an obvious scene of crime. Although it is a murder mystery, it involves only a suspected case of poisoning which might have been administered in any one of a variety of locations. The death might even be suicide. The vagueness surrounding the crime, despite the fact that a female writer of detective fiction and former lover of the victim

Harriet Vane is facing conviction for it, lends the novel its rather unusual edge.

Since the principal scene of crime is unknown for much of the narrative, the method of detection involves the use of spies and infiltrators rather than close, empirical investigation of the crime scene. The former are necessary to a modern nation state, in its international politics as well as its maintenance of internal civil order. But they also represent a negative aspect of modern democracy and remind us that the early nineteenth-century detectives were associated with spies. In *The Murder at the Vicarage*, Miss Marple is the physically passive but mentally the agile centre of the novel; most of the leg work and interviewing is undertaken by male associates, occasionally by a female friend or associate, or by the police. In *Strong Poison*, Lord Wimsey is physically more active than Miss Marple but much of the work, and especially that which borders on the criminal, is undertaken by his female associates. For example, one of them is taught to pick locks by a reformed burglar and is planted as an informant in the suspect Norman Urquhart's office; she clandestinely picks the lock of a confidential box and breaks into his wall safe. Another female assistant poses as a medium and uses information obtained by deception to lift documents from a safe. A third woman associate surreptitiously obtains hair and nail clippings from the suspect to establish that he has absorbed enough arsenic into his body to build up immunity to it.

The involvement of women in what is, albeit morally justified, crime is commensurate with the high profile given independently minded and somewhat unconventional women in this novel. We are first introduced to the spinster Miss Climpson who runs what masquerades as Lord Wimsey's Typing Bureau, referred to rather chauvinistically by him as the 'Cattery', as a member of the jury that fails to convict Harriet Vane. Like Christie's Miss Marple, she is an intelligent and determined woman; she resolutely refuses to agree with the other jurors and is described as of 'tough conscience' (26). The women employed in the so-called Typing Bureau demonstrate a capacity to deceive others, to manipulate situations to their advantage, to remain calm under pressure, and to think and act quickly when things do not go according to plan. In other words, they would make very good criminals themselves. The effect of this is to elide their independence and marginalisation – they are elderly, widowed or deserted women or out-of-work actresses – with criminality.

In the biography of Lord Peter Wimsey which introduces the reprint of Sayers's novel, his uncle reveals that Lord Peter 'never got on with his father, he was a ruthless young critic of the paternal misdemeanours, and his sympathy for his mother had a destructive effect upon his sense of humour'. Wimsey seems to be a man with 'feminine' qualities, at times appearing as the stereotypical passive, frustrated female waiting for something to happen. He reflects perhaps the 'feminisation' of masculinity which occurred in the period after the First World War, whereas, if we think in stereotypical terms, many of the women, in their single-mindedness, determination to see projects to a successful conclusion and their assertiveness, appear more masculine.

The cumulative result of these reversals of gender stereotypes is to make masculinity and femininity in this novel appear something of a masquerade. This is highlighted by specific 'performances' such as that of Mrs Bullfinch who offers evidence to Wimsey and the police. She is described as 'the life and soul of the saloon bar at the Nine Rings ... and well known to all for her charm and wit' (71). When we are first introduced to her, we are told that she 'dabbed her large, blonde face with powder' (71); in the course of her tale, she looks 'archly round for applause' (73) and seems 'pleased with the effect she was producing' (74). By comparison, Lord Wimsey appears anxious about the mask that he wears, confessing to Harriet Vane: 'I know I've got a silly face, but I can't help that' (33).

At one level, the Typing Bureau confirms a stereotype of women in business, but because it is a 'front' this is to some extent undermined and the novel as a whole offers a number of positive role models for women. The Bureau, as a female identified subversive space, provides women with a ready camaraderie and an alternative to the conventional male world that surrounds them. However, one of the points that the novel makes is that the female world is not in any sense homogeneous and the concept of essentialist female traits is called into question. The séance in which Miss Climpson becomes involved reminds us that, in the nineteenth century, women were associated with spiritualism and the occult – the majority of mediums were women – while men tended to be associated with rationalism and science. However, Miss Climpson herself does not exhibit any empathy for the other women present. Beneath the masquerade that she assumes for the investigation, she is extremely sceptical, unlike the nurse she dupes, about spiritualism. Rather than taking the investigation to a metaphysical plane, the séance betrays her rationality and preference for evidence-based assumptions.

There is also evidence in the text of the wide spread, social anxiety about the 'New Woman' that emerged in the 1920s and 1930s. Eilund Price, one of Harriet's friends, epitomises the threat which such women were perceived as offering to male privilege and authority; she 'scorns everything in trousers' (56). Harriet Vane is described glowingly by the judge at her trial for the independence and determination she has shown:

> You have been told that she is a young woman of great ability, brought up on strictly religious principles, who through no fault of her own, was left, at the age of twenty-three, to make her own way in the world. Since that time – and she is now twenty-nine years old – she has worked industriously to keep herself, and it is very much to her credit that she has, by her own exertions, made herself independent in a legitimate way, owing nothing to anybody and accepting help from no one. (7)

But she is also criticised for submitting to pressure and agreeing to live with a bohemian writer, the victim in the poison case, to whom she was not married:

> Now you may feel, quite properly, that this was a very wrong thing to do. You may, after making all allowances for this young woman's unprotected position, still feel that she was a person of unstable moral character. You will not be led away by the false glamour which certain writers contrive to throw about 'free love' into thinking that it is anything but an ordinary vulgar act of misbehaviour. (7)

The unequivocal nature of the judge's language – 'this was a very wrong thing to do' – is undermined when Harriet tells her own story, of passion, frustration and moral conflict to Lord Wimsey. It is an opposition signified at the outset where the reader is told that the judge's 'scarlet robe clashed harsh with the crimson of the roses' on the bench (5).

Any 'threat' that Harriet poses is associated with her passion for learning and knowledge. She finds herself in the dock through the circumstantial evidence of her research into arsenic and poisoning. This emphasis upon Harriet's research signifies how women in the 1920s and 1930s were acquiring knowledge that was changing their position in relation to gender politics. Indeed, the novel suggests that the history of women might be read in terms of their acquisition of knowledge and education against cultural forces that denied their intellectual and social advancement. The most radical, eccentric female in the novel is Urquhart's great aunt, Rosana Wrayburn. She is said to be 'a wicked old woman' (70), who in her youth had a notorious stage career which in turn invokes the novel's central linking of femininity with performance.

Hannah, Urquhart's maid, alleges that 'Queen Victoria wouldn't never allow her to act before the Royal Family – she knew too much about her goings-on' (70). Suffering a stroke she is silenced and paralysed – reduced in other words to a trance maiden which in many respect symbolised the Victorian ideal of womanhood. This is reinforced by the final impression we have of her as 'a doll ... with unblinking, unseeing eyes' and having a face like 'a child's balloon, from which nearly all the air has leaked away' (139). In other words, Hannah as performer, on stage and offstage, had an energy and sense of being that denied the doll-like mask that women as 'woman' were expected to assume. Like Christie's *Murder at the Vicarage*, *Strong Poison* is a product of the 1920s when women, and especially young women, acquired greater control of their performances, making masks to meet the masquerades they faced. And like Christie's novel, it is haunted by the Victorian, culturally sanctioned, masquerade of 'womanhood'.

Warshawski's Woolf

As we said at the outset of this chapter, the hard-boiled American detective fiction of Sara Paretsky is linked to the two earlier twentieth-century English detective writers discussed in this chapter by her reclamation of women's struggle with the Victorian ideals of womanhood derived from her reading of Virginia Woolf. Woolf provides her work with a different literary ancestry from the one that is usually invoked: the American hard-boiled, masculine, crime writing tradition associated with Raymond Chandler. As argued in Chapter 2, by the time Chandler was writing, this tradition had already lost much of its vitality and verisimilitude. Tracing Paretsky's work to the English feminism of Woolf, and comparing her representation of women with that of women crime writers of the 1920s, suggests that Paretsky's radical feminism has a more vibrant historical source than has generally been acknowledged.

Paretsky's heroine V. I. Warshawski, like the male detective in interwar crime fiction, is divorced after a short and troubled marriage and has neither children nor living parents. But whilst critics have seen these aspects of her characterisation as a transference of the traditional traits of the male PI to a female detective, Warshawski's similarity with radical women in women's crime writing in the early and mid-twentieth century has been ignored. Like Christie's Lucy, she frees herself from the traditional, maternal/domestic destiny of women. In doing so, like Christie's Lucy and Sayers's Harriet Vane, she invokes what she is struggling against: an ideal of the family which Paretsky realised in her reading of

Woolf can be traced back to the masquerade of the traditional, patriarchal family and its concept of the role of the daughter.

As has often been pointed out in feminist criticism of Paretsky's fiction, she offers women readers an assertive and powerful role model. But her first non-Warshawski novel, *Ghost Country* (1998), encourages us to see her crime thrillers as more than feminist versions of inter-war, hard-boiled detective fiction. It draws our attention to a kind of 'shadow land' which has always existed in the Warshawski oeuvre but which has never been explored. *Ghost Country*, like the Warshawski novels, is concerned with women who are outside the ideal, or the masquerade, of the traditional family. Its key protagonists are two half-sisters, Harriet and Mara Stonds, whose home is with Dr Abraham Stonds – ostensibly their grandfather. Initially, the half-sisters appear to be drawn around a familiar binarism in American dynasty narratives: Harriet, who is pale and petite, is the legitimate granddaughter while Mara, who is dark, is the illegitimate granddaughter, whom Dr Stonds's housekeeper resents. They might be envisaged as a projection of two aspects of V. I. Warshawski: her 'legitimacy' as a professional, independent woman – Harriet aged 32 is a senior associate in a law firm – and her 'illegitimacy' as a radical who, unlike Harriet, refuses to work in a male-dominated hierarchy, and who, like Mara, is something of a free spirit. They also reflect the binarism which Paretsky found in Woolf's writing about the 'angel in the house'.

The private I

Feminist criticism of Paretsky's feminist, hard-boiled, detective fiction has tended to stress the positive role models that it provides for women. However, it often implies that the texts have a conceptually limited view of the 'self'. One reason for this is that it is possible to think of Warshawski herself as having a stable, coherent and fixed sense of self. Ostensibly, this would appear to be supported by the coherent biographical framework that informs the Warshawski novels. But the biographical unity of the Warshawski oeuvre stands in contradistinction to the fluid and complex sense of self which is at the heart of the texts. Paretsky has herself observed 'that there is no one way to view women. Nor is there one way women see themselves' (xiv). The numerous women characters in Christie's and Sayers's fiction, discussed earlier in this chapter, are employed to make a similar point, creating a kaleidoscope of different female subjectivities. While Warshawski displays a degree of stability, toughness and courage, redolent of the hard-boiled, male detective, she moves through a range of female subject positions: surrogate mother, outspoken feminist, caring surrogate sister, guilt-ridden daughter, sexually independent female and female professional. This movement through and among various female roles mirrors the shifting spatial focus of the narrative between various work places, eating places and homes.

At the confluence of two competing conceptions of the self in the mid-twentieth century – autonomous, free thinker and socially inscribed subject – the Warshawski novels, like Christie and Sayers's work, examine the fictitious nature of identity. Paretsky's Warshawski novels are located in, and written from, an imaginative space conflicted by traditional and shifting concepts of the private 'I' (s). Explicitly, they direct the reader to the complexity of corporate and urban crime, but, implicitly, they address the complex cultural, familial and personal influences which determine self-expression.

Warshawski's labelling of herself as a 'private investigator' can be read in more than one way, as she is usually cast as the investigator of the 'private' in her own life and in the lives of others. The women that she comes into contact with have private lives which echo aspects of her own. For example, both Warshawski and Anita McGraw in *Indemnity Only* lost their mothers before their fathers and this influenced the relationship they subsequently had with their fathers. As in Woolf's work, and Christie and Sayers's murder mysteries, in-depth relationships between women in Paretsky's fiction constitute an alternative imaginative space to male-oriented public and corporate spheres.

This aspect of Paretsky's writings provides an important link between her crime novels and *Ghost Country*. The principal alternative space in this text is provided by a community of homeless women. As in the Warshawski novels, it is a space which only men who have acquired essentially feminine qualities may enter. In *Ghost Country*, the man with the right sensibilities is an idealistic, young doctor, Hector Tammuz. In some respects, he is comparable to Malcolm Tregierre in *Bitter Medicine*, and to Warshawski's principal female friend Lotty, for he runs a clinic for the mentally ill and homeless in 'a converted coal cellar at the Orleans St. Church' (50). Indeed, healing is at the centre of the female space in this book, as it is in all the Warshawski novels. But whereas the centre of healing in the Warshawski novels is Lotty's woman's clinic, in *Ghost Country*, it is healing of a more miraculous kind that in Rafe Lowrie's sermon is opposed to orthodox medicine. Starr is alleged to have raised Luisa from the dead and the wall at the hotel Pleiades has special healing powers. These powers have to do with restoring to women control of their bodies, evident from the various stories about the wall, including a woman who has stopped haemorrhaging, an infertile woman who becomes pregnant and a woman with an unwanted pregnancy who has a miscarriage (253).

The female spaces in *Ghost Country* are more contentious than those to be found in the Warshawski novels for several reasons, one of which is that there are no heroic female figures such as Lotty associated with them. Luisa Montcrief is an alcoholic and Starr, too, has spent time in a psychiatric hospital. But these women act as vehicles for the exploration of how women who establish themselves outside conventional discourses are (mis) represented by men such as Pastor Emerson:

> And the public should be fully aware that Starr was a dangerous cult leader. Whether Starr was a kind of genuine medium, speaking in grunts that only Luisa Montcrief could interpret, or whether she was a charlatan cynically playing with the emotion of women like Mara, Emerson didn't care. The point was that Starr threatened the stability of his parish, of the city – really, of all human relationships. (318)

In the open air with Starr and Luisa, Mara feels 'not just happy, but strong, as if she could run the length of the city and not be winded' (296). This new-found personal strength is juxtaposed with the attack upon them by the police when they venture into the Northern suburbs. As in the Warshawski novels, where Lotty and her women's clinic come under pressure – in *Bitter Medicine* it is attacked by anti-abortion protesters – the female space in *Ghost Country* exists in opposition to some of the dominant forces in society. These forces include what Lontano identifies, 'money, sex, the usual deities' of America (95) and 'a small battalion of Chicago cops' who force women to line up against a wall and turn on anyone who tries to escape from 'their tightly defined boundaries' (260).

The absent presence

Given Paretsky's interest in Woolf's exposure of gendered, social identity as masquerade, the similarities between her feminism and that in the writings of Christie and Sayers are not surprising. However, the stronger psychoanalytic element in her work, referred to at the outset of this chapter, gives a different slant to the masquerade of femininity in her fiction, compared with theirs.

The Warshawski fiction can be seen as employing the hard-boiled tradition itself as masquerade because of the way in which the reader is frequently given glimpses into something that lies beneath the surface.

Encouraging the reader to probe deeper and to think about what is beneath the mask of the text is invariably focussed upon the figure of Warshawski herself.

Despite appearing tough and resolute, there is always an element of Warshawski that remains lingeringly elusive. In *Indemnity Only*, for example, Jill Thayer brings out the caring side of Warshawski who clearly treats her like a daughter: 'Something about her pierced my heart, made me long for the child I'd never had, and I watched her carefully until she was in a deep sleep' (138). We have already argued that Paretsky's novels are distinguishable from the hard-boiled tradition in the emotional intimacy that Warshawski achieves with other women. At its most negative, at least initially, this is demonstrated in the turbulent relationship between Warshawski and her Aunt Elena. Her arrival at Warshawski's door in *Burn Marks* makes her believe that the 'familiar childhood nightmare' from which she had been awakened 'had been caused by some murky vibrations emanating from Elena to my bedroom door' (2). But the most complex of Warshawski's relationships with other women is that between herself and Lotty. After Warshawski, masquerading as the tough Private I, has been beaten up by Sergio and her face has been slashed, she is taken to hospital by Lotty. The title of this chapter, 'Needle Work', might be taken as referring not only to the hospital stitches but, taking the colloquial meaning of 'needle', the way in which Warshawski and Lotty 'needle' each other on the way to the hospital. Hallucinating, Warshawski believes that she is visiting her sick mother in hospital after a state high-school basketball championship and, cutting through the fog, Lotty and her mother's voices are blurred.

In *Bitter Medicine*, Warshawski admits that there had been times when Lotty 'filled in for my mother' (183), a situation explored further in *Burn Marks*. In this novel, Lotty's Viennese stew brings back 'the comforts of my own childhood'. In caring for Warshawski's blistered hands, she becomes her mother: 'She put more salve on them and tucked me into her cool scented sheets. My last thought was that the smell of lavender was the smell of home' (287). Indeed, there is a gradual regression in this episode through various stages of a daughter's relationship to her mother. Initially, Warshawski desires to be cared for as her mother used to protect her. She then regresses to childhood submissiveness, surrendering responsibility for her life, as Lotty commands: 'Now a bath for you and bed' (287). Ultimately, Lotty's bed becomes a surrogate for the mother's body as the cryptic reference to 'the hum of the bedside clock, an oddly comforting sound' suggests (288). However, in *Bitter Medicine*, Warshawski becomes a mother to

Lotty. When Lotty is grieving her nurse's sister Consuelo's death, Warshawski takes her to a chair that is similar to the one in which her own mother used to hold her: 'Lotty sat with me a long while, her head pushing into the soft flesh of my breast, the ultimate comfort, spreading through giver and receiver both' (42).

The identity of Warshawski as a Private I is simultaneously a product of her radical feminism and a mask which detracts attention from her private 'I' which the reader glimpses in her relationship with Lotty, her parents and her really close friends. Her private self can be represented as three zones. The first is her innermost, private self which is disclosed to the reader more often than to other characters in the novel, and then usually only obliquely. The dominant relationships in this zone, which is largely concerned with the past and memory, are those with her mother and father. Beyond this zone, and overlapping in some respects, are her relationships with close female friends such as Lotty. Outside of this larger centre, there are the more casual male and female friendships, including sexual relationships with men. Around these zones are those in which her more public selves are located. Whilst these are integrated to some extent with her private self, there is also, as one would expect of a writer interested in Woolf, a greater propensity for masquerade.

Dream texts

In Paretsky's Warshawski novels, dreams are frequently employed as a means of taking the reader behind the public façades. The most appropriate text to turn to in this respect is *Bitter Medicine* where what Warshawski refers to as 'the quicksand of dreams' pull her into a quagmire of anxieties, conflicts and guilt. To begin with the obvious, what we have in the novel are fictions written as if they are Warshawski's accounts of her dreams. Clearly, we are meant to suspend this knowledge and read them as if they are genuine accounts of her dreams that provide us with insights into Warshawski's private self. They are cryptically written, presupposing that we accept that dreams, as Freud argued in his essay 'The Interpretation of Dreams', have a 'manifest' and a 'latent' content, and that it is from the latent content, 'dream-thoughts', that we disentangle there meaning.

Having left Consuelo in the hospital in *Bitter Medicine*, Warshawski returns home to dream of hearing Consuelo's child, named after her, crying in her parent's house. In this dream the baby is both Warshawski's child and Warshawski herself for prior to sleeping, she was 'picturing the baby, a small V. I.' (40). The suggestion in the text is that this dream is an expression of her guilt in not having provided her parents with the grandchild that they had hoped for.

Warshawski's parents' house is also the centre of the nightmare which follows the murder of Lotty's associate Malcolm Tregierre. In this dream, the streets of South Chicago are flooded, signifying at some level the breaking of amniotic fluids, and she is able to make her way to her parents' house only with difficulty. This psychologically difficult journey leads her to a crib in which her baby is lying. But the child has no name and can only come to life if Warshawski provides her with one. This is the child, and the conventional maternal destiny it signifies, that so far Warshawski has avoided. In other words, Paretsky suggests that, even in the late-twentieth century, the prolonged persistence of female sexuality outside of marriage can still be an uncomfortable signifier within Euro-American culture, and one that induces guilt.

On waking, Warshawski is unable to return to sleep and jogs at the lake. The water is a reminder of the feminine but it is also 'mirror still'. Here, as elsewhere in the Warshawski novels, the mirror signifies the distinction between the self that speaks and the subject that is spoken. It is dawn, not the feminine, caressing twilight she favours. The sky, 'bathed in coppery red, a dull angry color' (49), might be taken to signify the symbolic order which Warshawski, as a woman choosing not to be a mother, fears she is offending. Unlike in her twilight swim, the water is unwelcoming, as if 'some action of wind and rain had stirred the cold depths of the lake' (40). These cold depths are analogous of her own doubts and anxieties, her guilt at not having fulfilled her parents' ambitions for her and her own anxieties over her unconventional life style:

> I gasped with shock as the freezing water hit my skin, chilling my blood, and I flailed my way back to the shore. The fisherman no doubt thinking drowning a fitting end for those who disturb the perch, continued to concentrate on his line. (50)

Not only is 'line' ambiguous, suggesting family line as well as fishing line, but a fish is a phallic symbol. This connotation is underscored by the presence of a fisherman on whom Warshawski projects disdain and censure of herself. But conventionally, the fish is a symbol of life renewed and sustained, while fish gods typify independence of motion in the water, the all-possible.

The conflicts raised in the dream and in Warshawski's subsequent thoughts are the subjects of a further dream which she has following her interviews with the police. Pressurised by them, and verbally attacked by Detective Rawlings for not revealing herself as a P I when she accompanied Lotty as her attorney, Warshawski dreams of being at a high-school baseball game, from which she is separated by a high, cyclone fence. One of the boys calls on her to join him at third base; on climbing the fence she sees the mute, mournful face of a baby, who is clinging to her pantleg. She cannot dislodge the baby without hurting her. Once again, the dream is triggered by the circumstances immediately prior to it. Warshawski has not only been criticised for not revealing that she is a P I but also for being one. The ambiguity of Private I, suggesting both private detective and private self, is clearly relevant here. The high, cyclone fence is what separates Warshawski as a woman from the male-dominated, symbolic order signified by the baseball game. While the boy has got to third base, Warshawski can only watch the game. In climbing the fence, she has to reject the maternal feelings that still haunt her.

The dreams in the Warshawski fiction mirror the structure of the novels. Associative paths lead us from one dream thought to another. The novels, like dreams, have a number of associative paths that lead to their deeper structures or preoccupations and combine the different aspects of the text. While up to a point this may be true of any novel, the Warshawski novels mirror dreams in the emphasis they places on these associative paths and in their strong, repetitive element. They double back upon, sometimes against, their own articulated ideas.

Self-divided

We have already observed that the Warshawski novels are poised on the cusp of two opposing views of the subject: the free-choosing self and the socially inscribed subject. Within frameworks derived from psychoanalysis, especially the notion of 'working through', it is possible to see the subject as achieving coherence by weaving around 'rememorated' events a network of meaningful relationships that are integrated with their view of themselves.[4] In Warshawski's case, an important 'rememorated' event is her relationship with her parents, especially her mother, and this is 'worked through' a range of relationships, those I have placed in the second zone in the graphic representation above, and are integrated with her sense of who she is.

Paretsky may well have assumed the trope of having to 'work through' a relationship with one's deceased mother from Virginia Woolf. There are parallels between Woolf and Warshawski. Both lost their mothers when they were teenagers: Woolf's mother died when she was 13, Warshawski's when she was 15. In the wake of her mother's death, Woolf suffered her first nervous breakdown. Warshawski's life, like Woolf's, is haunted by her mother's absent presence. This theme of the mother as absent presence emerges even more strongly in *Ghost Country*.

Like Warshawski's mother, Harriet and Mara's mother, Beatrix, is an absent presence in the narrative. After the death of her husband in a car accident with a medical student with whom he was having an affair, Beatrix begins to drift so that her father has to assume responsibility for Harriet. Beatrix eventually returns, pregnant with Mara, only to disappear again after the birth, leaving Harriet with a half-sister. The other important absent presence in the narrative, Beatrix's own mother is killed in a car accident. Harriet admits: 'If only Grannie Salena hadn't vanished, everything would have been different, they would have had a female protector against grandfather's laws' (294). Harriet's phrase 'grandfather's laws' is redolent of the Victorian patriarchal family against which Woolf pitched her radical feminist perspective. Paretsky has created an empty space around the mother figure, which not only Harriet and Mara's grandfather cannot fill but, with the complicity of hostile women such as Dr. Stonds's housekeeper, turns into an oppressive space. The novels do what Woolf did and what Christie and Sayers do in their fiction: they express the 'reality' beneath the masquerade of the traditional, ideal family.

Paretsky's fiction can be usefully traced back to Woolf also in its concern with what lies beneath the feminist idealisation of the mother and daughter relationship. In the Warshawski novels, there are numerous traces of Warshawski's mother which provide continuity between the two women. As Warshawski observes in *Bitter Medicine*: 'I guess my mother's hot-weather Italian genes dominate my dad's ice-bearing Polish ones' (223). In *Indemnity Only*, Warshawski admits that she types on an Olivetti portable typewriter that had been her mother's (6), and the same point is made in *Bitter Medicine* (61) and *Burn Marks* (18). In other words, she is using her mother's keys to communicate, although her mother wanted her to communicate in different, operatic keys. Having named her daughter Victoria Iphigenia – after an Opera singer Victor Emmanuel (49) – she wanted her to be an opera singer or a professional of some kind. Warshawski also has her Italian mother's olive skin colouring (14) and her mother's 'drive' (36). Indeed, Warshawski's mother is recalled frequently throughout Paretsky's Private I oeuvre, although often quite incidentally. In *Bitter Medicine*, when Lotty brings news of Consuelo's death, Warshawski has to pull on a T-shirt and shorts quickly, reflecting, almost irrelevantly in terms of the plot: 'I was fifteen when I last wore a nightgown – after my mother died there was no one to make me put one on' (41).

Consuelo, more understandably, reminds Warshawski of when she'd last seen her mother: 'small, fragile, overshadowed by the machinery of an indifferent technology' (40). Her prized possessions are a set of red glasses that her mother brought from Italy wrapped in her underwear, a fact which associates the glasses not only with her mother but her vagina/womb.

However, if the glasses remind us that Warshawski is a product of her mother's body, their twisted stems suggest not only the umbilical cord that still binds mother and daughter but also the problematic nature of that bond. Harriet and Mara in *Ghost Country* may be seen as the two aspects of Warshawski's relationship with her mother and, perhaps, of the relationship of all women with their mothers: Harriet, who admits to her grandfather that she has only painful memories of her mother, is an exaggerated version of the problematic aspects of the mother–daughter dyad. Warshawski's desire to be closer to her mother finds an exaggerated expression in Mara who 'keeps wishing she had a mother' (99). As in Warshawski's case, her deepest desires surface while she is swimming in a warm lake at sundown: 'Tonight the water was calm and gentle as a cradle ... . right now it was warm, caressing her naked body like silk' (299). But her desire is not only for her mother, as in Warshawski's case, but for her sister, for whom she suddenly feels 'a pang of longing'.

In *Indemnity Only* some of the glasses that Warshawski has inherited from her mother are broken when Warshawski's flat is overturned and some of her mother's jewellery is also stolen. The loss of her mother's possessions or fear of their loss is a trope that occurs more than once in the Warshawski novels. In *Bitter Medicine*, when her apartment is burgled, she is concerned about the copies of *Little Women* and *Black Beauty* that her mother gave her for her ninth birthday (94). Warshawski's dream of the glasses is especially significant: The red Venetian glasses lined up on her mother's dining room table break when Warshawski sings a high note, signifying the guilt she feels about becoming something her mother did not want for her. The glasses dissolve in a pool of blood, her mother's blood (116).

Warshawski's mother is often a censorious presence in her daughter's present; a disruption of her continuous, lived temporality. In *Burn*

Marks, which opens with a dream of Warshawski and her mother trapped in her bedroom, Warshawski is not free of her mother's censorship years after her death. Even when she buys 'domestic Parmesan' in the grocery store, she observes: 'Gabriella would have upbraided me sharply – but then she wouldn't have approved of my buying pasta in a store to begin with' (33).

It is through the representation of Warshawski's relation with her mother that the psychic tensions and conflicts on which the Warshawski novels are posited are actually 'worked through'. The novels return us to a commonplace distinction in twentieth-century psychoanalytic theories on gender formation: while the emphasis in Freudian theory is on how men have to separate themselves from their mothers in order to enter fully into patriarchy, feminist psychoanalytic theory usually stresses women's association with their mothers as the closest person to them. Implicit in the latter are tendencies to essentialise the bond between mother and daughter and to essentialise women as 'caring' because their ties to physical being are perceived as less severed than those of men. The Warshawski novels challenge both these assumptions: the mother and daughter bond is depicted in the novels as problematic; the texts recognise the need for the daughter to break free of her mother's influence if she is to become an autonomous being; relations between, and among, women are complex, contradictory and diverse; and the caring role is perceived as only one dimension of women's identity and relationships.

Like Christie and Sayers's detective fiction, the Warshawski novels pursue the notion that the female subject is always temporally self-divided. 1970s and 1980s feminist criticism posited an essentialism that was as much linguistic and psychoanalytic as biological. It stressed that women were set apart from men because of their distinct bodily experiences, such as birthing, lactation and menstruation. Within this context, the question that the Warshawski novels pose is: Where does this leave women like Warshawski? In some respects, she can be seen as abstracting herself from direct links to the maternal world in women's bodies. This, in turn, associates her with the male world in which she can never be other than 'other'.

Paretsky's fiction absorbs early-twentieth-century feminism in different ways and alongside a different range of further literary and cultural influences from Christie and Sayers. But reading them together within this context highlights their shared concern with the ways in which women can occupy 'alternative' imaginative spaces to those occupied by, and assigned to them. However, Paretsky's work demonstrates the way in which psychoanalysis became an increasingly important element in feminist crime fiction. Chapter 6 discusses how a contemporary African-American writer, herself influenced by Woolf, explores, from an African-American perspective, the masquerades which women are coerced into accepting as 'reality' or are forced to assume in order to discover freedom of being.

6
Masquerade, Criminality and Desire in Toni Morrison's *Love*

Bodily masquerades

Love (2003) is the eighth novel by the Nobel prize-winning, African-American writer Toni Morrison. Her fiction draws on African-American, American, African and European literary traditions. Like Sara Paretsky, she is indebted to Virginia Woolf, only more so. She completed a Masters thesis on Woolf and William Faulkner and her writings betray the influence of many of the characteristic of Woolf's non-realistic fiction.

Unlike Sara Paretsky, she is not a crime writer, although crimes from child rape to murder feature in her texts. These include Cholly's rape of his own daughter in *The Bluest Eye*, Sula's complicity in the death of a child, Jade's involvement with a fugitive in *Tar Baby*, the murder with which *Jazz* opens and the massacre of a female commune in *Paradise*. Criminality enters *Love* through the activities and the pasts of some of its principal characters. It includes a criminal assault on a child and on an elderly woman by a young woman whilst its central motif of criminality recalls one of the earliest examples of crime narrative, of which Dickens's *Bleak House* is a spectacularly complex example: the crime mystery based upon disputed inheritance and involving forgery or an attempt at forgery. The novel begins with the way in which the lives of two women in particular, Heed and Christine, have become entwined in a dispute as to which of them is the rightful heir to the estate of a reasonably wealthy man, William Cosey, with whom they had become involved. Heed employs a young woman to write a will in Cosey's hand. Like Sula and Nel in *Sula* (1973), the relationship between Heed and Christine, who were once very close childhood friends, is central to the text. Despite the animosity that develops between them, they have an unspoken affection for each other that neither admits to the other until one of them is seriously injured at the end of the book. Like her earlier novel *Jazz* (1992), which it specifically recalls in places, *Love* turns from the present into pasts that are slowly unravelled.

The character whom Heed engages to forge a more recent version of Cosey's will, Junior Viviane, is fresh from the 'Correctional'. In some respects, she is reminiscent of Sula, the sexual independent female and trickster figure who is implicated in the killing of a child in Morrison's second novel. In Part Two of *Sula*, the titular protagonist returns from a period of being mysteriously absent from the Bottom, as the community was known:

> Sula stepped off the Cincinnati Flyer into the robin shit and began the long climb up into the Bottom. She was dressed in a manner that was as close to a movie star as anyone would ever see ... Walking up the hill toward Carpenter's Road, the heels and sides of her pumps edged with drying bird shit, she attracted the glances of old men sitting on stone benches in front of the courthouse, housewives throwing buckets of water on their sidewalks, and high school students on their way home for lunch. (90–1)

She attracts stares that are admiring, envious and disapproving or masquerade as one whilst meaning another. Like Junior's arrival, Sula's return quickly becomes the subject of gossip and speculation: 'By the time she reached the Bottom, the news of her return had brought the black people out on their porches or to their windows. There were scattered hellos and nods but mostly stares' (91). Like Junior, she conveys a sense of bodily, sexual freedom which, as for Junior, attracts the displeasure of the older women. Her mother speaks for them when she warns Sula: 'Ain't no woman got no business floatin' around without no man' (92). But what separates Junior from Sula is the emphasis in her representation upon the use that she makes of clothes and on fetish, to which I will return later. Sula conveys physical and sexual freedom but, despite appearing dressed like a movie star, that impression seems somehow independent of her clothes:

> Sula would come by of an afternoon, walking along with her fluid stride, wearing a plain yellow dress the same way her mother, Hannah, had worn those too-big house dresses – with a distance, an absence of a relationship to clothes which emphasised everything the fabric covered. (95)

The portrayal of Junior is also different from Sula in the even greater emphasis upon the riskier kind of sexuality that also informs *Jazz*. In that novel, the City is a place of 'windows where sweethearts, free and illegal, tell each other things' (36) and people 'are not so much new as themselves: their stronger, riskier selves' (33).

The risky, at times violent, sexuality of *Jazz* comes to the fore in *Love* in incidents such as the one in which Christine takes revenge upon a man who cheats on her by vandalizing his prized Cadillac with a switch blade. *Jazz* opens with an episode in which Violet interrupts the funeral of her husband's young lover and attempts to slash the corpse's face. What she tries to cut open is 'a creamy little face' which 'nothing would have come out but straw' (5). The implicit comparison here between a prepared corpse and a mannequin is appropriate because Violet attacks the body of a girl whom she has constructed, even haunting the school that she had attended and pestering her aunt. Violet and Christine in different contexts both attack what for them is a phantasm.

The city as performance space

It hardly needs pointing out today that Morrison's individual works reflect Jazz composition in which various themes enter and re-enter the text at different times and are played against each other. But now that she has written eight novels, it is clear that this is true also of Morrison's oeuvre as a whole, as particular novels pick up and develop motifs and subjects from earlier works. One significant theme that enters her oeuvre in her first novel, *The Bluest Eye*, which is about the way in which light-skinned African-American women masqueraded as white, is performance itself. The subject recurs in *Sula*, has a prominent part in *Jazz* and is taken up again in *Love*. Whilst the City in *Jazz*, as mentioned above, is depicted as a place where people can be themselves, they are often nevertheless engaged in performance, albeit one that permits newfound freedoms of being. For in the City, women 'put the tiniest stitches in their hose', girls straighten their sisters' hair, and the 'citysky' makes 'the clothes of the people on the streets glow like dance-hall costumes' (36).

It is the emphasis upon 'performance' and upon opportunities for people to reinvent themselves that distinguishes Morrison's representation of the City in *Jazz* from the way in which Harlem has been traditionally represented in black crime fiction. It is closer to that of Claude McKay's *Home to Harlem* (1926) and *Negro Metropolis* (1940) than the more sceptical writings which emerged during and immediately after the Depression that fuelled the less idealistic crime writers' view of what they saw essentially as a ghetto. In Chester Himes's Harlem Cycle (1957–69), Harlem is a dangerous and eccentric place. As in Morrison's novel, it is a place of masquerade where, in *A Rage in Harlem* (1957) focussed upon two rival, confidence 'stings', there are:

> Hepped-cats who lived by their wits – smooth Harlem hustlers with shiny straightened hair, dressed in lurid elegance, along with their tightly draped queens, chorus girls and models – which meant anything – sparkling with iridescent glass jewellery, rolling dark mascaraed eyes, flashing crimson fingernails, smiling with pearl-white teeth encircled by purple-red lips, exhibiting the hot excitement that money could buy. (60)

However, Himes stresses more than Morrison the degradation and debasement. Himes's Harlem is a place of 'fetid tenements, a city of black people who are convulsed in desperate living, like the voracious churning of millions of hungry cannibal fish' (93). It may be similar to the City in *Jazz* in that 'honeysuckle-blues voices dripped stickily through jungle cries of wailing saxophones, screaming trumpets, and buckdancing piano-notes' but it is also a place where 'someone was either fighting, or had just stopped fighting, or was just starting to fight, or drinking ruckess juice and talking about fighting' (36). Acknowledging the crime and the violence, Morrison celebrates the performative aspect of the city whereas black crime fiction and novels involving crime by black male writers such as Himes, Herbert Simmons and Richard Wright tend to stress the violence of ghettoised black life.

In many respects, the most dominant masquerade in *Jazz* is the City itself in the 1920s:

> The City is smart at this: smelling and good and looking raunchy; sending secret messages disguised as public signs; this way, open here, danger to let colored only single men on sale women wanted private room stop dog on premises absolutely no money down fresh chicken free delivery fast. And good at opening locks, dimming stairways. Covering your moans with its own. (64)

Here, as in other passages where the City appears to be the novel's main protagonist, the language mirrors the blurring of masquerade and reality. Indeed, in *Jazz*, the City is not simply a character but a performance: 'The City thinks about and arranges itself for the weekend: the day before payday, the day after payday, the pre-Sabbath activity, the closed shop and the quiet school hall; barred bank vaults and offices locked in darkness' (50). The boundaries between the City and its people are elided around the way in which City life is essentially a matter of arranging and configuring oneself. The City's exhilarating diversity is depicted as a series of 'bodies' which it wears to meet its weekly rhythm, its buildings and its inhabitants.

This figurative way of looking at the City, seemingly standing and masquerading in a variety of physical guises, is extended to its inhabitants who themselves appear to become a bodily performance that they can inhabit rather than own for themselves. The young friends Dorcas and Felice believe that 'they know before the music does what their hands, their feet are to do, but that illusion is the music's secret drive: the control it tricks them into being is theirs' (65). Dorcas at sixteen is said to have 'stood in her body and offered it' to boys at a dance whilst she and her young friend come to learn 'that a badly dressed body is nobody at all' (65).

The maid as masquerade

Love is a novel where what the City is good at in *Jazz* – 'sending secret messages disguised as public signs' (64) – is an attribute of many of the individual characters. Junior noticing Heed's servant Christine's twelve diamonds realises that she has 'caught the other one's pose' (29) while her own blunt speech is said to be 'something of an act' (26). This notion of an 'act' communicating with what is a 'pose' is at the heart of female relationships in *Love* which are treated differently from in *Sula* because of the emphasis this time upon the masquerade or 'persona' that women assume in relation to each other. In this regard, *Love* offers a fresh perspective on Joan Riviere's thesis that some women 'put on a mask of womanliness to avert anxiety and the retribution feared from men'.[1]

In entering employment as Heed's personal companion and maid, Junior can be placed within a wider cultural framework in which the maid is associated with masquerade at a number of levels. Although the maid and the criminal may seem light years apart, history and literature have elided the two. Usually, the maid was associated with what is classed as petty larceny such as stealing alcohol, china and even feathers from pillows. This in itself underscores the way in which lower or working-class women who became servants were unable to 'buy into' the consumer society that turned them into a commodity, a status symbol. Unable to enjoy the benefits of capitalist society, some servants stole from it. For African-American servants, there were additional cultural anxieties in this respect. Black people with possessions were even more likely than whites to be presumed to have stolen them. It goes without saying that even in the twenty-first century, black people are more likely than whites to be subject to stop and search by the police.

It almost goes without saying, too, that the maid is a vulnerable figure in a male dominated household because she is susceptible to her employer's advances. Maids who were sexually abused and often made pregnant by their employers before being turned out on the street or sent to the workhouse are familiar subjects in the Victorian novel and a fact of history. The maid is a figure that exposes the hypocrisy behind the façade of middle- and upper-class respectability. The African-American who suffered criminal assaults from her white employer also became a signifier of the taboo of mixed-race sex. Moreover, within the wider cultural framework in which the maid is constructed, the mistress's personal maid is also an unstable and somewhat slippery cultural signifier in ways to which Victorian texts alluded and twentieth-century fiction often makes more explicit. At one level, both maid and mistress may be seen as indulging in a masquerade because each in her own way assumes a role. The maid conducts herself in a way in which she believes she is expected to behave with her mistress and in her presence she assumes a persona appropriate to the position she occupies. Her employer behaves in a way in which she perceives she is expected to behave as a mistress. This in turn raises questions about the relationship between them. Both are configured by the social reality in which they find themselves and ultimately are signifiers of socio-political difference. But they are always 'not quite' the mistress and 'not quite' the servant.

A recurring trope in writing about the mistress and maid relationship is the level of intimacy between them, especially in the case of a maid who, like Junior, performs personal services for her employer such as washing her hair or bathing her. Since the maid enters the mistress's most intimate body space she acquires a potential for power over her, as Junior comes to possess over Heed, and has access to her most intimate secrets. Although the maid becomes ultimately a functional body within a household, the fact that she is always, like Junior, never quite the servant and has access to her mistress's most intimate secrets restores to her a symbolic power that is otherwise denied her.

Language, performance and identity

Intriguingly, as Heed lies seriously injured at the end of *Love*, Christine and Heed revert to the language of their childhood, employing the word 'idagay' to express intimacy. In doing so, they reveal how their childhood, linguistic masquerade, whilst giving voice to what they wanted to hide, actually articulated what more 'normal' language hid, returning the reader to one of the novel's central motifs, talk as masquerade.

In their employment of the principles of jazz composition, even Morrison's most serious novels have an element of 'play' or 'masquerade' about them. At the heart of this is the concept of language itself as performance. In this respect, Morrison's use of language reflects an important aspect of American English between the World Wars and the trans-national influence of New York's Broadway. Words like 'Turkey', 'whoopee', 'hip' and 'fan' coming out of Broadway in the 1920s and 1930s that constituted what became known as Broadway slang were rich in codified meanings and seemed themselves a kind of masquerade. This was especially the case when, disseminated through the media, they were adopted in other parts of America and in other nations. But behind the masquerade not only the speaker but the nation also acquired a new freedom of being and a language for which it had been searching for decades to capture the rhythms of its seaboard cities and the concept of America as the great melting pot.

The performative element that entered American language in the 1920s and 1930s reflected the wider cultural power that performance and Broadway itself acquired in the first half of the twentieth century. All black musicals such as 'Shuffle Along' (1921), which introduced rising singers and dancers Florence Mils, Paul Robeson and the fifteen-year old Josephine Baker to the American and European public, and 'Runnin' Wild' (1923), which produced the worldwide hit dance the Charleston, gave a new impetus to the performing arts which led eventually to the formation of an all-black ballet company, Ballet Negre, and in 1931, the First Negro Dance Recital in America. But they also stimulated the development of other African-American arts, including painting, sculpture, literature and poetry. 'Shuffle Along' spawned what at the time was seen as risky stage performances including emotionally intimate scenes between black people. It was inspired by, and in turn, inspired the Harlem nightclubs that both pushed back the boundaries of black creativity and mocked the traditional ways in which black culture had been presented on the American stage.

The direct influence of the way in which the performing arts brought together the political, social and artistic climates of early twentieth-century America could be seen in the poetry of Langston Hughes and the black crime writing of Rudolph Fisher, Herbert Simmons, Iceberg Slim and Chester Himes. This interleaving of the arts and politics gave creativity and performance a special place in the formation of African-American identity encapsulated in the title of the Harlem writer's Alan Le Roy Locke's acclaimed anthology of stories, *The New Negro*. *Love* is a novel which, in its concern with performance and masquerade, exploits the way in which black identity and performance became synonymous and looks back to the Harlem Renaissance and the subsequent decades which it influenced. People are said to seek to undo the 'showpiece' of the world, put 'everything they feel on stage' and are 'busy showing off'. In earlier years, Heed is said to have 'paraded around like an ignorant version of Scarlett O'Hara (36), a performance based on a masquerade that is a performance. Junior finds herself watching 'for the face behind the face' (28).

More than any of Morrison's earlier novels, *Love* brings the notion of masquerade into the language of the text itself. Indeed, Junior finds herself listening 'to words hiding behind talk'. In the novel, Morrison exploits talk as masquerade. The conversation about Junior between Romen and his grandfather is an important example of this in the book. In coyly seeking the details of Romen's relationship with Junior, he is vicariously enjoying her body himself. *Love* is a novel in which conversations are often 'played'; they take the participants by surprise, involve them in highs and lows, and, as in the first exchange between Junior and Christine, have an edge to them.

The need to listen to the words behind the talk is especially obvious in the masquerade Cosey creates around his desire for Heed, defending himself by drawing attention to the story of a black girl who, running behind the cart to which her father has been tied by Whites, falls humiliatingly into a pile of manure. Describing his relationship with Heed to his friend Sandler, he gives him the impression that he is talking of a fashion model rather than a child (148). But the reality seems to be that he is excited by having a bride who is a child.

Female masquerade, sexuality and fetish

That the relationship between Heed and Christine is not what it seems is central to *Love*. Initially, they appear to be employer and employee, but then, as one character suggests, they appear to be cousins, only to turn out to be grandmother and granddaughter, Heed having married Christine's grandfather when she was eleven years old. This kind of twist is typical of many of Morrison's novels which keep the reader hooked through setting up conundrums or constantly hinting at deeper levels of meaning beneath surface.

The masquerade in the relationships between Heed and Christine, who become embroiled in a dispute over Cosey's supposed will, erupts through the language in which it is masqueraded into violence at his funeral. Heed's 'false tears' and 'exaggerated shuddering shoulders' (98) arouse Christine and her mother's anger. The duplicity is stressed in May's description of Heed as a snake. However, typically of this text, the dispute between the two women is configured as part of a larger masquerade at which the others present pretend to be shocked while secretly 'delighted' by the 'graveside entertainment' (99).

What emerges from *Sula, Jazz* and *Love* in particular is an interest in the way in which the fetishism of twentieth- and twenty-first century icons of female sexuality turns assertive, independent sexuality into a masquerade which is both socially determined and an act of performance. In this respect, these works share with the very different texts discussed in Chapter 4 an interest in the way in which women may be seen as implicated in fantasies that are oppressive but may be experienced as thrilling, even dangerously exciting. Indeed, Junior's presence in *Love* is itself a theatre of iconic female sexuality: her high heel boots and the crack that they make as she walks, the 'angle of her hips', the 'pleasure' in her voice, her tiny skirt, her long legs and her short leather jacket. The importance of fetishism to her sense of self and her involvement in fantasies that are oppressive yet thrilling are evident also in the way in which she always makes love to her boyfriend Romen – naked apart from her boots. Although she keeps her boots on to hide the merged toes, the result of violence against her when she was a child, she is only too aware of the fetish which she offers Romen. He responds by giving her his grandfather's officer cap, which she readily accepts, to complete the uniform and the fantasy.

The officer's cap is a provocative symbol in many respects. Transferred from a military context, where it traditionally signifies authority, power and respect, to the bedroom, the officer's cap reconfigures domination and obedience. But the transformation raises questions about the extent to which fantasy is not only part of sexuality but social reality more generally. The cap brings to the bedroom a repertoire of cultural associations that determine the nature of the fantasy but they are themselves creatively reinterpreted. The fantasy permits a freedom of being that the cap in its military context denies. Moreover, Morrison complicates the scenario in so far as the cap belongs to Romen's grandfather who has his own secret longings and for whom, too, Junior is a fetishised object. The officer's cap worn by Junior in a sexual fetish becomes a surrogate symbol of Romen's grandfather's secret desires.

The extent to which Junior is complicit in the fantasy and is led by or leads Romen brings a myriad of cultural associations to bear on the text including Eve, the temptress in the garden of Eden, the trickster figure upon which Sula in Morrison's earlier novel is based and the African-American or mixed race music hall dancers, like the legendary Josephine Baker, whose performances acted out or, as in Baker's case, took control of culturally determined images of black women. The image of Junior in the officer's cap might well bring Josephine Baker to mind as she was decorated for her work in helping the French Resistance during the war. But what also brings Junior and Josephine together is their subversion. Josephine Baker, whose most famous routine involved her dancing virtually naked apart from a grass skirt and bananas tied around her, mocked traditional Western images of black sexuality and frequently mocked the dance routines in which she participated. Both Josephine and Junior participate in cultural fantasies that fetishise black and mixed race women while turning themselves mockingly on the oppressive male gaze.

A point that is seldom made about African-American dancers, such as Josephine Baker, who pushed back the boundaries of black sexuality and sought to demonstrate ownership of their own bodies as African-American women is that they were dependent, like Junior in boots and officer's cap, upon a combination of naked and fetish. They performed often to largely white audiences and would cause society to ask itself whether the fantasies that they apparently acted out were in their bodies or in the heads of the predominantly white males who watched them. This was a question Morrison began to ask in her earlier novel *Tar Baby*, in which a young, light-skinned, African-American woman enjoys success as a photographic model. In the bedroom, Junior raises similar questions about the location of the fantasy in which she participates.

Romen is transformed through his relationship with Junior, who as the more confident and determined sexual partner appears to be in control. But she, too, stands more revealed, literally and metaphorically, through her relationship with him. An enigma in the text is whether Junior, who frequently masquerades in her social relationships, is more herself in her relationship with Romen. Is she revealed through her sexual behaviour or is this, too, essentially, a performance?

The way in which the novel moves from fetishism of the sexualised woman into the acting out of sexual fantasy is typical of the way in which crime and criminality is frequently employed in both popular and literary fiction to create an aesthetic space in which to explore the role of masquerade and pretence in sexuality and in gender relations. In particular, it creates a space in which to analyse, often from a psychoanalytic perspective, how women become complicit in fantasies that are thrilling but also oppressive and even dangerous. The boots and officer cap fantasy may appear reasonably innocuous, but it is integrated in the novel with Romen's anxiety about Junior's desire to have violent sex and to be hurt.

In the previous chapters, we have already seen that many of the fetishes and fantasies into which criminality in literature and much crime fiction takes us involve the secret acting out of sadomasochistic fantasy. This is the case, literally, in Colin Dexter's last Inspector Morse novel, *The Remorseful Day*, where, as we have seen, Morse's suspected involvement and his superior's certain participation in sadomasochistic scenarios offer the reader inverse mirror images of the unequivocal lines of authority and obedience followed (or acted out?) in their public lives. The focus is often not upon the violence but the scenario itself and the extent to which it involves assuming roles. Or upon the way in which the discovery of this acting out, overturns accepted interpretations of people and relationships and makes everything appear to have been, and to be, a masquerade.

For an African-American writer there is a long legacy of texts concerned with sexual violence and perversity that can be traced back to the slave narratives where white plantation owners availed themselves of black female slaves, even children, and male black slaves risked everything in succumbing to the desires of their white mistresses. What is often alluded to in the early slave narratives is more explicit in the twentieth-century African-American novel. The reader might think of the violent and sordid love story of Rufus and Leonora in James Baldwin's *Another Country* (1962) or the incest in his *Just Above My Head* (1979) or the train of events begun by Bigger Thomas taking advantage of the drunken Mary Dalton in *Native Son* (1940). Texts by twentieth-century African-American women writers, such as Ntozake Shange, Ann Shockley, Alice Walker and Gloria Naylor, are generally less charitable than male writers have been in their representation of the culpability of black men in crimes against women. In their novels, issues of race and caste are interleaved with family taboos such as incest. Whilst critics have generally stressed the more explicit violence and sexuality in these works, less attention has been paid to how the themes are embedded, as in the earlier slave narratives, in all kinds of masquerade. This is boldly exemplified in Gloria Naylor's *Linden Hills* (1985) which can be seen as an African-American version of the white community novel that sought to look behind the façade of middle-class, suburban respectability. Through the experiences of two young, odd-job men, the novel exposes the hypocrisy and masquerade in a middle-class, black suburb.

The fantasy, whether based upon sadomasochism, fetish or both, that frequently enters into the crime novel or the literary novel like *Love* based in some way upon criminality, permits a greater degree of fluidity in relationships and within an individual's sexuality than that person's conventional or public life would seem to allow. Whilst this is suggested to be true of the evolving sexual relationship between Junior and Romen, *Love* hints at desire that not only finds expression in fantasy and 'acting out' but in a type of sexuality that is thrilling because it is also, in a term Morrison uses in *Sula*, 'cutting edge'. In *Sula*, Morrison began exploring what this concept meant:

> [Sula] went to bed with men as frequently as she could. It was the only place where she could find what she was looking for: misery and the ability to feel deep sorrow. She had not always been aware that it was sadness that she yearned for. Lovemaking seemed to her, at first, the creation of a special kind of joy. She thought she liked the sootiness of sex and its comedy; she laughed a great deal during the raucous beginnings, and rejected those lovers who regarded sex as healthy or beautiful. Sexual aesthetics bored her. Although she did not regard sex as ugly (ugliness was boring also), she liked to think of it as wicked. But as her experiences multiplied she realized that not only was it not wicked, it was not necessary for her to conjure up the idea of wickedness in order to participate fully. During the lovemaking she found and needed to find the cutting edge. (122)

In *Jazz* and in *Love*, the concept of 'cutting edge' is associated with a sexuality that is thrilling because it is dangerous and violent. Junior's apparent craving for 'dangerous' sex, however, remains a covert trope, another enigmatic element in her mysterious characterisation.

In other feminist novels, the trope of dangerous and violent sex is much more explicit than in *Love* or even *Jazz*, as in the British writer Jenny Dixi's *Nothing Natural* in which a woman becomes involved with a serial rapist who in turn becomes the vehicle whereby not only his but her secret, sadomasochistic fantasies are acted out through scenarios which increasingly push back the boundaries between 'real' and 'performance'. But what *Love* has in common with many other texts that conflate criminality and fetish, even those that do so more overtly like Dixi's, in addition to the points made so far, is the way the tropes are often employed to suggest the unfathomability even of those who are

Josephine Baker in shaping African-American female identity. But he also invokes the way that dancers, as Graham Greene pointed out in *A Gun for Sale*, were frequently associated on both sides of the Atlantic with prostitutes, especially 'amateur' or 'occasional' prostitutes. L sees Junior as one of 'these modern tramps' (67) and Vida later says that she 'dresses like a street woman' (145). Heed calls Junior a 'sexpot' (72) and knows that she is using her to 'satisfy and hide her cravings' (72). These cravings, as Thomas suggests of the unadjusted girl, are ostensibly criminalised. In Junior's case this happens through the linking of her 'cravings' to her 'correctional' past; she is said to have had 'thief smarts' (72). By comparison, Romen is too adjusted, 'so tight around the mouth' (72). The occasional prostitute motif is also exemplified at one point in Christine's life. Her 'dream of privacy, of independence' (92), as in the case of some of the unadjusted young women discussed earlier, leads her into prostitution at Manila's whorehouse.

It is made clear through the characterisation of Christine and Junior that their involvement in professional, or what 1920s criminologists called 'occasional', prostitution was a product of a social environment 'organized around the pressing needs of men' (93). However, prostitution does not have the same negative connotations in Morrison's fiction as in the texts discussed in the previous chapters because of the way in which prostitutes are associated with 'style'. This is evident, quite literally, in the figure of Crystal who, walking naked into the sea, takes 'on the shape of the cloud dragging the moon' (106).

'Unadjustment' in Junior's case is also different from that examined in Chapter 4 with reference to White American and British literature because of the way in which it is linked to 'sass' (81) which whites are said to have hated, and feared when associated with separatism and Black Nationalism. 'Sass' disturbs some African-Americans; Sula who clearly has 'sass' earns her mother's reproach, in a clever piece of word play upon the absent noun: 'Well, don't let your mouth start nothing that your ass can't stand' (92). On the whole, though, 'sass' is admired by African-Americans because, as Heed observes, it has a 'winning' that 'took a brain' (79). In this respect 'sass' is not dissimilar from the 'unadjustment' exemplified by independent, sexually assertive women who become embroiled in the crime discussed in Chapter 4. If Junior is a 'criminal', it is an intelligent, controlled criminality that she is guilty of which is different from the kind exemplified by those who, like Christine, are said to live a 'sloppy life' that degenerates into 'brawls, arrests, torching cars, and prostitution' (73). In her intelligence, Junior echoes female criminals discussed in Chapter 4, such as Irene Adler in close to us. In fact, Junior appears in a variety of disguises. At one point, dressed in a red suit lent her by Heed, she looks like a 'Sunday migrant'. 'Migrant', an image of rootlessness, suggests the lack of a real centre within Junior's performance of herself. Romen observes in the course of his relationship with her that she has thirty eight ways of smiling, each with a different meaning.

'Unadjustment' and the African-American

In *Sula, Jazz* and *Love*, women seduce men for gain as much as pleasure. At one level, Junior, like Sula, might appear to be an African-American example of Thomas's 'unadjusted girl' discussed in Chapter 4 and might seem to recall his thesis that masquerade is used by many criminal women to realise other ambitions and desires. In *Sula*, Morrison describes:

> [Sula] came to their church suppers without underwear, bought their steaming platters of food and merely picked at it – relishing nothing, exclaiming over no one's ribs or cobbler. They believed that she was laughing at their God. (114–15)

Despite their shared preference for not wearing underwear, Junior seems to be more rooted than Sula in modern consumer society, as Thomas argued of the young criminal woman, and the fetishisation of women as woman. But, as the nineteenth-century criminologist Mayhew argued of women who became part of the spectacle of modern society, as we saw in Chapter 4, Junior is energised by the masquerade she assumes.

Both Junior and Sula would also appear to be examples of what Thomas labelled 'occasional prostitutes'. Sula follows her mother's example but brings to 'amateur prostitution' her own twist:

> And the fury she created in the women of the town was incredible – for she would lay their husbands once and then no more. Hannah had been a nuisance, but she was complimenting the women, in a way, by wanting their husbands. Sula was trying them out and discarding them without any excuse the men could swallow. (114–15)

As far as Junior is concerned, her ostensible role as an 'amateur prostitute' is perhaps evident in the manner in which she first 'takes' Romen. At one level, when Sandler describes how Junior has 'dancers' legs', he is associating her with the importance of the black performers like

Conan Doyle's 'A Scandal in Bohemia' who is one of the few women to outwit Holmes.

Like the unadjusted female in white Euro-American crime narratives, Junior enjoys the sense of power that her 'style' gives her. Her 'pose', like that of the young female criminal mentioned previously, is based on distance and disrespect, evident in the way in which, imitating Heed in a conversation with Christine, she cruelly pronounces 'memoir' as an illiterate person would. The 'sassy' young woman is distinguished from the 'sporting woman' who is driven by anarchic desire, for 'there is nothing a sporting woman won't do' (188). In the course of the novel, Junior is transformed from 'sassy' to 'sporting', evident in the way in which she reminds people of Celestial. However, the 'sporting' woman is as much a performer as the 'sassy' woman. As children, Heed and Christine name their 'playhouse' 'Celestial Playhouse' after Celestial (188). The image compounds the extent to which it is divorced from its reality, an overturned rowing boat. Under Celestial's influence, Heed and Christine talk in code using words like 'idegay', 'cidagay' and 'slidagay' as a masquerade. But the 'sporting' woman's performance is more sinister than that of the 'sassy' woman. Christine and Heed see Celestial as the devil with which Junior is also linked through her foot which, to Romen when he sees her naked, looks like 'a cloven hoof'. As we have seen in Chapter 4, the association of criminal women with the devil or his manifestation as the serpent in the Garden of Eden is a traditional trope in British crime fiction where it is part of the demonisation of assertive, female sexuality.

Thus, 'performance' is as important a characteristic of 'sass' as 'intelligence'. The two are specifically connected when assertive black people are described as 'acting-out negroes' (96). 'Acting-out' reminds us that those who are socially subservient in a particular society like slaves and servants are only ever partially controlled, as figures in nineteenth-century literature such as the 'swellman', discussed in Chapter 1, suggest. The phrase 'acting-out' suggests it is a variance of the colloquialism 'acting-up' which more readily encapsulates the African-American ambition that is at the heart of White society's fear of 'acting-out' negroes. At a lunch, Heed remembers a tomato slice with the kind of 'seedy smile' associated in the novel with young, 'acting-out' African Americans and those like Junior of mixed race. Heed's memory is used in the novel to reinforce, albeit obliquely this time, the link between 'unadjustment' and 'performance', for she also remembers listening at that moment, to the conversation of her neighbours who are actresses and singers.

Under Junior's influence, Romen begins to 'act-out', acquiring initially 'strut' instead of his 'skulk' (109). Later, he acquires a 'knowing smile' that in its impact upon young black women suggests the 'seedy smile' that Heed remembers seeing, a 'condescension in his tone' (110), and a look that 'appraised and dared' (114). In other words, he assumes a masquerade that is one of a number of different masculine masquerades in the book that stand in contrast to the 'suave' and 'unhip gloss for teenagers disguised as men' which men's magazines offer.

Female masquerade and masculinity

Junior's masquerade, based upon the fetishism of icons of female sexuality, plays into and against masquerades of masculinity, as Sandler guiltily realises. Faye's high-heeled shoes with an X of pink leather on the top encourage the reader to compare her with Junior. Although she has some of the signs of the fetishised 'unadjusted' female, she does not have the masquerade of unadjustment that Junior does. She has bitten-down fingernails compared with the manicured, boldly coloured nails of Junior. She comes, of course, from within the local community whereas Junior is able to position herself more easily in opposition to it. Although of a different kind and much more traumatically in Faye's case, both their displays of femininity, as part of a wider masquerade of 'dancing and showing off' (47), release hostility and violence in some of the men with whom they come into contact.

Faced with the prospect of going along with his male friends in the gang rape of Faye, Romen hesitates between what he thinks would be the outcome if he went through with it – himself as 'chiseled, dangerous, loose' (46) – and a humanitarianism that undoes the masquerade in which he and his friends are participants. What Romen thinks he believes turns the notion of criminality itself into a masquerade. Whilst the rape of Faye is a criminal act, he becomes in his own mind, and in the perception of his male peers, a 'criminal' for protecting her and denying the behaviours and values upon which their masculinity is based. Similarly, Junior becomes a 'criminal' by wanting to leave the rural settlement in which she has grown up. The criminal act of her uncles, referred to earlier in driving their truck over her bare feet as a punishment for escaping is perceived, even by Junior who refuses to betray them, as less criminal than her act of fleeing the settlement.

In *Love* the majority of women who are involved in or have memories of 'acting-out' have lives that in one way or another revolve around the principal African-American male character who 'acts out', Bill Cosey.

The notion of a promiscuous man who is so attractive to women that they find themselves fighting over him is one that Morrison once again introduced but did not fully develop in *Sula*. In a passage that anticipates the highly charged, violent, sexual City of *Jazz*, Ajax is said to have provoked women 'into murderous battles over him in the streets, brawling thick-thighed women with knives disturbed many a Friday night with their bloodletting and attracted whooping crowds' (125). Ajax himself stands apart from it all, realising that they are fighting not over him but their fantasy of him. At the end of *Love*, Heed and Christine finally admit that Cosey was what he himself made up, or what they made up.

An enigmatic, spectral example of Cosey as a construct in the minds of others is Junior's sense of his ghostly presence. When Junior makes love to Romen in Cosey's bed, it would seem that imaginatively she might be having sex with Cosey whose photograph hangs above them. But there is the possibility of a further ghostly presence, in the suggestion that Junior has in mind her own father which helps explain Junior's interest in Heed's older husband.

As a figure who is conspicuously a product of those around him, Cosey is comparable to F. Scott Fitzgerald's protagonist in *The Great Gatsby*. Indeed, the link between masquerade and performance in *Love* is principally signified by Cosey's parties which are reminiscent of those of Jay Gatsby. Both Cosey and Gatsby are also linked to gangsters as performers; Gatsby because he is reputedly linked to criminal activity in the 1920s and Cosey because he is said to have 'liked George raft clothes and gangster cars' (103). Both enjoy display; Gatsby has a library in which the pages of the books have not even been cut, a magnificent wardrobe of shirts and an eye-catching car while Cosey wants his hotel to be a 'showplace' and a 'playground for folk who felt the way he did' (103), linking the hotel through words that are associated with theatre, 'play' and 'show' to performance. His famous boat parties offer a 'counterfeit world' fuelled by talk.

Both Cosey and Gatsby host parties that are the centres of their communities. Each has an 'instinctive knowledge of his guests' needs' (34), but each is not what he appears. Women fall in love with their finesse, money and example; in other words the masquerade. Jay Gatsby's parties camouflage a profound spiritual emptiness that is at the heart of modern America. In *Love*, the masquerade – women in chiffon and jasmine scent and the men in beautiful, smart clothes – gives expression to a riskier sexuality that is always not quite fully present until it takes control and turns the masquerade into a performance in which dancers do steps with 'outrageous names' and the musicians 'confuse' and 'excite' the guests. Indeed, Cosey's parties symbolise how dance reflected wider social changes in the first half of the twentieth century. As older styles gave way to new forms, the former were preserved in formal balls. But what really brought people to the dance floor was the new styles epitomised by dances such as the Lindy Hop, named after Charles Lindberger's flight across the Atlantic, in which women were tossed through the air. In these dances, as in the music, movement became much more overtly a performance. This was especially the case in the 1950s and 1960s when dancers often danced face to face in solo improvisations based on African-American body rhythms and hip rotations, mimicking the jazz to which they moved. In presenting performances to each other, they really danced for themselves, discovering in the shared public space a liberating and expressive private space.

The performance motif is further developed in *Love* in the terms in which casual sex is talked about. Men who have casual relationships are described, as Cosey is, of 'playing around' (104) and the element of masquerade implied in the phrase is underscored in Cosey's case by the description of him: 'Even in those days, when men wore hats ... he was something to see' (104). There is probably no more poignant masquerade associated with Cosey than that on his gravestone: 'Ideal husband. Perfect father' (201).

The conflation of jazz and masquerade highlights 'performances' that are dependent, like jazz itself, upon mimicry, parody and 'play' which have an aggressive edge or a hint of melancholy to them. From her first novel, *The Bluest Eye*, Morrison confessed to admiring prostitutes because, as L says in her narrative in *Love*, they 'have always set the style' (4). *Love* explores, like *Sula* and *Jazz*, the boundary between 'style' and 'masquerade'. Inevitably, as when Heed assumes a 'posture' to interview Junior, the focus of this investigation falls upon 'pose' or 'persona'. Junior herself is named after her father Ethan Payne Jr and her mother Vivian; her addition of the 'e' for style suggests that her identity is a self-conscious persona. Her mixed race, signified by her merged toes, adds another dimension which she absorbs, for her style like what she calls her 'Colour' is constructed around difference. Located in difference, her 'persona' is also performative in that Junior Viviane is a masquerade in which she can react against social forces that seek to determine her, such as those in the Settlement into which she was born and brought up or in the Correctional institution to which she was eventually sent, and in which she can invent and reinvent herself.

When Junior goes out to meet Romen for the first time, she prepares herself by changing back into her leather jacket. This releases a sexuality and confidence inside her which would not otherwise have been possible. Ironically, and appropriately, L, 'remembered as 'the woman in the chef's hat, priestly', who recognises the extent of Junior's masquerade is a masquerade herself. In fact, no one is sure what her real name is. She responds to Junior's clothes, but she sees them differently and less admiringly from Sandler. Junior appears to her as a member of a motorcycle gang and she sees her in terms of 'Boots. Leather. Wild Hair.' The changes that she observes in Junior are perceived in terms of the fetishised icons of overt femininity: blue finger nails, dark black lipstick, leather jacket and boots, and long, see-through flowery skirt (66).

Thus, *Love* shares with the texts about female sexuality and criminality examined previously an interest in the male gaze in which female sexuality is constructed as simultaneously desirable and threatening. Morrison's interest in conflicts within the female psyche is matched in this book with a wider concern with the sexual fetishism of the female. In this respect, *Love* follows a trope which Morrison introduces in *Jazz*:

> The woman who churned a man's blood as she leaned all alone on a fence by a country road might not expect even to catch his eye in the City. But if she is clipping quickly down the big-city street in heels, swinging her purse, or sitting on a stoop with a cool beer in her hand, dangling her shoe from her the toes of her foot, the man, reacting to her posture, to soft skin on stone, the weight of the building stressing the delicate, dangling shoe, is captured. And he'd think it was the woman he wanted, and not some combination of curved stone, and a swinging, high-heeled shoe moving in and out of sunlight. He would know right away the deception, the trick of shapes and light and movement, but it wouldn't matter at all because the deception was part of it too. (34)

In particular, Morrison pursues the elements of deception and complicity which are raised here.

At one level, the representation of Junior is an analytic fetish in so far as Morrison is clearly exploring Woman as sexual fantasy, particularly the way in which women as Woman are integrated into culturally determined concepts of masculinity. Women as objects of culturally determined, sexual fantasy are complicit in those fantasies as is evident from the young, city woman in the passage from *Jazz* above. But, as in the texts discussed in the previous chapters, Morrison is interested in the way in which the fetishised woman becomes a mask behind which she is able to acquire a degree of freedom of being. From a Marxist perspective, the clothes that change a woman into a fetishised spectacle hide the fact that she has been reduced to an object of exchange. In other words, commodity fetishism reflects the way women become a commodity themselves.

However, in *Jazz* and *Love*, Morrison explores the way in which spectacle can paradoxically, as in Junior's case, empower women. In *Jazz*, Dorcas, with the help of her friend Felice, seeks the body and, what is more, the persona of an adult woman:

> But both girls have expectations made higher by the trouble they'd had planning outfits for the escapade. Dorcas, at sixteen, has yet to wear silk hose and her shoes are those of someone much younger or very old. Felice has helped her loosen two braids behind her ears and her fingertip is stained with the rouge she has stroked across her lips. With her collar turned under, her dress is more adult-looking, but the hard hand of a warning grown-up shows everywhere else: in the hem, the waist-centred belt, the short, puffy, sleeves. (65)

Whilst the situation in which Dorcas finds herself is typical of the experience of probably all young girls growing into adulthood and sexuality, the masquerade that she and Felice seek to assume is made all the more risky because they live in a City where sweethearts behave 'free and illegal' (36).

In this respect, the figure of Junior returns us in *Love* to Morrison's interest in how fetishised objects cohere or do not cohere in a dominating sexual female presence. Junior is effective in ways in which Dorcas in *Jazz* is not:

> Dorcas should have been prettier than she was. She just missed. She had all the ingredients of pretty too. Long hair, wavy, half good, half bad. Light skinned. Never used skin bleach. Nice shape. But it missed somehow. If you looked at each thing, you could admire that thing – the hair, the colour, the shape. All together it didn't fit. (201)

But Junior has a more developed sense of Dorcas's 'sass'. Despite not having the physical presence of Junior there is something 'dangerous' about Dorcas which attracts men to her as to Junior:

> I mean it was like she wanted them to do something scary all the time. Steal things, or go back in the store and slap the face of a white salesgirl who wouldn't wait on her, or cuss out somebody who had snubbed her. (202)

Dorcas, too, may be seen, like Junior and Sula, as an example of an 'unadjusted female'. But this passage makes clear that, as an African-American writer, Morrison configures 'unadjustment' as an act of political assertiveness in an oppressive white society and economy. In wanting revenge on a shop girl who is contemptuous towards her, Dorcas has more in common with Graham Greene's Raven than Josephine Tey's Betty.

Both Dorcas and Junior, of course, are more complicated characterisations than Tey's Betty. The representation of Junior as a fetishised object is rendered particularly complex because Morrison's approach is also psychoanalytic. Her high-heeled shoes are a symbol of the phallus. This is integrated in the text with Junior's search for her father. However, the boots that she wears are a more dominant sexual symbol than the high-heeled shoes hanging from the feet of the young woman in the passage above from *Jazz*. At one level a fetishised object, as in the scenario referred to above with the officer's hat, Junior's boots also disguise what disrupts her presence as a fetishised object and is itself a product of male violence. But in both the description of the young woman in *Jazz* and of the episode in which Junior wears only boots and an officer's cap, the fetish is dependent upon a contrast between naked and not naked. The young woman's foot is not quite naked as is Junior's body. This image of being both naked and not naked is associated with Junior throughout the novel, underscoring the sense in which, like the criminal(ised) young women discussed previously, she is always 'not quite' what she seems. Although she has been to a correctional institution, she is not quite a criminal; she is not quite a servant; she is not quite Romen's girlfriend and she is not quite empowered. The trope of 'not quite' draws together a number of larger themes including the issue of mixed race, but more particularly, the way in which the African-American stands in relation to white, consumer society.

7
Writing the Serial and Callous Killer into (Post) Modernity

Serial writing

Serial criminality is an appropriate subject for the final chapter of this book. If there are parallels to be drawn between the critic and the detective, there are others that link the writer and the serial criminal. Both are often the subjects of an obsession that totally dominates and determines their lives. Writing, like serial criminality, is posited upon an unending sequence of rehearsal and 'improvement'.

As the narratives of fictitious and 'real' serial criminals have proliferated and, in many cases, have become more sophisticated, the emphasis has fallen upon the repetitive methods and compulsive psychologies involved. The serial killer or callous killer narrative has changed from semi-theological narratives of the late-nineteenth century through existentialist thrillers to socio-psychological and socio-psychoanalytic studies. In the most sophisticated accounts, the interest has shifted from the horror of the crimes to the performance of the criminal and the masquerades which they assume in undertaking the crimes and in melting back into 'ordinary' society afterwards.

Nineteenth-century accounts of serial criminality demonised the criminal and stressed the horrors of serial killing. Robert Louis Stevenson's shilling shocker *The Strange Case of Doctor Jekyll and Mr Hyde* (1886) is a frequently studied text, often read psychoanalytically in relation to the Gothic and the fantastic. It was influenced by French writings on the multiple personality and Lombrosian theories of criminal anthropology; his case study approach links the novel with Richard Krafft-Ebbing's case histories of sexual deviants, *Psychopathia Sexualis* (1886), a 'medico-forensic study' of the 'abnormal'. Dr Jekyll's release of the dark forces within himself through the person of Hyde is analogous of the chaos within the text which threatens the structure and stability of the narrative itself. Pre-dating the development of psychoanalysis which provided a language in which to discuss the relationship between the conscious and the subconscious, Stevenson employs religious language. In a reference to the tabernacle, Jekyll remembers that 'the veil of self-indulgence was rent from head to foot' (50). Recalling that 'my devil had been long caged, he came out roaring' (49), he remembers, too, how 'instantly the spirit of hell awoke in me and raged' (49). The experience is conceptualised in terms of hell, the devil and possession. Religion and the Bible are invoked not only as a way of articulating but containing what is released: 'I sought with leas and prayers to smother down the crowd of hideous images and sounds with which my memory swarmed against me' (50).

However, the novel has been marginalised in discussions of criminality and violence. Its significance as a Victorian criminological text lay not only in its indebtedness to medical and forensic studies but its perception of how crimes of assault were often grist to the press and the reading public. When Dr Jekyll admits that 'I stood at times aghast before the acts of Edward Hyde' (46), one suspects that he speaks for the average middle-class Victorian reader who was becoming intolerant of, and yet remained attracted by, violence. The moral voice which Dickens allocates Magwitch in *Great Expectations* is clearly more sparing of his more sensitive readers than Stevenson. It keeps the criminal within the boundaries of the civilised whereas the lack of boundaries which Dickens configures in the opening chapters of *Great Expectations* is realised in Stevenson's Hyde. Jekyll laments: 'I had voluntarily stripped myself of all those balancing instincts by which even the worst of us continues to walk with some degree of steadiness among temptations' (49).

There were links between *The Strange Case of Doctor Jekyll and Mr Hyde* and the infamous murderer of prostitutes in London in the 1880s, Jack the Ripper. Initial newspaper coverage of the Ripper murders stressed the violence and the demon nature of whoever it was had committed the murders. The actor Richard Mansfield opened in the theatre version of Stevenson's work in the West End in August 1888, the month of the first murder and the play was actually shut down because Mansfield's very convincing portrayal of Hyde was seen as a model for the Ripper. Although the original story is somewhat vague about the object of Hyde's desire, the nocturnal adventures of Hyde were illicitly and violently erotic, drawing, like the Ripper murders in the public mind, on cultural fantasies of the sadistic sex criminal. The brutality of the Ripper murders is comparable to the murder of Sir Danvers Carew in Stevenson's novel, even though this is not the murder of a prostitute but of one 'gentleman' by another. Despite the differences, the hideous crime is envisaged in the novel, like the Ripper murders, as an act of 'insensate cruelty' (16); the body is left 'incredibly mangled' (16). Carew's murder, we are told, 'broke out of all bounds'. It is not difficult to find echoes here of press outrage at the Ripper murders. But the description of Carew's murder is also redolent of the killings in Poe's 'The Murders in the Rue Morgue'. The fact that the crimes in Poe's stories are committed by an orang-utan is echoed in Stevenson's description of how Hyde trampled his victim underfoot with 'ape-like fury' (16).

Despite the horror associated with Hyde and with the Ripper, the narratives of their exploits eventually turned implicitly to the concept of masquerade. As was argued in Chapter 3, Poe's 'The Murders in the Rue Morgue' indirectly exposed the masquerade of ostensibly 'respectable' men who used and abused prostitutes and the domestic violence that lay behind the masquerade of respectable marriages. Stevenson's novel and the newspaper accounts of the Ripper can also be seen as asking questions about the nature of so-called 'respectable' society. As 'other' to the gentlemanly Dr Jekyll, Hyde is the negative of Victorian middle-class respectability. But the way in which he articulates with Jekyll exemplifies an increasing scepticism in the Victorian period towards middle-class and professional men. As it became clearer to the contemporaneous press that the Ripper was what later periods would have identified as a 'serial killer', public attention increasingly shifted from the crime scenes, although these were always reported in as much graphic detail as was possible, to the way in which they exposed the masquerade of, for example, the medical profession and the middle classes. As we saw in Chapter 3, the contemporaneous theory that Jack the Ripper was a surgeon betrayed wider anxieties, especially on the part of women, concerning the medical profession while the conviction that he was a 'gentleman' highlighted the duplicity exemplified by men who used prostitutes and risked bringing sexually transmitted disease home to their own wives.

Indeed, in late Victorian crime fiction generally, it is possible to discern a shift in interest from the detective and the method of investigation by which the criminal is brought to justice to the masquerade which the criminal assumes. Conan Doyle's stories provided the Victorian reading classes with numerous examples of middle-class criminals and by implication of respectable masquerades. Frequently, they, too, highlighted public anxieties about particular professions. That the criminal in *The Hound of the Baskervilles* turns out to be a scientist with the knowledge to create a beast that glows with phosphorous reflects wider public concern about science and scientists. In the twentieth century, concern with masquerade in accounts of serial criminality shifted again. This time, as was suggested earlier, to the masquerade and performance that was necessary for the crimes to be carried out.

The Psychopath as text

In the twentieth century, interest in masquerade as an essential element in the act of serial criminality developed in tandem with a psychoanalytic approach to, or psychoanalytic profiling of, the serial criminal. In many respects, psychoanalysis has determined the way in which human motivation is approached in many twentieth-century texts. One cultural critic has observed that in the twentieth century, psychoanalysis became a 'social force' to such an extent that representations of the unconscious were determined by psychoanalysis itself.[1]

Not surprisingly, psychoanalytically determined models of the unconscious, together with the many complex hypothesises that followed them, have informed many fictional representations of the serial murderer. Thus, cultural representations of serial criminality often stressed masquerade and turned the serial performance into a thrilling text at the same time as they sought to explain both in psychoanalytic terms. Whilst the performance of serial criminality stressed the serial criminal as actively in control and consciously shaping his behaviour, the analysis of those behaviours emphasised the serial killer as the object of a psychoanalytic narrative and of psychically determined behaviours. Indeed, much serial criminal fiction, such as Robert Bloch's *Psycho* and William Trevor's *Felicia's Journey* to which we will return shortly, is written in the space between these two dimensions, pursuing the extent to which the serial criminal is subject or object of his own narrative.

The term 'psychopath' which is frequently invoked in relation to the serial murderer, is an especially difficult one because of all the popular connotations that the term has acquired. The World Health Organisation has sought to demythicise the psychopath by redefining the condition in terms of clinical characteristics:

- callous unconcern for the feelings of others and lack of capacity for empathy;
- gross and persistent attitude of irresponsibility and disregard for social norms;
- incapacity to maintain enduring relationships;

- very low tolerance to frustration and a low threshold for discharge of aggression, including violence;
- incapacity to experience guilt, and to profit from experience, particularly punishment;
- marked proneness to blame others, or to offer plausible rationalisations for the behaviour bringing the subject into conflict with society;
- persistent irritability.[2]

At one level, this is redolent of nineteenth-century criminological attempts to objectify and categorise criminal behaviour. At another level, it inadvertently demonstrates literature's interest in the 'psychopath' in relation to modernity, for it is against the positive character traits or ideals of modernity that the psychopath is defined: responsibility, self-restraint, rationality, stability and the capacity to learn from experience. The interest in the psychopath in the course of the nineteenth century undergoes a shift in emphasis from a pariah figure on whom cultural fears and anxieties are projected to a more inclusive social presence, signifying fault lines between the ideals of modernity and its realisation in practice.

Marie Lowndes's novel, *The Lodger* (1913), based on the Ripper murders, was the first attempt to place the phenomenon of a callous killer in a socio-biographical context. *The Lodger* is an expanded version of a short story of the same name published two years earlier. It is a subversive text that relocates the murders to the West End of London and focusses as much on the psychology of the person sheltering the Ripper as on the Ripper himself. Despite the notoriety that the murders and the crime scenes acquired, the killings only enter the novel through newspaper reports, gossip and snippets of information from a policeman involved in the investigation, and it teasingly calls the murderer, Mr Sleuth.

The Lodger is also the first text based on a sustained focus upon the serial criminal as living out a masquerade. Lowndes is interested in the kind of psychology that supported and was displayed in the serial criminal's performance as an 'ordinary' citizen. In fact, the 'ordinary' performance is itself disturbing, betraying many of the character traits of the serial criminal, including those that were later employed to identify the psychopath in the twentieth century.

Lowndes's Sleuth and Stevenson's Hyde are comparable. Both live in lodgings, and appear to lead solitary lives. It is difficult to imagine either of them feeling remorse or empathy with another human being. Both have a disturbing and disturbed quality about them. Hyde impresses people with 'the haunting sense of unexpressed deformity' and disappears 'as though he had never existed' (22). Both are 'protected' by women who keep their silence and in both cases they are not very familiar to the men associated with these women. An important difference is that while Sleuth prefers bare rooms, Hyde wants well-furnished and luxurious accommodation.

One of the salient narratives circulating at the time of the murders which Lowndes develops was based on the hypothesis that the Ripper was a religious fanatic. The principal exponent of this view was Dr Forbes Winslow, a specialist in mental diseases, who believed that the murderer laboured under the morbid belief that he had a destiny to fulfil. Sleuth reads regularly from the Bible in which he apparently finds support for his views. That the female sex and the flesh are an anathema to him is established as soon as he arrives at his lodgings. One of the first things he does is to turn the portraits of Victorian belles which his landlady actually admires to the wall. The deed is an obvious suggestion of his misogynism, but also perhaps of his fear of sex, and even of a sense of guilt – he cannot stand their eyes following him. Some of the words which he is heard repeating during his reading sessions are indeed sinister: 'A strange woman is a narrow gate. She also lieth in wait as for a prey, and increaseth the transgressors among men' (26).

The hired gun

The extent to which psychoanalysis became a social force in the twentieth century, referred to in the previous section, has led to psychoanalytic models of the unconscious being accepted uncritically by some writers but being seen as masquerading as verisimilitude by others. The latter was not generally the case when Graham Greene wrote *A Gun for Sale* which demonstrates the extent to which psychoanalysis produced psychoanalytically determined models of the unconscious in crime fiction. This sustained exploration of the psychology of a fictitious, callous killer, a hired gun rather than a serial killer, anticipates an area of criminological theorising that became important in the 1940s, and spawned more sophisticated studies of the link between callous murder and the criminal's emotional and family background.

The role of the mother was an important element in psychoanalytic thinking in the 1920s and 1930s, not only through the influence of the psychoanalytic theories of Sigmund Freud but also through what came to be known as 'object relations theory' developed by Melanie Klein. Whereas Freud tended to highlight the role of the father figure in a child's early consciousness, Klein emphasised the child's relation with the mother, understandably since for good or ill this is the child's first experience of a relationship with another being. Not uncontroversially, she stressed that the way in which the child related to the mother, particularly through breast feeding, determined the kind of person she or he became in adult life. One of the most contentious aspects of her theory was the importance that she attached to how the child came to associate their mother's breasts with positive and negative emotions through the twin experiences of satisfaction and frustration. In other words, according to Klein, breast feeding helped determine a child's responses to the world around her or him later in life. The child learns to see the offered breast as positive but the withdrawn breast as negative. The infant responds to the world in stark binarisms; the adult learns that things are not simply good and bad but that the world is more complex than that.

The idea that there was a link between criminality and one's early childhood experiences forcefully entered criminological thinking in the late 1930s and the 1940s when an unbroken relationship between child and mother was perceived as essential for the child's future mental health. Indeed, some criminologists went further in suggesting that separation from, and rejection of, the mother led to anti-social behaviour. In many respects, Raven in *A Gun for Sale* would seem to have been written according to a psychoanalytic blue print. In stressing the importance of early maternal deprivation in explaining adult criminality, Greene is a product of the psychoanalytic and criminological thinking of his time. Raven's violence outside of his contract killings is generally triggered by the way others treat him, especially those he believes look down on him for his hare-lip, and it is credible within the narrative that Raven's mental health and low self-esteem are traceable to his relationship with his mother.

An unfulfilling, primary relation between the criminal and his parents is an element in Greene's earlier novel *Brighton Rock*, too, discussed in Chapter 2. It may be that this preoccupation seeped into Greene's work through the biographies of the American gangsters of the 1930s which, as may be seen in the case of Clyde Barrow, tended to stress the indifference and/or cruelty of their early lives. But although Greene appears to be interested in this aspect of Pinkie and Ravens's psychic biographies, his texts establish a dialectic between this approach and a more existentialist emphasis upon the killer as the embodiment of a cold, calculating evil. For example, Pinkie is responsible for razor slashing Kite and for the death of Hale. It is this streak which distinguishes him from the mob leader Colleoni.

In *A Gun for Sale*, the emphasis is upon the possibility that extreme sadism is the product of a psychoanalytic rather than existential reality. Anne, with whom Raven enters into a complex relation after he has kidnapped her, stimulates him to think about his childhood. His memories of his mother reveal a frustrated sense of loss, not just of her specifically but of the act of being loved: 'Three minutes in bed or against a wall, and then a lifetime for the one that's born' (121). Although Greene emphasises Raven's total experiences in moulding his hatred, the point is that nothing that has happened to him since his childhood has really compensated for the loss of a meaningful relationship with his mother. For him, deep down in his subconscious, his mother is associated in Kleinian terms with a breast that has never been offered him in love. Despite the details of his mother's life, as a prostitute, her attempted suicide and his father's execution, the novel suggests it is her association in his mind with a lack of love that is fundamental to his own inhibited subjective development. Raven's hatred, as his behaviour toward the hunchbacked Alice reveals, is primarily directed at women. The description of his cruelty – 'he let his hare-lip loose on the girl' (14) – suggests that what he is projecting on her, as a representative female, is the distorted, primary relation between himself and his mother. He also forces his physical, and hence psychic, disfigurement on Anne but he is 'disconcerted when she showed no repulsion' (42).

As Raven develops a close relationship with Anne, the first woman to have shown him any affection, he assumes the position of a child with its mother, at one point crying before her. The novel appears to have two interlocking narratives: a linear, forward plot line concerned with Anne's single-handed mission to prevent a war and a backward, cyclical movement into Raven's childhood, which is also a movement toward 'rebirth'. When Raven lies beside Anne after he has rescued her from behind the fireplace, he can 'feel her breathing under his hand it was like beginning life over again'(98). One of his hands is on Anne's breast and the other is on his gun, which, apart from its obvious phallic connotations, is indicative of how rediscovering the female/mother is the basis of redefining an identity which has until now been configured largely in relation to violence.

Much of the novel is posited on what we might think of as negative images. The subject, a hired gun, is a negative version of the heroic soldier, as Dr Yogel's assistant is of the nursing profession. Although Anne Crowder is the fiancée of a police detective, she becomes cast as the moll of the criminal he is hunting. At one level, Greene is asking, what are the implications for our view of modernity if it is envisaged solely in terms of its negative underside. Raven has such a negative view of the modern nation state based upon his childhood experiences that the ideals of modernity held by Anne appear to him as a masquerade. *A Gun for Sale* reveals a country characterised by division, cruelty and 'otherness'. One of the major ironies in the novel is that the hired gun, like the criminal generally, is the 'other' of the nation state while mimicking its preoccupation with self-motivation and independence.

How far the text is structured around negative and positive perspectives is evident, for example, in the episode in which Raven goes into a shop to buy his friend Alice a dress, not out of love or generosity but in an act of cruelty. He is confronted by the sight of an assistant dressing a mannequin, and here the text invites us to consider the relationship between the two: 'A girl with a neat curved figure bent over a dummy. He fed his eyes contemptuously on her legs and hips; so much flesh, he thought, on sale in the Christmas window' (14). The mannequin might be considered as a masquerade; the negative ideal or the reductive phantasm on which women are encouraged to model themselves. The young assistant almost merges with the dummy. Together they represent the commodification of the female body which is the reverse image of the independent woman of the 1930s featured in Christie and Sayers's detective fiction discussed in Chapter 5. Moreover, she is linked not only to the dummy but the turkeys offered for sale in the butcher's shop window. A further connotation is the link between the mannequin, the girl and the prostitute. The assistant is complicit in the business of dressing the female body to be desirable to men, the reductive phantasm of which is the prostitute, as Raven cryptically observes: 'She was a woman, she knew all about it, she knew how cheap and vulgar the little shop really was'(14). At times, Greene seems provocatively to entertain the notion that hatred is a more authentic notion than love of humankind which spills over into a false sentimentality exemplified in the record that Anne purchases – 'It's only Kew to you' – and the numerous allusions to Christmas which has itself been culturally configured so that it is more capitalist masquerade than social reality.

Callous murder

The texts discussed so far in this chapter have highlighted how the serial or callous criminal has been represented in terms of different explanatory models of behaviour; one, deriving its metaphysical framework from theology, concerned with the demonisation of the killer and, the other, based on twentieth-century psychoanalytic theory, seeing the callous or serial killer as a product of a dreadful childhood. Although each text has an interest in one or the other, there is also a degree of scepticism as to whether the explanation of the callous killer in question is itself a kind of masquerade.

A dialectic between the socio-psychic and the existential links Greene's novels with a much later Irish work, John Banville's *The Book of Evidence* (1989), the first part of a trilogy. Banville's novel is based on a real event; in this case, the callous murder of a young nurse Bridie Gargan in Dublin in July, 1982, by the son of a prosperous Dublin family Malcolm Macarthur. Like Macarthur, Banville's protagonist, Freddie Montgomery, commits a violent crime apparently with no motivation. There are actually two crimes in the novel: the theft of one of the paintings that had adorned the walls of the Montgomery ancestral home at Coolgrange but had been sold by his mother; and the murder of Josie Bell, a young maid at the house from which the painting is stolen. Like Macarthur, Freddie forces his young victim into a car and shortly afterwards beats her to death with a hammer. A further parallel between Montgomery and Macarthur is that both are connected to the Government of the day; Macarthur was eventually apprehended at the home of the Irish Attorney-General and both masqueraded as cultured men-about-town.

In exploring the kind of psyche that would commit such a ruthless and brutal crime with no apparent sign of remorse, Banville appears to have turned for a model to Camus's *The Outsider* (1942). *The Outsider*, like Banville's novel, is a prison-memoir, an attempt by a murderer to represent his identity and his crime as he sees them. The representation of the key protagonist in both novels stresses the apparent, unprecedented nature of their crimes and, especially in Meursault's case, their cold bloodedness in response to what has happened. Freddie's act of murder lasts much longer and is far less efficient and clean; in the course of the killing, he becomes confused, emotional yet also callous at the same time.

An antecedent for these narratives is the murder in France in 1933 of Madame Lancelin and her daughter which, in its brutality was reminiscent of Poe's 'The Murders in the Rue Morgue'. But what caught the public attention at the time was the incongruity between the savagery at the scene of crime and the mild-mannered nature of the two maids, the Papin sisters, who were found huddled together and naked in a single bed upstairs. The press became fascinated in how they could have acted in the way they did without apparent provocation. In 1947, Jean Genet, who began writing for the theatre in 1943, made the case the subject of a play, *Les Bonnes* in 1947.

Ostensibly, the crime and the protagonists in Camus and Banville's novels are very different. In Camus's novel the French–Algerian Meursault shoots dead an Arab who threatens him with a knife. However, both crimes are apparently motiveless. The issue is not that Meursault shot the Arab in self defence but that while he was lying on the ground fired four more shots needlessly into the body. Both murderers baffle the authorities because they do not show the kind of remorse expected of them, and go on to commit murder even though they appeared rational enough to stop. Thus, the issue becomes not the number of shots that Meusault fired but that he paused between them:

> Next, without any apparent logical connexion, the magistrate sprang another question.
> I thought for a bit; then explained that they weren't quite consecutive. I fired one at first, and the other four after a short interval.
> 'Why did you pause between the first and second shot?'
> … .
> 'But why, *why* did you go on firing at a prostrate man?'
> Again I found nothing to reply.
> The magistrate drew his hand across his forehead and repeated in a slightly different tone:
> 'I ask you "*Why?*"I insist on your telling me.'
> I still kept silent. (71–2)

Freddie's interrogation similarly hinges on the subject of motivation:

> Listen, [Sergeant] Hogg said, tell us, why did you do it?
> I stared at him, startled, and at a loss. It was the one thing I had never asked myself, not with such simple, unavoidable force.
> [... .]
> I had not the heart to confess to him that there was nothing to confess, that there had been no plan worthy of the name, that I had acted almost without thinking from the start.
> [... .]
> I killed her because I could I said, I said, what more can I say? We were all startled by that, I as much as they. (196–9)

Montgomery, like Raven and Pinkie, is caught in a 'reality' which is revealed to the reader/audience as consisting of his own distorted reflections. Montgomery thinks of himself as a schizophrenic as have a number of murderers in post-Second World War crime fiction. He is both an intelligent, cultured man-about-town, and a brutal monster he calls 'Bunter'. However, an important distinction between Banville and Camus's novel is that Banville is more prepared to recognise that although the individual must assume responsibility for his actions, these are part of a wider world in which art, culture and criminality are fused. The point is made in the contrast between the way Freddie tries to imagine the life of the woman in the Dutch painting he has stolen and his failure to conceive of the life of Josie until he sees a newspaper photograph of her mother:

> A reporter had been sent down to the country to talk to Mrs Brigid Bell, the mother. She was a widow. There was a photograph of her standing awkwardly in front of her cottage, a big, raw-faced woman in an apron and an old cardigan, peering at the camera in a kind of stolid dismay. Her Josie, she said, was a good girl, a decent girl, why would anyone want to kill her. And suddenly I was back there, I saw her sitting in the mess of her own blood, looking at me, a bleb of pink spittle bursting on her lips. *Mammy* was what she said, that was the word, not Tommy, I've just this moment realised it. *Mammy*, and then: *Love*. (148)

At the end of *The Book of Evidence*, Freddie, unlike Meursault, realises that his salvation lies in the way in which he imagines others; in this case, his need to imagine Josie Bell, a lower-working-class woman, as a real person, and to understand that he was able to beat and eventually kill her because he was able to do so. In this respect, the novel is locked into the increasing awareness in the twentieth century as to how perceiving, and being encouraged to perceive, individuals in reductive ways, in, for example, war-time propaganda or racialist discourse, permits violence.

Ultimately, the subject of these two prison memoirs is not the crime but the discourse of criminality itself. Banville's protagonist raises and rejects many of the frameworks within which those who commit serious crimes are placed. In both novels the killer's relationship with their mothers is raised. However, in each the psychoanalytically driven killer is a convenient façade detracting attention from complex metaphysical truths. Meursault admits that he had been fond of his mother 'but really that didn't mean much' (69). Montgomery, sceptical of psychologists, cautions that 'when it comes to the subject of mothers, simplicity is not permitted' (41). Although Montgomery invokes at one point the Catholic notion of a sin so transgressive that it cannot be forgiven, he draws attention to the 'poverty of language when it comes to naming or describing badness'. What literature, language and the discourse of criminality have not come to terms with, in his view, is 'the bad in its inert, neutral, self-sustaining state' (54). Both texts argue against the way conceptions such as innocence and guilt, goodness and evil, sanity and insanity are imposed upon criminals and criminal acts in literature, aesthetics and law. Both narratives are based on the opposition of two discourses: one in which the identity and crime of the protagonists are perceived by themselves and another in which both are perceived by their observers. Again betraying the influence of mid-twentieth-century existentialist thought, when Montgomery looks at himself and his behaviour from the perspective of the 'outsider' it all seems absurd. His explanations for buying a hammer, taking the car and leaving his accommodation without paying are not as rational as the police account which places them into a causal narrative would suggest.

A mother's son

The way in which the callous murderer is written into modernity through socio-psychoanalytic theories and yet written out of it by scepticism about them is central to Robert Bloch's study of a serial killer, *Psycho*, discussed in Chapter 3. One of the differences between Robert Bloch's novel *Psycho* and Alfred Hitchcock's film adaptation is that Bloch stresses in more detail the relation between Norman Bates and his mother. This is an aspect of the late 1950s true-life American serial killer, Ed Gein, which Bloch appropriates. Despite the obvious differences between Gein and Bates – Gein fashioned objects from the corpses of his victims, skinned them and ate their organs – Bates shares Gein's fixation with an authoritarian mother. Like Bates's mother, she appears to have been responsible for repressing her son's sexual instincts and ultimately for his warped view of women. Bloch also appropriated the way Gein kept his mother's room preserved as a shrine after her death.

Although Hitchcock's film highlights Bates's mother fixation, her censorious presence during his childhood is revealed only fragmentarily. The novel offers a more sustained, Freudian explanation for Norman's relationship with his mother. In the opening chapter which blurs fantasy and reality, Norman apparently reveals that he has approached his mother about his 'Oedipus situation', using it as a basis to have sex with her. Later in the novel, Norman muses about the relationship, specifically recalling the mirror stage in which children first become aware that they have a body that is distinct from their mother's. Particularly influential was the occasion upon which his mother discovered him standing naked before the mirror and struck him across the head with a silver hairbrush, thwarting his attempts to see himself as separate from her and making him feel ashamed of his sexuality. The object of his Oedipal desire, she is also the mythical castrating mother figure. Unlike in the film, Norman attempts to articulate what is wrong with him in psychoanalytic terms:

> It was like being two people, really – the child and the adult. Whenever he thought about Mother, he became a child again, with a child's vocabulary, frames of reference, and emotional reactions. But when he was by himself – not actually by himself, but off in a book – he was a mature individual. Mature enough to understand that he might even be the victim of a mild form of schizophrenia, most likely some form of borderline neurosis. (67)

His self-assessment understates the situation: only 'a mild form of schizophrenia' and a 'borderline neurosis'.

At one level, the novel is more convincing than the film in tracing how the psychological fixations and anxieties of his early years were exacerbated through his reading in studies of the body in violent and pornographic contexts. His library consists of esoteric books on aspects of psychology and anthropology and volumes that are 'pathologically pornographic' (114). Here, Bloch has appropriated Gein's morbid interest in the female anatomy. But the mother fixation in the novel is more complex than in Hitchcock's film. Norman incorporates her rejection of his advance to her in more generalised censorious behaviour. He appears to have been jealous of her lover whom it is implied he has killed, and seems to project her condemnation of his sexuality and manhood onto women in general: 'That's what the bitches did to you, they perverted you, and [Mary] was a bitch, they were all bitches, Mother was a ....' (35). Through his peephole, Norman witnesses not simply Mary getting undressed but Mary admiring the sexual power of her body: 'Maybe the face was twenty-seven, but the body was free, white, and twenty-one. She had a good figure. A *damned* good figure' (30). 'Damned' in this context is double-edged, a colloquialism and reminder that in the climate of America in the 1950s women were 'damned' if they thought of their bodies as free and their sexuality as their own. The notion of damnation is ominously picked up again when Mary starts to think about her sexuality: 'She wished he was here to admire [her body] now. It was going to be hell to wait another two years. But then she'd make up for lost time. They say a woman isn't fully mature, sexually, until she's thirty' (31).

The three narratives – Norman, Mary and Norman's mother – are better integrated in the novel than Hitchcock's film of it. There is a correlation between the oppressive climate of the 1950s and the censorious voice of the mother-figure in both Norman and Mary's life. Yet the novel stresses the disparity between the configuration of Mrs Bates in this role and her true life romance which scandalised the community when Norman was growing up. Ironically, Mary cavorting before the mirror is redolent of the younger, sexual, devil-may-care Mrs Bates.

In the novel, Norman is even more disturbed by his mother's duplicity, which leaves him confused, than by her censor of his sexuality. She presents herself to him not only as the castrating mother but the sphinx. What has not received enough attention in the criticism of the novel, or of the film, is Norman's decision to preserve in his mind the image of the mother who criticised and humiliated him. The point is that she is preserved in the role of castrator mother-figure rather than in the contradictory role which is what worries him more but is even harder for him to deal with.

Preserved in death, Norman's mother is the silent object of his fixation. But he ventriloquises her censoring of him. In this sense, he displays a masochistic sense of agency. When he talks with Marion in his parlour, the birds of prey in Hitchcock's film are all caught in the moment before they fall on their prey. In the novel, a single squirrel peers down at them. Sitting in his room in the film, he is always surrounded by their cruel eyes, redolent of those of his mother as she, presumably in the film but explicitly in the novel, swooped on him on occasions such as the one on which she found him naked at the mirror. Mary, in both the novel and the film is the sexual body he desires, the object of his mother's and his own disgust, and the female figure with the potential to condemn and humiliate him.

The different roles in which Mary masquerades in Norman's mind are interleaved in the episode of her murder. Norman's attack on Mary is triggered more obviously in the novel by her performance in front of the mirror which, it is suggested later, made him think that she was acting for him. In contrast to his unease before the mirror, she is provocatively confident: 'Mary giggled, then executed an amateurish bump and grind, tossed her image a kiss and received one in return' (31). At this point, Mary has repented stealing her employer's money and has decided to wait until she and Sam can live together. Norman kills her after she has decided to go straight, as Bill Sikes did Nancy in *Oliver Twist*, one of the first of the better known brutal murders of women in fiction referred to in Chapter 2.

Ironically, it is Norman's remark that 'perhaps all of us go a little crazy at times' (29) that causes Mary to rein herself in. The punishment that he inflicts on her, in the guise of his censorious mother, is emblematic of how older generations of women have been complicit in keeping younger women in check. There are a number of allusions in the novel that interleave the way Norman and society in general regard unlicensed female sexuality: Mary's behaviour before the mirror recalls a striptease artist's performance; on his bookshelf Norman has a copy of *The Witch-Cult in Western Europe*, reminding us of how witchcraft was a way of controlling women's sexual independence. There is also a reference to Lady Macbeth, typical of the way in which ambition in a woman is 'othered' as something 'evil', and the scandal that the widowed Mrs Bates caused through having a relationship with a man before they were married.

The parlour in which the birds look down on Norman is significantly located in the film in the motel. In the novel, Mary goes up to the house for supper. The motel masquerades as a place of work where Norman as a man should make money to support his family. But, in Norman's case, this is his mother. Of course, the motel is a failure. In the novel, Norman comes down the stairs to greet Mary after having tucked his mother into bed. Norman's role in this respect is more traditionally associated, and certainly in the 1950s, with women as carers rather than with men. Norman is emasculated by his failure to be a financially dependable male and by his submission to an over-dominant mother. But shifting the parlour to the motel in the film associates it with sexual licence, since motels are also places where men and women have affairs. Here Norman is policed by his mother, whose gaze is signified by those of the stuffed birds. In the film, Norman, brings Marion his child's supper of sandwiches and milk. In agreeing to sit down with him, Marion is complicit in his humiliation. The supper in the novel is one of sausage, cheese and pickles, accompanied by the more adult coffee rather than milk. While the film appears to masquerade Norman as child and mother's boy, the novel highlights how Norman is constantly located on the border between adult independence and childlike dependency. The former is evident in the fact that he ostensibly entertains a woman in the kitchen of the house and the latter in the way in which the kitchen smacks of his mother's influence. This border territory is also evident in the figure of the stuffed squirrel, which at one level, signifies the manly pursuits of hunting and shooting but, at another, masquerades as a child's toy when Norman describes it as 'cute'.

Murder, modernity and discontinuities

Although written many years apart and in different cultural contexts, Lowndes's *The Lodger*, Banville's *The Book of Evidence* and Bloch's *Psycho* use schizophrenia, in one form or another, not only as a way of configuring how a callous murderer can exist in society but conceptualising what this kind of criminality tells us about modernity. A key late twentieth-century text in this respect is Angela Carter's short prose work, 'The Fall River Axe Murders', based on the murders of Andrew Jackson Borden and his second wife Abbey Borden by, allegedly, his daughter Lizzie Borden in Fall River, Massachusetts, in August 1892.

During the 'peculiar spells' from which Lizzie suffered, Carter surmises: 'Time opened in two. Suddenly she was not continuous anymore' (51). Like Norman Bates, Lizzie in Carter's account is aware that something is wrong. While Bates underestimates his condition, Lizzie tries not to think about it. Thus, she is always 'a stranger to herself' (51). But Carter's crime faction, like Lowndes, Banville and Bloch's novels, suggests that, since modern Euro-American culture tends to 'other' serious crime, it is always going to be a stranger to itself.

Division and separation – Carter emphasises how butter metaphorically separates (like the human mind and modernity itself?) into 'the liquid fat and the corrupt-smelling whey' (52) – is redolent of nineteenth-century approaches to criminology in the work of Lombroso and Mayhew, referred to in Chapter 1. This apparent 'continuity' with the previous century's concepts of criminality belies modernity as a product of the pre-eminence of the new over the old. Carter's work, like Lowndes, Banville and Bloch's, represents extreme criminality not as a rupture of modernity but a reminder that modernity is never the radical disruption it masquerades as. At one level, the ostensible, increasingly modern approaches to serial criminality and callous murder appear to underscore the way in which modernity represents the pre-eminence of the new over the old. But in invoking older continuities, such as the split personality of the serial criminal and entertaining scepticism as to whether the callous killer can ever be integrated into the wider social totality, so-called 'new' interpretations appear themselves to masquerade as the 'new'.

Murder and postmodernity

Postmodern American society masquerading as the realization of the ideal of modernity is at the heart of Bret Easton Ellis's *American Psycho*

(1991) which recalls Bloch's novel in its title and in the name of its central protagonist, Patrick Bateman. Whereas Norman Bates is ignorant of his true murderous identity, Patrick Bateman believes himself to be a psychopath. Although believing his mother to be the killer, Norman is aware of the hatred that he projects onto women, and of its origins in his own childhood, Bateman seems to be devoid of any authentic emotion; his definition of fear is turning up at a restaurant without a reservation. This apparently cold, calculating evil is inseparable from the so-called social 'normality' of Wall Street in the 1980s. This is reinforced in the way Bateman is frequently confused with someone else and his preoccupation with 'murders and executions' is misheard as 'mergers and acquisitions'.

The psychological terrain of the novel interweaves an obsession with primary orality – at one point Bateman confesses in a scenario which leads to murder that when he is in an edgy pre-coke state he chews nervously on things like a drink ticket – and an obsession with breasts. He is dismayed by his girlfriend's cold breasts, and has to phone one of his friends while watching the Patty Winters show so that they can ridicule a woman who wants a breast reduction. Orality and the vagina are, of course, closely linked but in this novel both are associated with abuse; through the substances that Bateman takes into his own body and the objects he uses to penetrate and mutilate the vaginas of the women he murders.

Bateman seems to embody the kind of stunted growth that in the work of post-Freudian psychoanalysts such as Melanie Klein would be associated with the child who does not move beyond projecting his anger and frustration onto what is perceived as the mother's 'bad' breast. He thinks of pizzas at one point in terms of a 'good' pizza which is yeasty, bready, cheesy and comparable to the mother's feeding breast, and a 'bad' pizza which is brittle, hard, overcooked, like the mother's withdrawn breast (46). Similarly, he is inclined to think in terms of 'good' and 'bad' coke. The kind of primal regression that Bateman exhibits characterises the environment in which he lives. Bad coke at one point drives Price, who, in taking in coke with a platinum Express card combines two forms of consumption, into an almost primal rage, 'furious, red-faced and sweating', and like a frustrated child he gives vent to his anger through screaming (58). The description of him sniffing coke is comparable to a child at its mother's breast: he 'shuts his eyes tightly, lips white, slight residue of cocaine under one nostril' (59). After taking coke, analogous of feeding at their mothers' breasts, they look at themselves in the mirror, redolent of the 'mirror' stage in childhood when a child begins to recognise that it has a separate identity from its mother.

The scene that follows this particular coke sniffing episode is one which repeats the cycle of 'need', 'rejection', 'frustration' and 'aggression'. Having difficulty attracting a waitress's attention, Bateman tries to make out that he knows her but is ignored for his trouble. When he is eventually served, the waitress is, in his view, cold, indifferent and contemptuous toward him. He responds like a child ignored by its mother. The imagined outburst on his part is not in keeping with what has happened, but it provides a clear indication of the kind of psychology which produces the murders, be they real or imagined: 'You are a fucking ugly bitch I want to stab you to death and play around with your blood' (59).

The extent to which psychoanalytic models of the unconscious determine Bateman's psychotic state is evident in Patricia's murder. The telephone and answer phone exchanges between them follow the 'need', 'rejection', 'frustration' and 'aggression' scenario. When he responds to the message she has left on his answer phone, she asks him to wait because she is on another line. When she then rings him back, he has to make her wait as a revenge, telling her that this time he is on another line. Eventually, he is able to manipulate her into having dinner with him in the fashionable restaurant Dorsia. However, failing to be able to book a table once again creates the 'need', 'rejection', 'frustration' and aggression' scenario. The fact that they do not have a table leaves him 'stunned, feverish, feeling empty' (75). At the Barcadia, he projects his frustration on to Patricia, now the 'Restaurant whore', who does not disguise her disappointment and frustration over not getting into Dorsias. Eventually she apologises. What is interesting, and significant in this episode, is that throughout he thinks of her as the 'good' Patricia when she is compliant and the 'bad' Patricia when she is resistant to him.

In *American Psycho*, Ellis not only creates a consciousness, or unconsciousness, determined by psychoanalysis but locates it at the heart of the self-referentiality of postmodernity. Bateman's narrative frequently slips unnervingly from what appears to be actual violence and imagined violence into mundane, humdrum activities. At the centre of the novel is the issue of what the young upwardly culture does to the individual sensibility – *Les Misérables* if we pick up on the advertisement on the side of a bus early in the text. Bateman admits at one point, that a waitress is 'looking at me as if I were some kind of monster – she actually looks *scared*' (45). Meaning is only derived from the relationships between the different elements from which it is configured. Thus, there is constant, overwhelming and oppressive reference to what people are wearing. Characters in the book are assaulted by designer labels. There is no world outside these signs and the different ways in which they are configured. Here we have a manifestation of how American consumer culture is based on a loop – advertising videos and signs repeat themselves endlessly and even television news is continuously repeated throughout the day. Indeed, Bateman himself appears to be caught inside some kind of loop. One of the earliest images with which the novel presents us is of 'gridlock':

> In one issue – in one issue – let's see here … strangled models, babies thrown from tenement rooftops, kids killed in the subway, a Communist rally, Mafia boss wiped out, Nazis' – he flips through the pages excitedly – baseball players with AIDS, more Mafia shit, gridlock, the homeless, various maniacs, faggots dropping like flies in the streets, surrogate mothers, the cancellation of a soap opera, kids who broke into a zoo and tortured and burned various animals alive, more Nazis … and the joke is, the punch line is, it's all in this city – nowhere else, just here, it sucks, whoa wait, more Nazis, gridlock, gridlock, baby-sellers, black-market babies, AIDS babies, baby junkies, building collapses on baby, maniac baby, gridlock, bridge collapses – (4)

The repetition indicates the loop of information in which individuals in this culture are caught up. One horrific event merges into another so that it becomes impossible to distinguish between them and the potential impact of one horror is mitigated by another falling soon after.

Like other texts of its kind, *American Psycho* offers a self-referential approach to criminality that integrates it with the larger sense of spectacle upon which late modernity in America appears to be based. The subject of the text is not so much the criminal as determined by psychoanalysis as the criminal determined by the wider self-referential cultural field. Within this context, the emphasis falls, as it does in William Trevor's *Felicia's Journey*, upon the different masquerades and performances assumed by the serial criminal.

Cat and mouse

Felicia's Journey is the story of an Irish girl who leaves her oppressive home environment to find her boyfriend who has joined the British army and by whom she is pregnant. In England, in the midlands, she is befriended by Hilditch, a serial killer who preys on young, homeless girls. The crime scene is something towards which the novel moves rather than starts out from and, in fact, Felicia, unlike Hilditch's previous victims, manages to escape his clutches, after which he commits suicide.

Hilditch prefers to pick up his victims at bus stations, cafés and service centres well away from where he lives and works. These are 'frontier' places in post-industrial Britain where Hilditch can rely on anonymity and achieve a level of surveillance that would not be possible in a close community. They also signify how post-industrial Britain is becoming a place where community is breaking down and more people, living and working in different places, travel considerable distances on a daily basis.

Unlike *American Psycho*, *Felicia's Journey* is a psychological, rather than a horror, crime thriller. In some respects, it is a contemporary version of the Red Riding Hood fairy story. Felicia's encounter with Hilditch seems to be presented at times as a punishment for her transgression – getting herself pregnant outside of marriage and having sex with a boyfriend who 'crosses over' into the British army. When Hilditch first meets her outside the factory where he works, she is wearing a red coat and hood, which she has on again over a nightgown in his house in the scene in which he attacks her. But in serial murder, coincidence is the key; the murder if it does not occur immediately can be traced back to the moment when the paths of the victim and the killer crossed. There is also the coincidence that triggers his decision to select a particular victim. While Felicia believes that she is the subject of her own narrative – searching for her boyfriend – she is the object in someone else's as she is manipulated and toyed with by Hilditch in the various roles he masquerades and is eventually brought to his home.

Thus, many of the episodes in which Felicia and Hilditch are together operate at different levels of meaning. For example, at Buddy's café, Felicia thinks that Hilditch is upset because, as he tells her, his wife Ada has just had a serious operation and is poorly. She also thinks that he is concerned for her welfare. However, this is all a performance. He manipulates the scene so that the café staff thinks that he has a girlfriend young enough to be his daughter. He also thinks of her as 'Beth' and 'Jakki', two of the other girls he has killed, thus blurring this location with his previous crime scenes. The novel brings together two 'outlawed' narratives, destined to fuse in the crime scene toward which it moves: that of a naive, young girl who has transgressed the rules of home and community, and the narrative of Hilditch who has failed to grow beyond his relationship with his mother and lives in a house which is very much like it was when he lived there as a child.

Like Ellis's Bateman, Hilditch regresses to a primary orality. Throughout the novel, his obsession with food is linked to his pursuit of the girls. Both are associated with meticulous planning, and, at one point, the litany of the names of the girls he has killed parallels the list of the different types of biscuit on his domestic biscuit barrel. At the end of the novel, we learn that his mother appeared to his young mind as a 'good' mother with whom he enjoyed a fairly normal, if obsessive, relationship until she took up with men and became the 'bad' mother. Eventually, when the men stopped coming, she resorted to dressing up and taking the young Hilditch in their place. Once again, we have a serial killer whose psychological profile suggests a damaging primary relationship with his mother.

In some respects, Hilditch is a rather feminine character, adopting, for example, a nurturing role toward Felicia. At home, he is associated with the kitchen, which was his mother's room more than any other. His employment as a Catering Manager continues the kitchen association into his adult, working life. Associating sexuality with his mother's promiscuity, and prostitution, he preys on young girls who appear to be pre-sexual. In his imagination, they are masqueraded as 'safe' partners. It would appear that he kills them when he thinks that they are behaving sexually towards him. The decision to kill Felicia is triggered when she appears in her nightgown and bare feet at the foot of his stairs and he thinks of her as leading him on. It does not matter whether they have behaved in a sexual manner towards him or not. Eventually, they become objects on which he projects his anger and frustration; in killing them he is really killing the 'bad' mother from his own childhood.

The central enigma in the novel, however, is based on the intended crime. Why did he break his rules of not picking up girls near his home or place of work and of not bringing them to his home? Did he want to be caught? At one level, he is excited by these departures from his normal practices, but he also senses that there is something different about Felicia from the other girls he has picked up. Does he want her to be the one who will bring every thing to an end? In each murder, through the typical serial process of rehearsal, repetition and improvement, referred to at the outset of this chapter, he is trying to eradicate more effectively each time the 'bad' mother. But she remains a presence in his memories and his consciousness. At one point, he tries to explain to Felicia, 'that people often want to do something that isn't in their best interests, that it often takes someone else to see what's what' (149).

Despite being a late twentieth-century novel, *Felicia's Journey* has at its heart the dialectic between the need to find an explanation for the behaviour of the serial killer and an interest in masquerade and performance, itself part of the rehearsal and improvement that drives the seriality. In this respect, the novel takes us back to the early serial killer fiction, and has much in common with the callous killer narrative. But in performing for an audience, such as the women working in the café, and implicitly mocking them and their values in the process, Hilditch takes us back to the nineteenth-century swellman where we began.

Conclusion

> When I speak of a 'conspiracy of art,' I am using a metaphor, as I do when I speak of the 'perfect crime.' You can no more identify the instigators of this plot than you can designate the victims. This conspiracy has no author and everyone is both victim and accomplice. The same thing happens in politics: we are all duped and complicit in this kind of showcasing. A sort of non-belief, of non-investment makes it so that everyone is playing a two-faced game.
>
> (Jean Baudrillard, *The Conspiracy of Art*)

Beginnings often masquerade as endings. When the Ripper murders ended in London in 1888 they did not stop there. The unknown killer, perhaps because he was never uncovered, influenced artists such as Otto Dix and Walter Sickert, inspired film directors, and attracted the attention of a host of writers from Marie Lowndes to Robert Bloch and Patricia Cornwell. He has been the subject of numerous studies and is frequently invoked in press coverage of similar crimes, most famously in the case of the British 1970s killer, the Yorkshire Ripper.

It may be possible to think of Jack the Ripper as a personification of evil but in cultural terms he has become a signifier within such a wide range of texts that he has ceased to have a meaningful relationship with any reality. He has become a 'sign' devoid of any meaning other than that invested in him by the texts in which he is invoked. As one of the better known yet unknown serial killers, the Ripper has entered twentieth-century popular culture, like many highly visible criminals, as a sign of where modernity fails.

This book has focussed upon a range of criminal activity from the Victorian swellman and rough, through the female confidence trickster, the American gangster, the mobster's moll, the female murderer, to the serial killer, and even to the cadaver. Many of these criminals have acquired the power to intimidate and disturb. But, as in the Ripper's case, it is not a power attached to reality. It is in excess of their actual status or the occurrence of the crimes with which they are associated and, as we have seen, has been called a 'transformational power' based upon their status as signs.

Without necessarily being fully aware of it, the representation of criminality, like many criminological studies, promulgate criminality as sign. This has proved especially true in the case of female criminals. The lurid covers of twentieth-century pot boilers fetishise the violent, female criminal, the mobster's moll and those whom we have seen labelled in American criminology as 'unadjusted girls' and 'amateur prostitutes'. The fetish object is the ultimate sign not tied to any reality.

In approaching criminality from the perspective of performance and masquerade, this book has sought to acknowledge its place in the social structures that give it meaning while reclaiming it from its potential reduction to only a cultural sign. The starting point has been how criminality operates in modernity where it is forever a symbol of its failings. As we have seen, criminality mimics and mocks modernity, holding a mirror up to its fragmentation, its excesses and what it mythicises and denies. The mimicry has been explored as part of a wider performance and masquerade in criminality.

Most forms of criminality, as we have highlighted, involve masquerade, performance and exhibitionism, from the Victorian swellman and rough to the confidence trickster and the serial killer. The confidence trickster takes us into their 'confidence' but destroys our confidence in whomsoever we meet thereafter as well as in modernity itself. Thus, configuring criminality in terms of masks and masquerades has many ramifications and offers fresh insights into how it is represented in literature. As soon as we begin to admit the performance of criminality into our consciousness, we find it difficult to be sure as to where the masked game begins and ends. Dickens, as we have seen, acknowledging that criminality is a masquerade, recognises the performances that are all around us.

But perhaps one of the most disturbing outcomes of the 'game of masks' that Dickens and others identify is that we begin to fear that we do not know even those whom we think we know. The Renaissance destroyed the unified sense of self on the dissection table. The contemporary forensic novel takes the anatomist's tools, the mirror and the scalpel, to a corpse whose fragmentation signifies the dismembered, postmodern self. Postmodern crime writers, like Thomas Pynchon and

Umberto Eco, most obviously make the fragmentation of postmodernity the subject of their narratives. However, the contemporary forensic novel does something different. It is less willing than the postmodern crime novel to accept that literature has little to offer in the face of the annihilation of the unified individual. The text, in moving forward in an investigation of the crime, usually travels backward into a life that is both less and more than at first appears in what is ultimately an attempt to reclaim the essential, non-fragmented self.

There is a permeable boundary between literary and cultural studies. Whilst the latter approaches criminality through its cultural signification, literature contributes to our cultural understanding of criminality but also reclaims its vibrancy as performance. In doing so, it takes us into the complexities, contradictions and ambivalences of criminality. Perhaps, the most important question is not who Jack the Ripper was but who the female prostitutes he (or even she) murdered thought he was. Did they think he was a gentleman? Did he masquerade as a doctor? What masks did they wear to meet the masquerade with which he presented them? As they led him to a secret place they knew, did the masquerade excite him?

This study has been concerned with what the cultural study of the criminal simply as a cultural sign has denied: our fascination with criminality as masquerade. Whereas the sign is definable, criminality in the literary text is usually not. This has been at the heart of the approach taken in this study to those texts that, in reaching indisputable answers, appear confident in the appearance of reality. In their work, the reality of appearance is anything but indisputable. Even some of the most ostensibly conservative crime stories, from Edgar Allan Poe's 'The Murders in the Rue Morgue' to Agatha Christie's murder mysteries, are riddled with tensions, contradictions and ambiguities. The best crime narratives are fascinated by transgression, as Agatha Christie was interested in what American criminologists called 'unadjusted women' and others we have discussed, such as Dorothy L. Sayers and Josephine Tey, were intrigued by limit and taboo. That level of explicit or implicit fascination with criminality and transgression is akin to the seductive power of performance and masquerade. It is one of the reasons that the language in which criminality is written is itself problematic: at the boundary of objectivism and fascination.

It is the combination of scientific investigation and fascination that the literary critic and the detective share not simply rational analysis. However, a more disturbing analogy is that between the serial killer and the writer, for both share an obsession with rehearsal and improvement.

The serial killer epitomises the paradoxical approach of modernity to serious crime that we highlighted at the outset of this study: at one level, writing it out of modernity and, at another, writing it into modernity in order to make sense of what ostensibly denies rational explanation. The book began by drawing attention to how press coverage of a 'real-life' killing in twenty-first century London placed it in a larger, cultural narrative derived from *A Clockwork Orange*. When the teenage girl who took photographs on her mobile phone of the violent attack, a form of crime known at the time as 'happy slapping', was sentenced, the press published a picture of her, usually on their front pages, with headlines like: 'The face of a killer, 14'. She looked like any other child, but the press seemed to think this should have been otherwise. Her face, the headline implied, was a mask and, if her face hid a ruthless, young killer then it seemed to ask what could be accepted, literally, at face value. This is one of the central dilemmas in crime writing that this study has sought to explore.

Criminology and psychoanalytic study have sought to write extreme criminality into modernity. But the criminal as pariah figure has intrigued authors seeking to get inside their minds whilst remaining sceptical of psychoanalytic explanations. One of the phenomena which this study has highlighted is the way in which psychoanalytic explanation has become a blue print for writing about the serial or callous killer. The best serial-killer fiction has refused to hang the criminal psyche on a ready-made hook. Entering the performance and the masquerade which serial murder must entail has provided crime writing with an opportunity to explore what mocks modernity's preference for the indisputable thesis from Robert Bloch's *Psycho* to Bret Easton Ellis's *American Psycho*.

This study has discussed writers who use performance as a vehicle for social satire and political criticism, others for whom it is a means of challenging psychoanalytic, explanatory narratives and those who recognise that in performance a 'freedom of being' is released. In literary writing about crime, criminality becomes a space to explore the fluid nature of gender identity. This study has brought us to what writers who have entertained criminality have known all along: performance is empowering. The African-American writer Toni Morrison's *Love* is included in this study because not only does its central protagonist, like many of Morrison's characters, appreciate the emancipatory nature of 'acting out' but African-American identity has also been reclaimed and developed through performance. As Junior in that novel discovers, criminality and 'unadjustment', because they are based on performance and masquerade, can be an inspiration.

Notes

1 Mocking Modernity

1. For a fuller discussion of the nation state and cultural difference, see Homi Bhabha, 'Dissemi/Nation: Time, Narrative, and the Margins of the Modern Nation', in *Nation and Narration* ed. Homi Bhabha (1990; rpt London and New York: Routledge, 1993).
2. Eamonn Carrabine et al., *Crime in Modern Britain* (Oxford: Oxford University Press, 2002), p. 76.
3. See, for example, D. A. Low, *The Regency Underworld* (London: Dent, 1994), p. 44.
4. See, Kevin Hetherington, *The Badlands of Modernity: Heterotopia and Social Ordering* (London and New York: Routledge, 1997), 65ff.
5. For example, Peter Nicholls, *Modernisms: A Literary Guide* (London: Macmillan, 1995), p. 16.
6. See, Robert Sindall, *Street Violence in the Nineteenth Century: Media Panic or Real Danger* (Leicester: Leicester University Press, 1990), pp. 95–110.
7. Stephen Knight has pointed out that in the nineteenth century 'the complexity of social life in its physical reality made it improbable that a criminal could be easily detected by the social group against which he or she sinned'. Stephen Knight, 'Regional Crime Squads: Location and Dislocation in the British Mystery', in *Peripheral Visions: Images of Nationhood in Contemporary British Fiction* ed. Ian A. Bell (Cardiff: University of Wales Press, 1995), p. 28.
8. For example, Deborah Cameron and Elizabeth Frazer point out that 'the varying forms of violence and crime are intimately connected to the forms of the wider culture – what societies believe, how they define things, what they do about them'. Deborah Cameron and Elizabeth Frazer, *The Lust to Kill: a Feminist Investigation of Sexual Murder* (Cambridge: Polity Press, 1987), p. 20.
9. Eamonn Carrabine *et al.*, *Crime in Modern Britain*, p. 19.
10. Cited Robert Sindall, *Street Violence in the Nineteenth Century*, p. 61.
11. Jean Baudrillard, *Symbolic Exchange and Death* (1976; rpt London: Sage, 1993), p. 114.
12. Cited Judih Walkowitz, *City of Dreadful Delight: Narratives of Sexual Danger in Late-Victorian London* (London: Virago, 1992), p. 81.
13. See, Michel Foucault, *Discipline and Punish: The Birth of the Prison* (1977; rpt Harmondsworth: Penguin, 1991), p. 27.
14. Henry Mayhew, *London Labour and the Labouring Poor* IV (1988–99; rpt *History of Criminology* ed. Paul Rock, Aldershot: Dartmouth Publishing Company, 1994), p. 335.
15. Low, *The Regency Underworld*, pp. 71–72.
16. J. J. Tobias, *Crime and Industrial Society in the Nineteenth Century* (1967; rpt Harmondsworth: Penguin, 1972), p. 61.
17. Polly Nicholls's body was found on 31 August in a doorway in Buck's Row; Annie Chapman was discovered on 8 September murdered in the back premises of 39 Hanbury Street where no fewer than six families resided; Catherine

Eddowes and Elizabeth Stride were found in a courtyard adjacent to the International Working Men's Educational Club on Berner Street on 30 September; and Mary Jane Kelly, the most brutally murdered woman, was discovered in her rented room on 9 November.
18. Walkowitz, *City of Dreadful Delight*, p. 193.
19. Cited R. Odell, *Jack the Ripper in Fact and Fiction* (London: Mayflower-Dell, 1966), pp. 18–19.
20. Cited L. James (ed.), *English Popular Literature 1819–51* (New York: Columbia University Press, 1976), p. 272.
21. See, David Jones, *Crime, Protest, Community and Police in Nineteenth-century Britain* (London: Routledge and Kegan Paul, 1982).
22. Jones, *Crime, Protest, Community and Police in Nineteenth-century Britain*, p. 33.
23. Jones, in *Crime, Protest, Community and Police Nineteenth-century Britain*, p. 62.

2 Gender and Performance in the Criminal Masquerade

1. Foucault, *Discipline and Punish*, pp. 25–26.
2. See, Homi Bhabha, 'Of Mimicry and Man: The Ambivalence of Colonial Discourse', in *Modern Literary Theory* ed. P. Rice and P. Waugh (1989; rpt London: Arnold, 2001), p. 381.
3. Foucault, *Discipline and Punish*, p. 26.
4. Lynn Pykett, *The Sensation Novel from The Woman in White to The Moonstone* (Northcote House, in association with the British Council, 1994), p. 7.
5. Sindall, *Street Violence in the Nineteenth Century*, p. 60.
6. See, for example, Barry Godfrey et al., *Comparative Histories of Crime* (Cullompton, Devon: Willan Publishing, 2003), p. 63.
7. Homi Bhabha, *Nation and Narration*, p. 299.
8. Walkowitz, *City of Dreadful Delight*, p. 129.
9. See, for example, Robert Connell, *Masculinities* (Cambridge: Polity Press, 1995), p. 45.
10. Connell, *Masculinities*, pp. 52–53.
11. Jones, *Crime, Protest, Community and Police in Nineteenth-Century Britain*, p. 178.
12. For a wider consideration of masculinity from a criminological perspective, see, Angus McLaren, *The Trials of Masculinity: Policing Sexual Boundaries 1870–1930* (Chicago: Chicago University Press, 1997) and Carrabine *et al.*, *Crime in Modern Britain*, 29–34, 67, 76–77, 116, 117–18, 137, 139, 144.
13. Alison Adburgham, *Shops and Shopping 1800–1914* (London; Barrie and Jenkins, 1989), p. 174.
14. Susan Casteras, *Images of Victorian Womanhood in English Art* (London and Toronto: Associated University Press, 1987), p. 159.
15. According to Dudley Edwards this aspect of Holmes may have been introduced after Doyle met with Oscar Wilde. O. Dudley Edwards, *The Quest for Sherlock Holmes* (Harmondsworth: Penguin, 1984), p. 55.
16. Anna Pukas, 'Torture and Terror by the English Goodfellas', *Daily Express*, 29 October, 2005, 40–41. The article publicises Eddie Richardson, *The Last Word* (London: Headline, 2005).
17. George Orwell, *The Decline of the English Murder and Other Essays* (1944 rpt Harmondsworth: Penguin, 1965), pp. 70, 76.
18. Pukas, 'Torture and Terror by the English Goodfellas', p. 40.

19. Pukas, 'Torture and Terror by the English Goodfellas', p. 40.
20. Judith Butler, *Gender Trouble: Feminism and the Subversion of Identity* (London and New York: Routledge: 1987), p. 128.
21. Lew Louderback, *Pretty Boy, Pretty face – I Love You: the Gangsters of the '30s and their Molls* (London: Coronet, 1969), p. 8.
22. Michael Hatt 'Muscles, Morals, Mind: The Male Body in Thomas Eakins's *Salutat*', in *The Body Imaged: The Human Form and Visual Culture Since the Renaissance* ed. K. Adler and M. Pointon (Cambridge: Cambridge University Press, 1993), pp. 57–9.
23. Edwin Woodhall, *Jack the Ripper or When London Walked in Terror* (London: Mellifont Press Ltd., 1937) and William Stewart, *Jack the Ripper: A New Theory* (London: Quality Press, 1939).
24. Stewart, *Jack the Ripper*, pp. 209, 207.
25. Walkowitz, *City of Dreadful Delight*, p. 128.

3 The Cadaver as Criminalised Text

1. Karen Halttunen, *Murder Most Foul: The Killer and the American Gothic Imagination* (Cambridge, MA: Harvard University Press, 1998), p. 66.
2. John Walsh, *Poe the Detective: The Curious Circumstances Behind the Mystery of Marie Roget* (New Brunswick, NJ: Rutgers University Press, 1968), p. 7 and Halttunen, *Murder Most Foul*, p. 144.
3. Cited Walsh, *Poe the Detective*, p. 13.
4. Walsh, *Poe the Detective*, p. 19.
5. Ronald Thomas, *Detective Fiction and the Rise of Forensic Science* (1999; rpt Cambridge: Cambridge University Press, 2000), pp. 51–2.
6. Halttunen, *Murder Most Foul*, p. 145.
7. Cited Walsh, *Poe the Detective*, p. 20.
8. Cited Odell, *Jack the Ripper in Fact and Fiction*, p. 31.
9. Cited, Odell, *Jack the Ripper in Fact and Fiction*, p. 106.
10. Odell, *Jack the Ripper in Fact and Fiction*, p. 70.
11. Jonathan Sawdry, *The Body Emblazoned* (London and New York: Routledge, 1995), pp. 183 and xi.
12. Karen Dale, 'Identity in a Culture of Dissection: Body, Self and Knowledge', in *Ideas of Difference: Social Spaces and the Labour of Division* ed. K. Hetherington and R. Munro (Oxford: Blackwell Publishers, in association with *The Sociological Review*, 1997), p. 109.

4 Where Does That Criminality Come From? Writing Women and Crime

1. Sigmund Freud, *An Outline of Psychoanalysis*, ed. James Stratchey (1949; rpt London: Hogarth Press, 1969), pp. 40–1.
2. W. I. Thomas, *The Unadjusted Girl with Cases and Standpoint for Behaviour* (Boston: Little, Brown and Company, 1923), p. 4ff.
3. Thomas, *The Unadjusted Girl*, pp. 230–1.
4. Thomas, *The Unadjusted Girl*, pp. 230–1.
5. Thomas, *The Unadjusted Girl*, p. 109.

6. Thomas, *The Unadjusted Girl*, p. 109.
7. Adburgham, *Shops and Shopping 1800–1914*, pp. 189: 146, 145, 143, and 96.
8. Walter Benjamin, 'Paris – The Capital of the Nineteenth Century', in *Charles Baudelaire: A Lyric Poet in the Era of High Capitalism* trans. Harry Zohn (London: NLB, 1973), p. 166.
9. Adburgham, *Shops and Shopping 1800–1914*, p. 103.
10. Mayhew, *London and the Labour Poor* IV, p. 342.
11. Gladys Mary Hall, *Prostitution: A Survey and a Challenge* (London: Williams and Northgate Ltd, 1933), p. 20.
12. Hall, *Prostitution*, p. 75.
13. Hall, *Prostitution*, p. 30.
14. Joanna Glenbrander, *A Portrait of Fryn* (London: Andre Deutsch, 1984), p. 190.
15. Sally Mitchell, *The New Girl: Girl's Culture in England 1880–1915* (New York: Columbia University Press, 1995), 1995, p. 3.
16. Gill Frith, 'The Time of Your Life: The Meaning of the School Story' in *Language, Gender and Childhood* ed. Carolyn Steedman, Cathy Unwin and Valerie Walkerdine (London: Routledge and Kegan Paul, 1985), pp. 121–2.
17. Thomas, *The Unadjusted Girl*, p. 119.

5 Agatha Christie, Dorothy L. Sayers and Sara Paretsky: The New Woman

1. Sara Paretsky, *Women on the Case: Original Crime Stories by Women* (New York and London: Delacorte and London; Virago, 1996), vii–viii.
2. Paretsky, *Women on the Case*, vii.
3. Paretsky, *Women on the Case*, ix.
4. Jean Laplanche and Serge Leclaire, *The Unconscious: A Psycho-analytic* Study (New Haven, CT: Yale University Press, Yale French Studies, 1972), p. 128.

6 Masquerade, Criminality and Desire in Toni Morrison's *Love*

1. Joan Riviere, 'Womanliness as a Masquerade', rpt in *Psychoanalysis and Woman: A Reader* ed. Shelley Saguaro (Basingstoke: Macmillan, 2000), pp. 70–8 [70].

7 Writing the Serial and Callous Killer into (Post) Modernity

1. Baudrillard, *Symbolic Exchange and Death*, p. 91.
2. Cited Wayne Morrison, *Theoretical Criminology: From Modernity to Post-modernism* (London: Cavendish Publishing, 1995), pp. 156–57.

Index

'Accusing Shadow, The', xiii, 84–5
Acid House, The, 20
'Adventure of the Beryl Coronet, The', 82–3
Aesthetic Movement, The, 40
Allingham, Margery, 2, 19, 54–5, 112–13
American Psycho, xv, xvi, 166–9, 170, 176
Another Country, 139
Arnott, Jake, 43, 44

Baker, Josephine, 135, 138, 142
Baldwin, James, 139
Banville, John, xv, 159–62, 166
Barnett, Mrs, 17–18
Baudrillard, Jean, 173, 177, 180
Beggar's Opera, The, 11, 13, 16
Berne, Suzanne, xii, 73
Bhabha, Homi, 177, 178
Bitter Medicine, xiv, 119, 120, 121–4, 125–6
Bleak House, 129
Bloch, Robert, xii, xv, xvi, 70, 78–9, 80, 153, 162–5, 166, 167, 173, 176
Bluest Eye, The, 129, 131, 146
Blyth, Harry, 84–5, xiii
Body in the Library, The, xii, xiii, 72–3, 74, 102–3, 108, 110
Book of Evidence, The, xv, 159–62, 166
Breaker, The xii, 73
Brighton Rock, xi, xiii, 42–4, 87, 156, 160
Burley, W. J., 21
Burn Marks, xiv, 121, 125, 126–7
Butcher Boy, The, 70
Butler, Judith, 179

Caleb Williams, 11
Camus, Albert, 159–62
Carter, Angela, xii, xv, 70, 72, 73–4, 166
Case of the Late Pig, The, 54–5

Chandler, Raymond, xi, 19, 20, 46, 47–50, 117
Christie, Agatha, xii, xiii, xiv, 2, 39, 57, 72–3, 74, 87, 92, 102–3, 104, 105, 106–13, 114, 117, 118, 119, 120, 125, 127, 158, 175
Cleft Chin Murder, The, 42, 87, 91, 94–6, 97, 103
Clockwork Orange, A, viii, ix, 176
Collins, Willkie, xiii, 84
Colquhoun, Patrick, 7
Cornwell, Patricia, xii, 70, 74–6, 77, 79–80, 173
Corpse, the, 11, 54, 59, 61, 70–4, 76–8, 103, 131, 162, 174
Crime in the Neighbourhood, A, xii, 73
Crime scene, 3, 9, 55, 16–61, 66, 70, 91, 97–8, 100, 101, 114, 152, 154, 169, 170
Criminology, 1, 3, 5, 6–7, 10, 15, 20, 21, 22, 23, 24, 30, 31, 36, 39, 41, 64, 86–7, 93, 166, 174, 176, 177, 180

Daughter of Fu Manchu, 51
Debt Collector, The, 70
Defoe, Daniel, 5, 13, 51
Dexter, Colin, 71–2, 74, 139
Dickens, Charles, x, xi, 1, 7, 12–14, 15–17, 18, 19, 21, 24, 26–8, 29, 35–8, 39, 40, 52, 53, 85–6, 129, 151, 164–5, 174
Dissection, 68, 77–9, 174, 179
Dixi, Jenny, 139
Donoghue, Emma, xi, 51–3
Doyle, Sir Arthur Conan, x, xiii, 2, 3, 9–10, 30, 38, 39, 40, 57, 72, 82, 111, 112, 142–3, 152–3
Du Maurier, Daphne, 74

Eco, Umberto, 175
Ellis, Brett Easton, xv, xvi, 166–9, 170, 176

Ellroy, James, 3
Eugene Aram, x, 11–12, 32

'Fall River Axe Murders, The', xv, 166
Farewell My Lovely, xi, 46, 47–50
Faulkner, William, 129
Felicia's Journey, xv, xvi, 2, 153, 169–72
Femininity, 29, 46, 50, 82, 84, 85, 92, 93, 103, 104, 110, 115, 116, 120, 144, 147
Fetishism, xv, 89, 137–8, 144, 147–8, 174
Fielding, Henry, 5
Fingersmith, xi, 26, 51–3
Fisher, Rudolph, 135
Fitzgerald, F. Scott, xi, 46–9, 145–6
Forensic crime fiction, 77–80
Forensic science, 55–6, 59–60, 70–1, 74, 76–80, 150, 151, 174, 175, 179
Foucault, Michel, 14, 177, 178
4.50 from Paddington, 39, 110, 111–13, 117
Franchise Affair, The, xiii, 87, 91, 96–102, 103, 149
Freud, Sigmund, 66, 86, 87–8, 89, 92, 93, 122, 127, 155, 162–3, 167

Galton, Francis, 8
Gangster, the, 3, 25, 42–49, 51, 96, 145, 156, 174, 179
Gay, John, 11, 13, 16
Ghost Country, xiv, 118–20, 125, 126
Girl from Cardigan, The, 23
Godwin, William, 11
Great Expectations, 12, 37–8, 39, 151
Great Gatsby, The, xi, 46–9, 145–6
Greene, Graham, xi, xiii, xv, 42–4, 87, 149, 155–8, 160
Gun for Sale, A, xv, 44, 149, 155–8, 160

Hall, Gladys, Mary, 90–1
Highsmith, Patricia, 53–4
Hightower, Lynn, 70
Himes, Chester, 19, 20, 132, 135
Hogarth, 5, 18
Home to Harlem, 131
Hornung, Ernest William, 2–3,
Hound of the Baskervilles, The, 39, 152–3
Hughes, Langston, 135

Indemnity Only, xiv, 119, 121, 125, 126
Inquiries into Human Faculty and Its Development, 8
'Ivy Cottage Mystery, The', 41, 56–7

Jack the Ripper, viii, 17, 19, 50–1, 58–9, 60, 67–70, 71, 75, 76, 78, 79, 151–2, 154–5, 173, 175, 177–8, 179
Jamaica Inn, 74
James, P. D., 70
Jazz, xv, 129, 130, 131, 132–3, 137, 140, 141, 145, 147, 148–9, 149
Jesse, F. Tennyson, 87, 91–4, 103
Just Above My Head, 139

Keen, Herbert, 29–30
Klein, Melanie, 155–6, 157, 167, 168, 170–1

L. A. Confidential, 3
Linden Hills, 139–40
Locke, Alan Le Roy, 136
Lodger, The, xv, 154–5, 166
Lombroso, Cesare, 8–9, 17, 150, 166
London, 5, 7, 11, 13, 15, 16–19, 20, 29, 34, 60–1, 67, 71, 76–7, 89, 93, 151, 154, 173, 176
'Long Arm, The', 57–8
Long Firm, The, 43, 44
Love, xv, 129–31, 133–49, 176
Los Angeles, 20, 47
Lowndes, Marie, xv, 154–5, 166, 173
L'Uomo Delinquente, 8
Lytton, Edward Bulwer, x, xi, 11–13, 21, 22, 32

Marshal's Own Case, The, xii, 73, 76–7, 80
Masculinity, 1, 17, 25, 26, 30, 32–3, 35, 37, 39, 40–2, 47–50, 55, 60, 65, 84, 98, 115, 144, 147, 178
Masquerade, 1–4, 12, 16, 19–22, 23, 29, 30, 39, 44–5, 50–5, 57–63, 65, 67, 69–72, 75–6, 79, 81–6, 88, 89–92, 95–6, 98, 100, 104–118, 120, 125, 128, 129–41, 143–8, 150–4, 158–9, 164–6, 169, 170–1, 173–6, 180

Mayhew, Henry, 14, 15, 20, 25, 26, 50, 89–90, 141, 166, 177
McBain, Ed, 19, 20
McCabe, Patrick, 70
Meade, L. T., 101
Merthyr, 31, 34, 38
McKay, Claude, 131
Mirror Crack'd from Side to Side, The, 110
Modernity, 2–5, 7, 8, 9, 10–11, 12, 14, 16, 19, 20–1, 24, 25–6, 32, 38, 41, 55–6, 58, 60, 65, 78–80, 86, 88–9, 96, 110–12, 154, 157–8, 162, 166, 173–4, 176, 177, 180
Moll, 29, 42, 45, 46, 51, 87, 96, 157, 174, 179
Moll Flanders, 13, 51
Morrison, Arthur, 41, 56–7
Morrison, Toni, xv, 20, 70, 129–149, 176
Murder, 2, 5, 6, 10, 11, 17, 18, 19, 32–3, 38, 39, 41, 42, 44, 49, 50, 53, 56, 57–73, 75–6, 80, 84, 87, 91, 92–3, 95, 96, 97, 103, 106–11, 113–14, 117, 119, 123, 129, 145, 151–5, 158–60, 162, 164–8, 170–1, 173–6, 177, 178, 179
Murder at the Vicarage, The, xiii, xiv, 87, 92, 106–13, 114, 117
Murder is Announced, A, 111
Murder of Roger Ackroyd, The, 109
Murder on the Orient Express, 39
'Murders in the Rue Morgue, The', xii, xiii, 19, 59–62, 63, 64–7, 69, 73, 97, 152, 159, 175
'Mystery at Number Seven, The', xiii, 83–4
'Mystery of Marie Roget, The', 62–4, 67
Mystery of the Blue Train, The, 108

Nabb, Magdalen, xii, 19, 73, 76–7, 80
Native Son, 139
Naylor, Gloria, 139
Negro Metropolis, 131
New Negro, The, 136
New York, 47, 53, 54, 59, 62–3, 67, 92, 135
No Name, 30,

Norris, Leslie, xi, 23–4, 34–5
Nothing Natural, 140

Oliver Twist, x, xi, 1, 12–14, 15–17, 18, 26–8, 29, 35–7, 40, 52, 53, 85–6, 164–5
Orlando, 53
Orwell, George, 34, 44–5, 95–6, 178
Outsider, The, 159–62

Pall Mall Gazette, 11, 33
Paradise, 70, 129
Paretsky, Sara, xiv, 104–5, 117–128, 129, 179
Parker, Alan, 27–8
Parker, Bonnie, 46, 47
Paul Clifford, 11, 12
Pickpocket, 1, 13–14, 25–8, 58, 89
Pin to See the Peepshow, A, xiii, 87, 91–4, 103
Poe, Edgar Allan, xii, 19, 59–67, 70, 73, 97, 152, 159, 175
Police at the Funeral, 112–13
Postmodernity, 77, 78–80, 166–7, 168, 175
Postmortem, xii, 70, 74–6, 77, 79–80
Power, 4, 10, 14, 28, 29, 31, 33–4, 35, 38–9, 42–5, 55, 58, 60, 64, 66, 74, 77, 104, 105, 106, 118, 119, 134–5, 137, 143, 148, 149, 163, 174, 175, 176
Prostitutes, 17, 25, 26, 29, 50–3, 62, 67, 69, 71, 76–8, 80, 85, 88, 90–1, 100, 102, 141–2, 146, 151–2, 157–8, 174–5
Prostitution, 31, 51, 53, 78, 86, 90, 108, 141–2, 171
Psycho, xii, xv, xvi, 70, 78–9, 153, 162–5, 166, 167, 176
Pulp fiction, 42–3, 47
Pynchon, Thomas, 174

Raffles, 2, 3
Rage in Harlem, A, 20, 132
Railway murder mysteries, 38–9
Rankin, Ian, 19
Raymond, R. Alwyn, 42, 87, 91, 94–6, 97, 103
Remorseful Day, The, 71–2, 74, 139

Rendell, Ruth, 21
Reynolds, G.W.M., 18
Rhomer, Sax, 51
Riviere, Joan, 133, 180
Road Rage, 21
Road to Wigan Pier, The, 34
'Rough', The, 31, 33, 34, 36, 38, 41, 42, 173–4
Rural, 4, 15, 18, 21–4, 30, 32, 106, 107, 109, 144

Sadomasochism, 69, 72, 74–5, 98, 140
Sayers, Dorothy L., xiv, 2, 104, 105, 113–17, 118, 119, 120, 125, 127, 158, 175
'Scandal in Bohemia, A', 30, 39, 82–3, 142–3, 82, 83, 142–3
Sensation novel, the, 11, 29–30, 41, 50, 82, 11
Serial Killer, 1, 3, 53, 67, 150, 152–3, 155, 159, 162, 170–6
Shadow Dance, xii, 70, 73–4
Shange, Ntozake, 139
Shockley, Ann, 139
Sign of the Four, The, x, xiii, 9–10, 40–1, 56, 82, 112
Simmons, Herbert, 43, 132, 135
'Skinning', 29
Slammerkin, xi, 51–3
Sliding, The, 23
Slim, Iceberg, 135
'Speckled Band, The', 82
Stead, W. T., 11
Stevenson, Robert Louis, xv, 150–2, 154–5
Stewart, William, 50, 179
Strange Case of Dr. Jekyll and Mr Hyde, The, xv, 150–2, 154–5
Strong Poison, xiv, 113–17

Suburban, 73, 75, 93, 109, 139
Sucker's Kiss, The, 27–8
Sula, xv, 129–31, 133, 137, 138, 140–2, 145, 146, 149
Swellman, 25–6, 28–9, 37, 51, 143, 172, 173, 174

Tabloid, 3
Talented Mr Ripley, The, 53–4
Tar Baby, 129, 138
Tey, Josephine, xiii, 87, 91, 96–102, 103, 149, 175
Theatre of pain, 43–4
Thomas, W. I., xiii, 87–8, 89, 91, 93, 95, 96, 100, 102, 41, 142
Tiger in the Smoke, The, 19
'Tin Box, The', 29–30
Trainspotting, 20
Treatise on the Police of the Metropolis, 7
Trevor, William, xv, xvi, 2, 153, 169–72

Urban, 2–6, 15–16, 18–24, 30–3, 73, 119

Walker, Alice, 139
Walkowitz, Judith, 17, 177, 178
Walters, Minette, xii, 73,
Waters, Sarah, xi, 26–7, 51–3
Watson, Colin, 21
Welsh, Irvine, 19, 20
'Who Killed Zebedee?', xiii, 84
Wilkins, Mary, 57–8
Woodhal, Edwin, 50, 179
Woods, Mrs Henry, xiii, 83–4
Woolf, Virginia, xi, 34, 53, 104–5, 117, 118, 119, 124–5, 128, 129
Wright, Richard, 132

Years, The, 34

Printed in the United States
133344LV00001B/255/P